Maybe once

By Bernard Spencer

CHAPTER ONE

Brushes with wild nature had been assumed by the Abstract painter, on the purchase of his property in far-off Aquitaine. Confronted daily by hardy farmer nonchalance, enthusiasm for the future, plenty had not been lessened by familiarity. Novelty never deserted a Fulham boy, virgin to the ways of the country.

One cherished early French confrontation had been with an owl. Accepted thereafter as guidance.

On the first recce day out from Stanstead, the whole of a three-hundred-year-old oak tree had been spotted in place as the support beam to the roof; master carpentry saved perfectly intact from another age, with little else of the house freed from the ravages of time.

Contiguously, for that whole special day, he had argued with himself to ever own such fragile beauty. Astonishingly, he had come down in its favour, considering the life-changing nature of his decision.

Summoned previously, after he had viewed agent photos in London with his daughters, craftsmen had arrived, boasting that forebearers probably had built the house, insisting they still had the skills to repair the near ruin. Without an architect if he had so desired. A process, to rely heavily on the new homeowner's design skills; coincidentally a miraculous speculation since college days.

Like could be replaced for like, had been

explained haltingly, after written estimates in French; his ex-wife's language, also his London-educated children's second. A comprehension he had always admitted he would never master. Nevertheless, after much arm waving, terms had been agreed, surprisingly quickly. A long job they had warned, ending with a small home in the south of France, in the tens not the hundreds of thousands of Euros.

Everything needed for the restoration had been available at the village builders' yard, less than a kilometre away. A convenient electric biking distance for him who had no car.

Or supplied through it, as a base by skilled others, intimate to the supplier. They had turned out an assortment of always skilled local rugby ragamuffins, who had recognised the enemy the moment they had seen him; to nickname him Wilkinson, like the fair-haired English captain, most revered and feared foreigner after Churchill.

At a wooden kidney-shaped desk, salvaged from his time in America, Thomas during restoration had taken to sitting in the precious space below his petrified tree, comfortable in a second self-ordained life job; not just on that day, but a storyteller from two decades back. Unpublished in a craft for which he had not been trained, he had promised himself that one day his words would make it to print. Albeit to explain his views on painting; an itch that had irritated him ever since he had finished Art school; deciding inaccurately that he could not paint.

Later one afternoon, with the tv link installed, on

for company, but muted, he had looked down onto unusual movement on the stripped wood floor.

Followed instantly by a shadow, it had become the tiny owl.

The he, or maybe she, with a small body resembling a feathered version of a Russian doll, seemed as surprised at someone else in the room.

The owl and the writer continued to stare at each other for a considerable amount of time.

Nudge by the legendary pussy-cat precedent beloved by John Lennon, written by Edward Lear, the painter felt the urge to confirm his experience for later re-telling. His small digital camera was on the desk beside his laptop. Reaching out for it, carefully, he had turned it on, conscious that any movement might startle the bird. Without seeing the image in the viewfinder, he had pointed to the machine and pressed the button. Alas, he had forgotten the self-regulating flash had been set. It lit up the tiny bird with claw feet, enormous to the size of its body, turning its large yellow eyes into headlights. In a gesture, clear as it was unrehearsed, it had blinked enormously and waddled out.

The checked snap was just a blur, the incident recognised, ever more, as a prod to his psyche.

Truth such a preposterously egotistical burden to carry, this little thing had confirmed his idea.

An honest two-front approach in his writing.

For the real and the imagined.

One tale is his own life story.

The second, a fictitious painter its hero.

Two able minds to claim identical sourcing, with

space, side by side.

CHAPTER TWO

An analogous blistering foreign afternoon, aeons later, the same sovereign sun bore down on the same delicate British skin, concluding the start to a typically oppressive August week. Most French were on vacation. Reflective T.H. Maher could not contain his smirk at a thought, a self-satisfied expat, currently in his own Aquitaine Garden. After thirty-odd years of sobriety, many suns passed, painting, in the land of the plenty. Any alcoholic alternative was long gone from a proud man, who could and would remember with clairvoyant clarity, the first moment the cold pink nectar had hit his tongue.

He grinned again.

"Could use a drink".

In English prescription bi-focal sunglasses, out on his deck under the protection of a large sun umbrella, he was in his favourite cushioned wrought-iron patio chair, reading. For added security, he had on a second application of an unmemorable French factor fifty sun lotion, strictly according to daughter's instructions. One act of defiance for a father who had never liked to be told anything, was the knitted sizzle hat. Bought at the village evening market and traditionally made, he had thought it just like the one Van Gough had worn when he had painted himself in his Mistral picture.

It had flopped interminably forward, covering his

face, making his mobile the more difficult to use.
Its ancient forerunner must have been a torture to
paint in.
New headgear, which was specifically banned by his
grown daughters Em and Av.
There in France or at his other home in Fulham.
Or indeed anywhere in the radius of twenty
thousand miles of dear old 'Blighty.'

Inbred miscellaneous British urges to anaesthetise
everything that moved in the heat, unfortunately,
Thomas's iced orange drink was finished.
Additionally, to his ear, he had the iPhone.

Sometimes admired, but more often hated for its
service to inclusion. A tricky younger brother was on
the other end of the line.
Generally, secure around his kins quasi-Socialist
rants by ignoring them, the insults had turned putrid
when they became slimy verbal assaults on other
family.

In fast turns, the artist became over-hot, outraged,
and then incandescent.

"Ungrateful little sod"

Among several acts of kindness performed by the
comfortably off middle-aged saints, who were their
two sisters, had been helping this brother on a
weekly basis, after a long-standing wife-in-law had
cut him loose.
Ending months of anguish by drawing the line at

rehousing him in their own homes, as he had demanded, the griping continued.
In barely microseconds, the live overseas call had been clicked to the clouds.

"Why don't you grow the fuck up."

Curious at the conjunction of his profanity, as he got up impatiently to refresh his juice, he had noted in his isolation that he might be watching a bit too much American tv on his French cable hook up.

Honestly, whenever a family problem had drifted into his consciousness, like today, all his brothers had aggravated him.
Even after the death of the youngest male, following his lengthy decline into alcoholic oblivion.

A second irascible child's new fight was with cancer.
Sisters were able to forgive; to help him in what were to be his last few months.

Refused contact before he died had been a challenge for the writer, who had battled long and hard to publish an autobiography.
Resisting because of hurting family feelings.

He had felt no inclination to delay it further.
Castigating had done little to reduce his well-developed guilt, when the poem about his kin him had seemed apposite. Totally the way to reply to people one loved, who had acted against family.

8

In childhood, if their late mother's stories were to be believed, Thomas had doted on his eldest sibling. Idolatry that was no longer a reality.

Maybe he had not always loathed his three brothers, but there were few in the world who could irritate him so viscerally.

Truthfully, the four Maher men all had been drinkers.

This middle brother had made claims he was on the wagon; but it was a boast without change in the disruptive conduct of a dry drunk, previously hospitalised.

Associating these days with either of the living pair had seemed to end only in anger.

So, they had hardly ever spoken.

Met up even less.

Brotherhood had not become the everlasting Emerita tradition promises.

And he would be the first to blame himself.

After another recent family upset, a wild- pony round up had been needed, to corral his furies. Searching to rid himself of the stinging angst, he had wanted to do more than just cover his pain.

With the intent to aim higher, the trained draughtsman had made an etching.

An abstract picture, drawn with only a little more patience.

Of their old family council-flat; a once new-home-build in which all six siblings had shared a youth.

One ferocious day before that, he had tried to dash off a pose poem. A craft in which as already

stated as a visual artist he was not well tutored,
though he had loved to write.

Its subject of course was the brother.

With reasoned resolve, the baby poet had fell
afoul of his fury, only in the last few bucking stanzas.

Currently, the sadistic source of all energy
seemed more than heartless to fair, English
discomfort. Thomas sat in the late morning
suffocation, wallowing in the cleverness of his own
spite.

He wondered how they had ever created an
Empire in the heat.

Costly domestic water drained from his small
dipping pool, adding a drip to paradise.

Needing only a one-hour-a-day replenishment
from the cold-water garden hose, made the feature
affordable in the intense thermals of summer. He
had refilled the tank that morning.

Without reason, he thought of England.

"ALICE"

Hardly able to admit, even to himself, his
unconscious desire was to splash again in the
dangerous depths of conjugal intimacy with a
disappeared lover.

Unfortunately, wife of a long-term friend.

Thomas was dedicated to saying no to the issue.
Often fiercely and out loud.

A quite separate obsession, he had sought to

disengage.

Still alas a regular thought on most days.

Hostile to any critique of him, the prospective 'laureate' lacked any cogent reply to his pleas.

Other than to rumble on like an overbearing London taxi driver, having no French fish wives to hold as comparison.

Hating himself all over again, for the ease with which he had turned nasty, Thomas got up with his empty pint glass, to refill it once more from the six-pack of cartons in the fridge.

Tomorrow, Thursday, he would replenish his supplies from the village's aptly named Super U store.

On his way to the kitchen, through the door, built by himself as a copy of the old farm one that had been there, he had been distracted.

"He needs to be spoken to."

Mobile still in his hand but previously culled, thoughtlessly, he brought it back to life.

The effortless thumb press bragged illusionary dominion over a shaky ego.

Inadvertently, he restarted the seven-year unpublished history, yet to be completed.

"He needs to be spoken to."

After so many warnings to others, not to engage,

glass refilled with orange and plenty of added cubes of ice, a repeating self-deceiver, reacted far, far too quickly. Flopping back into his desk chair inside, with the hat gone, overriding all fears of unjustness, he dispatched the e poem with all its awkward conjunctions, directly to the man who had inspired them.

Simultaneously, an attendant flash of an old art schoolmate added dazzle to the frisson.

Thomas understood he had sinned.

But it had been memory, for sure, not a phantom. It left a huge question hovering.

Why a man he once had called 'best friend' had continued to communicate with this angry middle brother all those years ago but never with him.
Inexplicably, and divine-like in the moment, Thomas intuited just how his early bigotry had harmed a special talented, and secret gay man.
After nearly half a lifetime, the vertiginous straight male confessed a huge self-loathing for just how hateful he once must have been, to someone who might have loved him.
Even, when unreciprocated and never properly empathised, it was important to recognise when you were loved.
Tough words were sought to construct a shade to cover his precipitous sense of loss.
But none could be found.
He looked up, to under his restored French red

tile roof, remembering tales of an old friend's later successful academic career.

An unsettling stick started to drum.

Of the chance, others seeing viciousness in his verses if they were read.

Until his brother had adumbrated him a second time by return email, denouncing him as an unpublished chancer.

Then, from the Tate and Lyle syrup tin of his youth, the drawing of a dead lion with bees exiting the honey in its mouth, words tattooed everlastingly, sang out their inspiration as fuel for an email of the discourse to his family.

' Out of the strong comes forth sweetness'.

CHAPTER THREE

On his Autumn visit to check the London house, his girls were on vacation in Greece.

Away from comfy French isolation, the Fulham building had felt evacuated.

Explaining somewhat; but not wholly, why two life members of the Tate Modern bar had been lingering, perilously long over second large lattes.

In a nervous call, Alice had agreed to meeting up in their once usual haunt; not verbalising past skills to fudge, if her husband found out.

The day after Thomas arrived from France, she hardly had time to case the empty bar stools, before he had dished his dirt about the poem.

Worse, accidentally mixing A's and endangering his sanity, he called her by his daughter's name.

"Av darling "

Such weedy pretension, while extending the hand of supposed friendship, would always have proved disastrous, eventually with her. This of course had instantly.

"I wrote a poem because my brother made me angry.
Stupidly I emailed it to him.
What do you think I should do?"

Following the unreal pause, an answer arrived,

very deliberately in separate parts.

"My name is Alice,

Thomas

Av is your youngest daughter.

Who doesn't like me.

Neither of them does.

Never, ever, ask me again about your family."

Candidly, the strident timbre and pauses were at no more than their general level after failed intimacy.
Frankly, when introduced to them at the same gallery, his girls had not taken to Alice.

"Way too much makeup pater"

"Battered haddock "

Basically, the issue was his and clearly the fault.
Simple enough contrition, for any sinner to admit.

Losers had never been Alice's thing.
Even though the one-time leggy adolescent, destined for classical dance, had been trained too tardily at boarding school, to have made the grade to the Royal Ballet school.
Later, she would complete a maths degree, for which she had a remarkable aptitude, but it gave her

15

little personal kudos.

Someone, unable to relinquish hold on an issue which vexed her, she had believed she was a step above the regular in dance and lived for her contact with it.

Exampled wordlessly, following the accusing ballerina's backward stare, by her dry cleaning or groceries, passing automatically for Thomas to carry. In 'life 'or seeing the ballet; she coexisted with the professionals; she believed were equals.

One repeating piece of theatre had been compelling.

After finding a favourite table, as they had that morning, trading barbs between the silences, they had sat overlooking the postcard view of St Paul's.

For no reason determinable, she had loosened a fibril to the universe.

"You have more brains than sense, *Thomas.* "

Speedily divested of her coat, she stood up, eyes to the horizon, full of avarice, to 'speak out' attending celebrants of any persuasion; without ever seeming to be searching. Her stealth dance was moves in a standing choreography to the four compass points: miming small adjustments of every moving skeletal part while settling the day's costume. A second act would follow the move back from the lady's room; another scout filled with imaginative diversionary feints, meant to mystify an ex-lover or everyone else she had assumed would be watching.

16

That morning, another round of expensive milky coffee had added unneeded caffeine to a temperamental confidant, allowing way too much time to badger him.

His poem had become the sweet-smelling apple pie with cloves, left sitting on the kitchen sill to cool.

A major temptation to a dancing blackbird.

"So now I suppose you want me to critique it. "

However unsatisfactory, this untitled verse might have been, the matter could have rested there, had he just said no.

Once introduced, despite her tone, he had liked the suggestion way too much.

For some reason, it had been intimate sharing difficult topics with her.

Over a home ground, much less powerful brew the following morning, Alice was permitted to read his short work, joining the cycle of foolishness on hugely masculine mistakes.

After edgy silence before the read, she had intoned it with a performer's empathy for his words.

Half-heartedly, he had attempted to stop the recitation, but she had sounded so professional, he had let her continue to the end.

Without the excuse of too much concentrated Museum caffeine, irradiating approval had inflated full discredit to a calumny, turning a vain part-time poet into a perilously stupid one.

"It's your poverty-stricken Catholic family, with five children in a council flat, isn't it.

"Six.
My brother died. "
"Wow, angry boy. Very cunning. "

"I made a drawing of the old place too.

"Really?
You must let me see that."

Directly, after accepting the praise, however warranted or not it may have been, he had let slip, word of the fuller prose tome of which his tempestuous friend was only instinctively aware.
She had hinted that she knew it; but it was a guess.

A notion well beyond her comprehension, when eventually told it.

Vicariously, and more characteristic than his silence, Thomas confessed his truth to her.
Fumbling for the words, which had flown so effortlessly onto his pages, he had explained her suspicions were correct.
But much worse.
A novel had been started.
The central character had been named after her.
A different character, but the same name.

Overriding patient resolve, the need for absolution was his reason.

A dizzy author had to end the strain put on a difficult friendship by not asking her permission.

The surprise shocked sulk out of the house of art, with coat and bag overly cuddled tightly into her arms, was fully choreographed without a full audience.

Total silence between the pair had been his compensation.

Alice was never a woman to cross.

Wilful according to most, even by her own account, she had never been obedient.

Even as a child.

A Vietnam war hero father would boast of her crossness with her first demands for breast milk; drawn from a mother's tepid source; to give up entirely on news of his test-pilot death.

Though not by many, or directly, to her worshipping mother's face, the spirited temper had been blamed on resulting maternal over-protection.

The single parent's lifelong self-castigation for an inability to nourish her baby girl would be exploited by the fully grown 'Madame', whenever the situation suited. Conscious of her dusky languid graces, the manipulative waves came as second nature.

Especially to someone with her own, hidden secret.

Soon he had mollified her first strop with the drawing he made in relation to his fraternal poetic rant.

Only then had communications been restored.

And not all.

That final disaster was achieved, after recompense of a read of the first part of the book to date.

A few sampling pages were wet finished, including the poem.

Reading them in one tortured afternoon, her fury had turned boundless.
A rage to continue at hells-fire-pace seemingly forever.
Approval always had been a prerequisite to starting the publishing process.
He would continue to assert; he was never published.

Ignorance of appearing in it without consent was by far the worst crime ever to be committed against her person.
Or any other.

Knowing it had put her at a disadvantage, she would erupt at the oddest times; at the thought of the betrayal; producing memorable attacks, spoken hatefully under her breath as if he was not present.

Remembering the insult, suddenly, as if given death's date, she would become inconsolable. Picking carefully, through every sentence, she had memorialised his dialogue to a surprisingly continuing relationship, which at the very least had been tricky.

CHAPTER ONE

" There is no such thing as a Painting without a subject." Mark Rothko.

Swaying, just perceptibly, painter Sam Lawrence was standing to rapturous attention, near to but not touching what had once been a pure white distempered wall. Subsequent years of working his larger canvases against it had taken their toll, for when the muse took him Sam was not an overly careful technician; the spill of his oil paint speckled and splashed, haphazardly all over the area in the multitudinous shades of a formidable double decade palate.

'Extraordinary.'

Presently, with his steel-rimmed 'specs,' held circumspectly by his side, he was in such proximity to the pock-marked wall he could not focus on it even with a lifetime of short-sightedness. From this odd viewpoint, he discovered, he could immerse himself in a spectacular pointillist oblivion, made by his own hand without the need of a single deliberate brush stroke, or the worry of one conscious colour choice. Truly, abstract Nirvana.

Maybe the representation of emptiness was the solution to his morning's riddle.

'Zero is an even number.'

Today's self-set task was to meditate on 'nothing.'

More simply put, he was trying to imagine what it might look like, so he could paint it.

"Really extraordinary.'

Blissfully, rocking his head to and fro, in time to Mahler's 1000 on his sound system, he had held the position for several satisfying minutes, congratulating himself on his genius.

Wanting to investigate the spectacular visual phenomenon further, instinctively replacing his glasses, he leant back slightly. Unfortunately, with this sudden shift in perspective, he was able to recognise the undeniable provenance of his painterly paradise.

"Oh, piss on it. That's Jackson Pollock."

With recognition of the American master, who already had attached the splattered visual high ground to himself for all time, Sam's imagined heavens came tumbling in on him. Tortuously, he pulled away from the old dried-paint surface in frustration, as he would have from a faithless lover. Not that there was any such person in his life at present.

Nor was there likely to be soon, according to his long-suffering wife Alice.

Citing her much-diminished libido as the reason for certainty.

"Jackson pissing Pollock".

Annoyingly, this could not be the path to any graphic analogy of emptiness. Above all else, Sam prided himself on his originality; a career-long striving turning the painter's life into a quest, much to his family's misfortune.

His highly trained eye normally would have recognised most any twentieth-century painter of note, immediately. Constantly studying styles, he had prided himself on naming names without the need for a gallery label. Willing himself into this accidental wonderland, so conveniently located on his studio wall, he had duped himself for well on ten minutes. A style he was not only familiar with but one he actively disliked and spoke out against. Not ready to reflect on this conundrum, or on his inability to complete what had looked like such a simple little task, abruptly, if temporarily, it interrupted a morning's search for the truth.

"Nothing."

Giving himself more 'seeing' space, he had turned away from the dunce's position in the corner and forced his spectacles back down on his strong but attractive nose,
Moving back into the heart of his large studio, he was ready to start work.
Even without an idea in his head, Sam had needed to paint.

Always at least one canvas positioned on his seven hundred pounds ("that's sterling not ounces") ratcheted oak- easel all the way from Rome. Presently, the canvas positioned there was an imposing four by four-foot virgin white one, without a mark on it.

He made his way to it, clumsily, aiming an air kick at an invisible diversionary devil on the way.

He shouted at no one in particular.

"Fucking nothing."

Given the task set for himself, he missed the irony of his eruption.

The chance reading of a newspaper article was the inspiration for his current preoccupation with vacuity. Temptingly, the previous day, between tube stops at Piccadilly Circus and Gloucester Road, occupying an otherwise vacant seat, had been a day's old, discarded Weekend Guardian. Its front page had been covered with deep brown circular stains, smelling heavily of cappuccino. This 'rag' of a newspaper, or so he believed, had 'savaged' him, in a review of his one-man exhibition the year before. The actual offence was running their few words on a single line while including the gallery opening times. Despite his ban on 'never ever reading it again', instinctively he grabbed at the free second-hand copy of the up-market broad-sheet, just beating a young Arab boy with piercing eyes to the draw. Taking the seat, it had occupied, Sam kept the body of the newspaper, while placing the unopened plastic bag with supplements between him and the glass side panel to the seat. Like its previous owner neither were huge buyers of perfume.

Despite his year-long boycott of the paper, he had devoured an entire article on "meditation on the single word."
Hence the current preoccupation.

Off the train again, he had stuffed the main newspaper securely deep into a council trash bin outside his station; so, no one else would be encouraged to read the filthy rag. Left to distract those more consumer-orientated travellers, the supplements are long forgotten.
Sam was able to think of little else but that single word 'nothing' for the next few hours.

Grumpily, and finally the artist recognised his creativity was a temporary deserter.

.

"Bullshit! That is a single word."

Smiling, momentarily, he accepted it was probably two.

"Buddhist bullshit."

The new avenging mantra brightened him. He repeated it.

"Buddhist bullshit."

Though disconsolate, but by no means defeated, he soon was back flying down the familiar thought path.

"Nothing?"

He sat down on a tall upright stool by his extensive mobile work desk; supplied plentifully, with paper, paint, conte chalk, and indeed any media, he had desired to work in.

"NOTHING."

Still unable to work, he sipped, contemplatively, at a mug of lukewarm green tea he made for himself, using a tea bag and his wife's electric kettle, a present to him at Christmas. He had read somewhere, it might even have been in the Guardian, this brew was a 'hedge' against Alzheimer's; the vegetative state he had nightmares about ending up in.

There followed further minutes of intense, moody introspection.
They had passed silently; save for his whistling breaths.

Then, rudely, a novel solution had squirrelled itself into his cortex; an idea, which made him hiss. An involuntary sound, very much like the wince, only angrier.

27

"Jesus no."

Being an artist and having long ago reasoned all such brothers were born different, not bound by common conventions, he had no problem conducting, loud, heated discussions with himself.

The preposterous new idea proposing itself immediately posited a further noisier problem.

"Maybe by making a film?"

Microseconds before he had delivered this awkward question to himself, he had already formed its disparaging reply, signalling the start of a regular tirade against 'Modernism'.

"I'm a painter."

Though his work, exclusively, was about the 'modern condition', where moving images were referenced, habitually, films per-say were not his kind of art.

"I'm a figurative painter."

He reassured himself in a tone, if he were not alone, would still not have allowed for any discussion.

Most of his pronouncements, even in company, were couched in a similar mocking fashion.

Sam reckoned you had to know your mind to be a successful Artist.

Be a bit selfish.

'Like a priest.' Cézanne had said.

For his whole lifetime, since grammar school certainly, oil painting had been his only calling; disparaging even the pencil or charcoal preparation.
After a glass or two of red wine, Sam would grudgingly admit drawing was not his forte.

Heavier even than the one he used to intensify the verb for the act of procreation, his finishing exhalation accentuated into a curse.

'And I don't do fucking installations."

Oil painting always had been his vocation; his religion.

"I'm a colourist."

Even his wife came second to it.

"I'm a painter."

Instinctively, though he was alone, he paused here for effect.
But with no audience for his views, bar himself, the victory for fine art received an

unexpected slowing.

" Video is shit."

Such 'shit', that the family Palm-corder deemed strictly the responsibility of his wife, invariably along for the ride, on research trips for his painting and lectures.

Unfortunately, there was nowhere else for the painterly spirit to go but down, into the vacant hanging silence of a studio with an unresolved problem and an empty canvas.

"God it's cold in here."

Truthfully, even cosseted by a second heavy jumper, it was freezing in his studio that morning. In a mid-winter cost-cutting measure he had turned off the central heating.
In anticipation of the frugality, his clothing comprised layers; recent impulse buys from the new Afghan mart at Bow, all ridiculously cheap and seemingly good quality.
The studio fuel bill, or at least part of it, was his responsibility.
Money was not all that tight.
He just liked to be careful, sensing that Alice was getting anxious again that he was not contributing to the household economy.
She had a well-paid job; even a little money behind her, when they had married, which had allowed them to buy the house thirty years ago.

A much grander property than his hired old school room. Presently, their mortgage-free home was worth more than he could ever earn in a lifetime; even if he were to start selling his paintings at the prices, he had deemed fair.

Sure, the council tax was heavy, but Alice's job with the N.H.S. gave her regular and quite large pay rises. How he had scoffed in those early days at all those dull people who had chosen this as their career path.

His top layer was a navy fleece giving him the retro look, not sported since Art school.

The fashion, then, was for Prussian-blue fisherman's polo-necks.

With distaste, he recalled the oil painting he had painted while wearing one. For years, right up to her death, this work had held a prime position in his mother's living room. The spot with the greatest OTS (opportunity to see) according to neighbour Jed who seemed to live in her house rather than his own next door. He had been once in Advertising. Dad was already long dead and buried. Against her Regency stripes that every two years changed colour and thickness but never direction, it had hung over the period mantelpiece, made of pale chocolate tiles, a colour he had found impossible to duplicate in oil paint. The portrait hair was black and shiny as coal, entirely foreign to the silver wire brush, grown in its place and that he had feared might be tonsuring at the back.

"I'm freezing"

Putting down his mug, he jumped up, instinctively, began to pump his arms rapidly, in huge bear hugs around himself to get the circulation going; instantly fathoming he was doing a very good imitation.

"Jesus. I've morphed into my father."

His voice flew aloft on clean breaths, transparent white from the cold.

After a check in the free-standing full-length Edwardian mirror inherited from Alice's family, set by his easel, he confirmed this undeniable parentage but avoided his search for a bald patch, flopping dejectedly, into the wheeled work office chair.

Just as he had with pigments, canvas and paper, Sam understood the materials for photography; he just had not approved of this kind of image-making.

For him, it was not art.

"Rubbish and a waste of money."

Film and video were expensive; he understood that, but not much else about them.

Nor had he care to.

Technology was for younger people and nerds.

Presently, his most cherished profanation.

"Nerds."

Momentarily, another thought enlightened, then instantly shamed him, remembering for several years he was the self-same way about computers; distrusting even ridiculing them before eventually Alice had persuaded him, they should buy one.
Then his whole attitude had changed completely.
Like a converted Catholic, he became the most fervent of believers, ultra-fond of roaming the Internet on his laptop baby. Soon his day was never complete till he had dealt with all his emails.
When his 'loved one' was not about, he had checked into the naughty stuff too. Truly there were images of people doing things on it he had never believed possible, let alone pleasurable.
Disturbingly, sunlight sliced abruptly into his private space through his tall windows kept spotless and by weekly cleaning. Loathing the Fulham filth, he had started a local group that paid for the whole street to be done, costing no more really than the once or twice-a-year jobs. Such fastidiousness, should, have welcomed this painterly source of all energy.
But while working or even looking at his pictures, he hated the sun shining directly on them.
It showed too many of the imperfections in the process of applying paint to canvas. Conversely, in other circumstances, he would

also argue, pictures were never supposed to be finished like the bodywork of a car.

Whirling his arms paternally at the luminous, "invisible" intruder, Sam stalked aggressively across his space, shooing away the offending god of light as if he was moving out a trespassing dog.

"Fuck off Metapotigue"

Dexterously, with the old shutters on each side of the windows, he deflected his unwanted intrusion.

"Fuck off"

Unfortunately, none of this was improving his mood.
Nor moving on his project.
Too many worldly things were invading the space in his brain where he wanted to see nothing.

It was a good hour before he could dare think about having a break.

Also, if anything, it was getting colder in the studio, so he thought to put on his dark blue woollen duffel coat.
Perhaps turning off the central heating was not such a wise choice.
Staring down hard at the polished hard floor between his legs, it might be an inviting place

from which to meditate on the world.

Moving off his chair, he went first onto his knees, then turning, he stretched himself out fully on his back, onto the floor.

He covered himself with his topcoat hung on the ratchet next to the easel.

Pulling over for an improvised pillow his copy of Ulysses, keeping the wheel of his desk stationary, it all felt very relaxing.

Years ago, he had spent a week trying to sand these hard slightly undulating pine floorboards, before giving up and paying a fortune to have the job finished, professionally.

Their high hard-gloss finish was pleasant on the back of his hands.

Momentarily, the aching all over his body ceased.

Supported firmly all the way along his back he felt he could sleep very easily here, like a Samurai warrior on his hard headrest.

Waking, after maybe a few milliseconds, somewhere close by the familiar sound of 'jingle bells' pierced the air.

It took a moment or two for him to remember it was his mobile.

It must be Alice calling.

For no reason he could remember, he felt hugely threatened but dared not ignore it.

Sitting upright, dexterously, he picked up the old but waring favourite and flipped it open with a click in a surprisingly fluid gesture for

someone, who was often gauche.
If there was a food spot to be flicked it would invariably end on his jumper.

"Just checking to see you had it switched on."

As usual, her tone was mild but with more than a hint of a determined teacher.

Bitterness never left her these days.

"Of course."

Though he could sometimes devastate her with his words,
Alice had come unresponsive to this arrogance.

Sam sounded more commanding than he had felt.
He adopted it over the years to keep people at bay.
Never understood, just how aggressive he came across.

"See ya later."

"And be nice to her."

"Yes dear."

Snapping dead the phone, he had no idea of

the "her" she was talking about.

Suddenly, the notion of nothing as a thousand mobile phones, with their cameras set inside a perfect sphere, viewing each other, jumped into his mind.

The new idea, immediately, consumed him.

"Wow, now that actually is nothing."

Standing up quickly, he headed straight for the work desk, pencil and paper.

Then diverted.

First, he would turn on the heating."

CHAPTER FIVE

Taking a breather at the end of her early morning route, a tall willowy blonde, anaemic rather than strawberry before treatment, grumbled to herself while doorstepping a hand delivery. A bad repeating rendition of Van Morisons 'like a ballerina 'tinkled on the door chime. Postman Zuleika's real concerns were on the seat placings for her and her friends at next month's Eurostar for a dance trip to Paris. In counterpoint, she began humming a catchy show tune; of an older balladeer than the gloomy Irish genius her client had favoured. After an impatient third push on the doorbell, the unwary blues fan had opened his stained-glass front door, and she was on him, ferocious as a timorous kitten, pouncing on its bobbling ball of wool.

Serenading in full school-girl contralto, she fanned him with a heavily stamped envelope.

"There may be trouble ahead.
but while there's moonlight and dancing.
let's face the music…and dance. "

His startled gaze shot to the busy thoroughfare at the end of the street, then back again, a pause long enough to cut dead any further attempts at humour.

Zu dispatched her special delivery.
Regrettably, with a full-lipped pout.

"Registered."

Forgetful in her eagerness to raise a smile, she had not reckoned with its damaging potential.

"I can see that Zu."

Sulkily, she checked the rim of her oversized postman's hat with two fingers to see if it was on straight. Hiding a short almost sheared haircut, it was without an adjustable- plastic back worn low as a dealer's eyeshade. Fortunately, the vogue of a 'catcher's' reverse mode had not predisposed this ex-Majesty's foot-soldier to any dated heterodoxy.

"Sorry mate; I forgot."

Grabbing at the letter more fiercely than he had intended, he grunted an inaudible acceptance of her apology.
Zuleika her birth name, same as a still active Gran, but no Dobson, a relocated, Bethnal Green Goldsmith, in the simpering discourse of what was and what was appropriate for the male of the species, she always felt able to speak to the contrary view.

"Same trouble as 'imeros Mate "

"'IMEROS?"

With irresistible winks to the lascivious brother to the great god Eros, her history had been garnered from an antiquities graduate turned woman's tailor.

"No, HIM mate; HIMEROS.
'Twin to man God of love.
Desire's ugly face.
Used to put it about all over the place regardless."

Ending a thought with an adjective and quoting obscurely was an affectation copied from the less-bosomed mate with whom she had tangoed as the girl half in a bi-weekly salsa class.

But such male roughness prompted its own properly aggressive repost.

"She loves her Irvine Berlin."

The "she"', was the never-seen guardian, identified by the 'Laura' tattoo, on the post-girl's wedding finger.
Often referenced in their morning chats together, both the client and her 'friend' were aged above thirty; so, assuming to enjoy similar older person activities.

Struggling to regain composure, Thomas was in sweaty running gear after a run and could only manage a mumble of his avocation to wariness; further stoking anguish, the envelope stamped franked and sealed according to its hostile protocol, the Borough logo identified in the bottom right-hand corner. Apprehension turned to real fury at the people responsible for his scrutiny.

Zu tried to be conciliatory.

"Have a nice jog mate?"

Innocence, protected by plenty of sunblock, mixed with the distinctive aroma of Vic vapour rub was apparent as she leaned toward him. Adding to the bitterness of a paid-up taxpayer, already hugely conspired against, the offending missive required a signature.

Aware, that happiness seldom travelled by registered mail, he believed he was forced into acknowledging the 'wretched thing' together with his current whereabouts.

"There, on that line, if you don't mind mate."

She offered him a tablet and a plastic pen to squiggle with.

Years in 'therapy' had taught him to avoid the perfect aspect.

Pausing for an embarrassed beat, he searched for inspiration in the gaze of his mail deliverer.

After so many hours on the internet, with ever more ways to identify himself, the homeowner could have argued he was too familiar with digit passwords to include one capital letter. Nodding a certain smile in her direction, he raised an imagined finger to nebulous authority, endorsing her package with a reproachful flourish, substituting his name with that of a notorious old joker.

"Bernard Manning."

The drollness of his new identity reinvigorated him.

Ever efficient at reading the signature on her slate, she re-presented it; accompanied by the stick. Despite her age, she knew the comic.

"He's dead mate."

"Really?"

No deviant child was ever so wide-eyed.

"Yea. Right old fascist."

Her copy resigned, this time with his own name, it was quickly, returned.

"He was me granddad's favourite too, mate."

Immediately, a characteristically responsive male was chilled by his choice of celebrity, worrying it had dated him.

Turning to head back to her colourful stroller parked on the pavement stuffed full of other people's mail, it was obvious the post could tarry no longer.
Confusingly, as it had been on previous mornings, after her farewell, he had received the familiar raised eyebrow, with the departing 'come-hither' shake, daring him to follow.

Grounding himself sensibly, an easily swayed amorist was attentive that this attractive person, much more inclined toward her own sex; unquestionably, was two decades out of the flexible age range permitted by his grown daughters.

Earnestly, clutching the delivery in his free hand, Thomas closed his heavy front door; thus, the warming view of a long, lean gently curving rear, further dangerous intercourse was brought to its conclusion.

Albeit with a heavy sigh.

After a deep intake of breath to relieve the tension, one 'Dear Citizen of the Borough' then had established the missive he held in his hand had said what he thought it would say.

Only to boil over again at the sight of its contents.

Giddily defensive whenever the use of their powers was questioned, and the reclusive committee overseeing all 'surveillance' issues in the West London area had replied negatively to the complaint made by him.

Several vociferous complaints but only one in writing.

The heavy blunt instrument wielded so effortlessly at 'Bernard Manning's' real concerns for privacy was caste from an alloy, one part police brass, the other local council steel.

The catalyst for its fusion a self-aggrandising view up its own rectitude.

At least according to his way of thinking.

The registered letter answer contained a single

formula-typed sheet of paper, tersely informing the homeowner he had not been successful in his written bid for a review of a 'security' judgement made against him.

CHAPTER SIX

'Amo, amas, amant,'

To the declining beat of the ancient verb to love, ingrained internally by his hated Latin master at Catholic Grammar School, the middle-aged creative, sat morosely at his desk, rhythmically dispatching flattened staples from a small pistol-like-machine for the clicks they had made. To this point in a long morning, he had succeeded in reviewing, only the preface to his short autobiographical parables in the form of a novel; inspirational categorising, after the late journalist Dominic Dunne.

Thomas would be publishing under his own name.

Instinctively, when questioned about his heritage, in his commercial film director career in America, T. H. Maher, would credit himself being one hundred percent British. With a Shavian lilt to the surname pronounced Ma as in mother, he would then explain an Irish Catholic inheritance, in which he had little pride.

"Amus, amatis, amant".

After retirement from making Advertising films, a business riddled with ageism, in his attempt at an early second vocation, he would gladly be free of the treasures passed down by a London-Irish grandfather. Same name, d the limited special education; most assuredly the pale sun-sensitive freckled skin with the hair of a potato farmer. A dry-humoured cinematographer on a Florida film shoot, to too much laughter, had asked him to put his shirt back on, during a sunny afternoon filming; claiming his director had been acting as a white reflector, thereby blinding his actress, making her unable to open her eyes for the close-up.

Truman Capote had been a blonde, but who honestly would have conceived of the dashing Byron as carrot-topped?

Shakespeare had been bald; according to the single known portrait.

Good modern world men Thomas felt, ought to have dark hair.

Like Harold Pinter.

Certainly, my favourite modern poets, Cohen and Dylan, both were black-haired Jews.

Momentarily, he considered whether either of them might have succumbed to the dye bottle and accepted the actuality. Without the courage to dwell, he had noted both wore hats on stage these days, often a sign of a balding musician.

"Amo, amas, amant, amamus, amatis,"

His own fair hair was far too long, mostly intact but grey.

For the artist-formerly just once known as 'Bernard Manning, was using no non-de-plume in his work.

After weeks of considering the highly charged

issue, nurturing the idea since art school that he had a novel in him, its time had come.

T. H. Mather would write this book.
That decided he had switched effortlessly to other innervations.

Currently easily available on the list, local civilian Council had been filed under 'obdurate'.

A bursting category diminishing by the monetary cost of work over the years since he had categorised it, to include doctor and dental receptionists, bank answer-phone personnel, branch bank managers; ministers; et al. A prejudice, to his shame, doubling in urgency, if the offender had been critical of him with a Scottish accent. Which in his defence they often had been. Endeavouring to curb his bent, indeed all unhealthy racist traits, his long-time therapist, Barbara, left long ago in downtown New York City, could not conceive of a reason for this bias; other than the Dundee-born lady he had divorced.

Though still talking, it had been twelve years of separation before they had divorced officially, and she took dual citizenship.

Having worked harmoniously for years in the most pulsating American City, Thomas had been a freelance commercial film director. His final contract had been with a company owned and staffed, excepting himself, by African Americans, who had liked to joke; he had been their token white.

Only a small contrition, but a whiff of evidence against serial racism.

47

With working-class beginnings, Thomas believed that he understood the London council people he had been fighting; didactic white, middle-class moderates to a man.

Well to a man, plus, one determined mid-life beauty.

A once New Labour Mayor from the Home Counties. She was of Swedish extraction, who once had been a live strip-a-gram and a fervent Buddhist. According assuredly this time by the Guardian.

Regrettably, the rest of the 'security gang' saw crooks and thieves everywhere; a growing national neurosis extended to include terrorists.

Recently, after he had worked for some considerable amount of time in America, the sometime painter had returned to live in the streets, where he had spent his childhood. Through several fortuitous, some torturous circumstances, he had become the owner of his old, once-rented family townhouse.

Council 'titled' but not council 'built'.

After he had made the extensive renovations needed to the good-sized Edwardian property, in a neighbourhood changed beyond all recognition, it carried a heavy mortgage.

At least, it had been heavy at the time he took it out.

By current, younger peoples' standards, it had been a pittance.

Paradoxically, he had bought his deceased parents' house, directly from the self-same council, after it had turned a loathed Tory blue.

On his regular returns from France to Fulham, long since they had flown the family nest, whenever his girls had 'visited', both were curious about the development of this 'work'; unafraid to offer help. Mostly in the form of acidic criticism.

They had felt it their duty, like all loving daughters to forbid things like the Vincent hat, otherwise to amuse the world and themselves at his expense.

Casually, but with learnt female precision, his poesy was discovered in his unlocked desk and dissected, in a trio that he was allowed no air.

Harshly it had concluded the verses made without the sense a fair man would have argued.

'Can't have you shaming us with any old rubbish Pops."

A silenced Thomas would have to be content that his angry song without music had made it into even its present limited circulation.

"Stick to your paintbrush, Pater"

It was agreed he could make drawings if he had so desired.

To illustrate the continuing fury, he had hoped to dampen with creativity.

Resting his tongue, wisely; he had not explained the etching that had been completed.

In his beloved home space, in what he had hoped
was an accessible way, the lifelong socialist,
occupied himself, rendering ancient ideas into
graphic modern-day, images.

The overall genus was to explain, how, someone
like himself might create.

Thinking about zero as an even number was a
current initiative.

This exploration for his youngest, Em, arguing
against fact, was for her more than a touch fey.

"Zero can't be even. Dah.

Nothing is nothing, papa."

Finding the notion something of a puzzle himself,
Thomas had moved from noughts to circles, then to
spheres, and finally to Pythagoras; to the
mathematician's theory of the divinity of a perfect
sphere provable theorem.

"If equal and similar spheres surrounded the
'sublime' form, their number will always be twelve".

"We did that for our second year at Uni.
V hard to draw."

Another genuine redhead, like her mother, Av
was his eldest.

A Philosophy graduate, she had gained a first in a
discipline chosen to study by default in a harried late

application to college.

Not entirely comfortable with so esoteric a life choice, on graduation she had decided to defer her 'Masters' till later. Which she had passed honourably.

Currently, she was pursuing a career as a stand-up, explaining her father's interest in reading anything on the topic, why Bernard Manning's name had tripped so easily from his tongue.

'Daddy' had been reading the comic's recent biography.

"You're 'elitist' papa."

Terms used by his daughters to define the relationship status to their parents, he had learnt over time, were an indication of their mood. Not entirely him.

"And very High end"

This charge would never be levelled at his offspring if her sister had been believed.

Thus far, 'dear old Pappé', to his intense relief, had not been allowed to attend a single of her 'gigs' to judge the filth for himself.

Pythagoras had made 'twelve' the root number of all his intimates.

Over the centuries, it would become the means for off-shoot faiths derived from his beliefs.

As many others had noted before, it was a dozen apostles to follow Christ, over two millennia later.

Thus far the ancient concept had been translated by him into a medicine-ball-sized tetrahedron, made of thirteen clear plastic balls with the centre, or God ball, realised in gold.

"Can you sit on it?"

Responding to Av's kookiness, not yet entirely, sure he was not caricaturing himself; he had agreed, it was a work in progress.

"I prefer the pinned-up stories you did for all your alchi friends."

"Especially the one on Mr Kent."

Mister Kent was a silver birch bought as a sapling at a nursery in Sandwich Kent and replanted in the garden.

"Stars and the Book of the Dead; v permissible legends."

Em worked in the film business, behind the cameras.

"Words from the virgin Mary herself."

Both sisters regarded all her views on Film entirely, unimpeachable.

"Virgin, sis?"

"So, to speak."

Even in the spring of their praise, it was not long before thorns of summer would appear amongst the roses.

"And comics with C.G.I."

"Otherwise, no one gets it."

"We have no attention span, dearest, old one."

"Written words' are for describing the special effects."

"Only way to make cash from all this art stuff."

Another of his recent written short works elaborated on the basic elements of visual art', exploring the old theories of light.
How they related to the visual world.
To 'improve' old concepts, in his view, you first needed to understand basic maths and have a clear idea of physics.

"Like the fact that light travels in a straight line?"

"Euclid c. 325-265 BC."

"To become, more 'lucid? eh, Pops."

"Shame you never made it."

Both girls had been curious about his communication from the council when they came upon the letter in a rummage through his mail. They had liked to check the bank statements in his case they had needed to borrow cash.

Before he discovered he could go 'paperless'.

"What's this letter from the council."

Three months before to further invade and clarify their near-sighted vision, the ever-suspicious Borough Security Committee had wanted to fix a wrinkle in their wobbly 'Maginot' line against crime. Unhappily for his peace of mind, its demarcation line came too close to home. A council review had ruled that the North-End- Road fruit market falling like his property, under their authority, should be beefed up by the addition of colour cameras with larger memory chips. Since its inception, its present system recorded only sporadic sightings of the dangerous flotsam it had been established to search out. Miraculously, having survived several decades without any security at all, the famous old street market had continued to function, even during the blitz; albeit, at a very low level, selling cans of government powdered egg and a few hard potatoes.

"Means you will have to put on your dress when you go shopping pater."

Used as a dressing gown over other clothes, Thomas owned a floor-length black Shin priest gown, custom-made for him in Hong Kong, which he had liked to work in.

They had hated it.

But he never, ever, went out in the street wearing it.

"Have to put on some make-up".

In the campaign for the garments burning, both the girls had found the idea of him wearing foundation unspeakably funny,

"And shave his legs".

After only minor protests, the orders to upgrade market security had been followed, with specified cameras duly installed.

To the random streams of shoppers, these efforts affected to protect, blinded by simple human serendipity, and sheer familiarity, continued as usual, ignoring them.

A trait, easy enough to predict, but one by which a growing multitude had encouraged the frittering away of a precious freedom.

The innocent right to remain anonymous; releasing its antithesis; the disease of specious celebrity.

In his creative work, he was not concerned just to be known.

His efforts were to satisfy the need for unique experience.

To explain ideas, primarily to himself.

Contemporaneously, fame was often only for recognition; of someone, or something.

In his view, this could never be art.

Nor something made by an artist.

"That's why you spend all day on the internet Poppa?"

Drinking at the heady internet fountains; or more appropriately a metaphor at its water coolers, he would not admit to immunity to the pleasures of the search for celebrity news.

He had found it relaxing.

"Half an hour at the very most I should think. ".

"You said we SHOULD never say 'should' daddy."

"Another way of saying you gotta."

Within the lattice of traditional wheeled barrow-stalls strung together down the east side between the cross streets, one of the new electronic eyes with a sharper focus and more precise site-lines was installed high up on a street corner lamppost. Uniquely, positioned there because of overcrowding on its designated home pole, it could see further than the market thoroughfare, into the end of the adjacent street, i.e. his street, by about the length of a cricket pitch.

For those unfamiliar with the great invented game; wicket to wicket on the shiny red leather ball bowling 'strip' was exactly 22 yards.

Or in metric currency, just a little over 20 meters.

A once considerate E.U. had allowed devotees in its collective to still think, legally, in dozens, pounds, or even leagues, if they had wished.

Though cubits, to his knowledge, wasn't assessed.

That magical measure was his endless ponder.

To make a work using its dimension. The exactness was known from a line carved into the limestone at Gaza when the pyramid was built.

After his morning jog, lazing on top of his large double bed with an extra firm mattress, a sweaty but house-proud owner was reading his morning Guardian. Before taking a shower, his attention was caught by a glint through his '' sash windows net-curtains and the London grime. Cleaned, professionally that very morning, it was a weekly occurrence paid for by someone who hated grime.

Alas, the energy of the sun god Ra bounced into his bedroom off the filtered front of a too closely situated lens.

"What the....."

To verify a dismally perceived perspective, he jumped up off his bed and fled downstairs, still in his long-running shorts, with his feet, hurriedly stuffed into knurled comfortable old trainers with the laces untied. Walking outside his front door, he 'long paced' the twenty-two strides, determinedly, to his street corner, careful not to trip on the ties.

Turning, when he had reached the previously detailed lamppost in the already heady buzz of the market, he looked back at his house, simply astounded. Even at this low level, there was much too clear a view up to a self-portrait he had painted while at Art College, which hung on the wall behind his bed. The higher-up camera's view must have been straight into his en-suite bedroom; the very same one he would give up to a daughter to use when they visited with a friend.

"Oh my god. Thank God we could never do it in there."

"Too much information sis."

By chance, incidental to its major job of hunting criminals and terrorists, the over-sensitive watcher was centred on his house. It gave him an unasked and unwanted twenty-four-hour surveillance, which h he had maintained, forcefully, would have been an encroachment on anyone's rights to privacy.

Recorded, electronically, 4.2 million, vigilant, moving-photo-opportunists, he learnt from further research, make imperishable digital images of almost every citizen walking the streets, lawbreaker or not, by their thousands, if not in their hundreds of thousands, every second, of every day in the kingdom. Clearly, the capacity to properly supervise such a growing mountain of information could not exist.

'Gait DNA', a new individual code for the way one walks, also had been recently enacted.

A system by which the facial image could be matched to gait, height and weight; so, a computer would be able to identify any person on its database; instantly. Just as Kubrick had predicted, these things did not need the cooperation of an individual and would run themselves.

When discovered, the new English Colonial had been the first to be exposed to 'the mother of all' visual recording devices, the Victorian 'stills' camera. Native victims had believed any photograph taken of a man, stole his soul, thus he would never be able to find his way to paradise. Igniting a magnesium powder flash at him was worse even than spiting off a few chambers of the service revolver. With such a faith, modern life would have been for him, merely, the preamble to everlasting Hell.

Feeling something important had been stolen from him, even an enthusiastic agnostic was filled with sympathy for those long-departed souls with a viewpoint allowing, only the housebound any chance at eternal resurrection.

Jostled by the flow and slightly red-faced, after kneeling and retying his laces, the angry anxious artist had stormed back to his home to make a few calls.

In the next few days, an undisputed homeowner, however much he had harassed the authorities was never allowed to access what had been filmed,
i.e. his house and its human activity.

These images, he had been told, were off-limits' to him or any regular civilian.

"Put up some net curtains if you don't like it."

This despite every available statistic confirming London town, his town, had become the highest remote-controlled-camera urban environment in the Universe.

The facts simply staggered.

"Unbelievable, Pops."

"You have to sue."

Truly, he felt, he needed to be acknowledged; somehow.

Hence his written request.

A curious visitor from the fashionable creative destination of Mars also might cite the unique checks on the British railway system, to exemplar the extremeness of our current national angst against their fellow countrymen.
Of suspecting ourselves to be a tribe of thieves in need of continuous monitoring.

Tickets on our trains were scrutinised at the beginning, at the end, and often in the middle of a journey; using up enormous amounts of passenger time, patience, money and their own railways' manpower; which maybe could be used, usefully, elsewhere.

Like checking that video footage.

Ticket collecting happens once and once only on the New York Subway; by passing through a barrier at the start of a journey, in the once dangerous and always neurotic City.

On the 'laissez faire' Metro in Paris, similar ticket collection methods apply.
This was a rail link he happened to use regularly, albeit briefly, to get across town when changing trains to southern France.

His English property, incidentally, was in a south-westerly London suburb; more correctly speaking, a borough. Property-wise, in easy reach by public transport of the notorious Chelsea district, the richest Borough in the UK, it too was 'desirable'.

Well before the worldwide financial crash, and therefore not to blame for it, large estates in Britain, mostly, had passed on to less Aristocratic birth lines.
A complex, for outsiders, an ultra-difficult, English ranking system includes townhouses in its overall 'class' league table.

Contrary to hopeful liberal media discourse, these classifications were up and running, as strong as they had ever been. Under the right circumstances, urban property in places south of Watford would score heavy points; but granted still not as high as the traditional old-school accent (badly modified by apparent cross-Atlantic and hip-hop connections).

After pregnancy, itself an almost essential for full class status, the correct, most expensive buggy was no longer a solely female status prerogative, but an absolute necessity. Even for the male of the couples in the far-flung outposts of the recolonised Wandsworth and Clapham Commons.

Suffice to conclude, the obsessive British pastime of talking house prices, done at all levels of society, was creating another chasm between the rich and the poor. His house done up, tastefully, with four beds, two reception rooms, and two baths, that for maximum profit should have been three, and with a kitchen extension, would have been the estate agent's dream: even in these terrible times.

In case, it appears otherwise, because of his two-house property 'portfolio,' these were the moves of a prudent 'creative' who had invested at the right time in his old family house.

He was not a rich, business, person.

He was a man who had worked all his life on associated things,

To allow himself to indulge in his art later, on a full-time basis.

However, as Euclid must have missed, when first he wrongly observed the straightness of the line in which light had travelled, the appearance of the objects it illuminates can sometimes be exceedingly, deceptive. As modern man knows, all energy including light travels in waves.

CHAPTER SEVEN

On a random search of the local station waste bin, few of the city-suited rush hour travellers, streaming passed in numbers, registered even a glance at the young Pakistani. Myopically concerned with hurrying home to well-insulated houses and expensive worker 'cottages, these were the majority which had encouraged the heavier security near Chelsea football club.

The universal expression of superior indifference carried by resident faces was accepted safety, needed on the club's home game days when the expensive streets had been overrun for a few hours by West London's football-loving masses; many of whom, barely, a generation before, had populated them, and still believed it their property.

Thomas had lived five streets away most of his early life.

Shiny imitation black-leather jacket off, sleeves rolled high up on pencil slim arms, dark skin exposed zero body fat and impossibly long muscles competed for thickness with his protruding bones. More of an oddity to the area, his intelligent face covered in a fine dark down thickened around his side-burns eyebrows lips and chin; indicating it would not be long before he was the owner of a first Muslim beard.

As he laboured, Benjamin had two expressions;

one, intense; with huge brown eyes, full of childish wonder with no apparent change in colour between iris and pupil; the other, beatific, and radiating pure pleasure, even at a time, when it might have seemed inappropriate.

Religiously, without tearing a single page he extricated the folded-up sections of the newspaper he had been searching for. Stained and still smelling strongly of coffee, the well-worn Guardian, obviously, was a highly prized find. Smoothing down his shirt sleeves, his bomber jacket had been on in a moment, the newspaper stuffed up under it. Moving with limber grace the school-boy jackal was soon invisible again amongst the swarming droves, surging after his afternoon prey. In no time at all, he had caught up with the man in the hairy Harris tweed suit, Nike boots and beacon red socks, the cause of so much trouble.

There was no inkling for Thomas that he was followed.

Worryingly, as it steadily darkened, the newspaper felt to the boy not bulky enough, slipping down under his jacket. Fear increasing with every bounding step, he had yanked it out for inspection. Still at an easy walking pace with his track in sight, knowing the exact number of pages, he was able to check the paper while on the move. All thirty-six were in place. Clutching again under his jacket, agonisingly he understood that the magazine section with all the ads had been missing. Certain he had extracted everything of value from the waste

65

bin, his loss would mean big trouble later, when he got home. Not from his parents, Allah forbid, for they knew nothing of his assignment. But from his elder sibling who had set up and paid for the operation.

Secretly, this special magazine edition had been spliced with hidden driver's licences and social security cards that he had helped his brother print; and sealed into a clear plastic bag with the edge of his mother's steam iron, when their sealer machine had broken down. The youngest son of an indulgent immigrant family had not properly internalised what it meant to play in his brother's dangerous games.

Till about half an hour before.

The childish notion it was 'cool', to play in a revolution, evaporated into the stuffy air of a crowded tube compartment, under the hated glares of three over-muscled policemen. Turned instantly to terror, the conspicuously un-Guardian reader, knew the fruits of his sibling's dishonest labour, the disruptive content, other than the opine of its Socialist scribes, tucked bulkily under his arm, needed to be speedily got rid of. Casually, as he could manage; dropped surreptitiously onto the train seat as someone else's discarded rubbish.

Of late there had been talk in the community of the stop and search of his Muslim brothers on the underground, The evil-looking group of black-clad, unmarked 'heavies' were further down the carriage looked ominous. After a lingering study, they had lost interest in him; dismissed him as just too young for a terrorist. Moving as one off the train as the doors closed at the next station, the last man out, confirmed his armed police identity by exposing a holstered side-arm to him with a smile. By the time the boy had looked back to his dangerous package, the 'British guy' had 'half-hitched' it.

Standing market side of Thomas's street corner, Benji had delivered the bad news to his brother on his iPhone. Purchased by his 'flush' relative for exactly this kind of emergency, it was a treasured and envied possession. But a secret one to his mother.

It was kept well-hidden and muted, to have been used in his murder if she had ever found it.

Hardly a year out of school himself, his elder sibling was working as a legitimate printer during the day. In the evenings had started making facsimiles of documents in his spare time. Mostly for money, because he could. After he had made a few replica car tax discs, the word spread of his facility through the less scrupulous car dealerships in the suburb. Bearded political 'friends' had come calling. They had money. Lots of it. They had wanted other things done. The stuff to breed revolution. With their help, an elaborate digital printer had been purchased. A scruffy one-bedroom room had been rented to store it in his real name.

After a fierce lingering telephone interrogation by his irate relative, and the inevitable dressing down, Benji was clicked off, abruptly, left to his own devices.

Replacing his handset in his pocket with the insolence of youth he smiled, broadly to himself.

Not unduly worried by the outburst, but thankful not to be in custody, he had had the foresight to get paid in advance for this job.

You could never be too sure with his big brother, who though always was flush would often get" forgetful" around people he owed money to. The price Benji bartered for this job was an official red Arsenal cap, which he had carefully drawn from his bomber jacket pocket and placed on his head, solemnly as a prelate's barrette. Worn in these fervent Chelsea streets, it might have been the most dangerous part of his mission. Unnecessarily, righted a second, then a third time, thus with full London Street incognito, he departed alien turf wearing the badge of his adored team. Heading home for a certain dressing down from his mother for arriving so late, another radiant white tooth grin broke out. It was Friday and was anticipating his favourite fish and chip tea.

CHAPTER EIGHT

Autobiography in the form of a novel.'

Following Dominic Dunne's style in his Simpson trial book, the category Thomas had chosen to write in was proving difficult. Eager to stay positive, he was imagining criticism for admitting lying in his preface, working himself into disproportionate misery. He had reassured with the thought he had never heard the journalist he was copying, disavow his own Truman Capote affectations.

An avid reader of new work critics, Thomas began recognizing his naiveite; that novel writing worked in other ways than inspirational, where real people were copied, not imagined. Unpacking the notion like he never had before, inventing a rounded human was hard; but more interesting to model people with the intentions he was pursuing. Indeed, it might have been a universal truth he had missed, to stub an uneducated toe upon.

Even amongst the greatest of authors, at the level which he had considered well above his own, straightest talking of all, Harold Pinter had based his play 'Betrayal' exclusively, word for word on a 'relationship he had had with broadcaster Joan Bakewell, when both were married to other people. A key element to this scripted work was the real-life confession of her husband, also a Pinter friend. A person Bakewell would continue to love. Early in the adultery, as subscribed in her autobiography, she had caught him in his own affair. Confronting him immediately over a friendly bottle of whiskey, whilst on a family holiday at the Lido, they had decided to stay together. Pinter had been told by Bakewell about this in an exchange of confidence, only well after his seven-year affair with her had ended.

Cussedly, the writer had taken huge male umbrage, and the poor husband's friend had been maligned; demanded an explanation as if he had not been the one sinned upon. The victim however would claim no rights in the matter, explaining that he too had been the sinner.

Stranger even, later day wife, Lady Antonia, following her own married affair with Pinter, wrote to Bakewell, on the arrival in the theatre of the written 'melange'. Facts changed only by substituting real names and reversing the order of events, she had claimed, the author, her beloved, had made his lead female character stronger than the man's, thereby, writing a feminist play, absolving Pinter of guilt. Again, referenced breathlessly in another lover's autobiography.

Though a fan of the TV journalist and a huge admirer of Pinter's last wife's historical writings, Thomas had neglected to finish reading either of the biographic ladies. None of the women in his life, though of huge importance to him, could stand up to the public relations scrutiny of those with whom Harold had bedded.

Regressing, to an over-familiar fear, Thomas was reminded, when flipping through an old school magazine, he had come across a divergent article on his Latin Master. The bulky stature of the diminutive Irishman Craven, he recalled, had resembled a pug in the after-world-war years to an underfed twelve-year-old; appearing in his updated fancy, as the gigantic thirteen-meter dog rendered in flowers by Jeff Koons at the Biennial.

"Think I need a pee.

'Report to Mister Craven, boy."

Never to be forgotten, those schoolboy words were ever the most feared uttered.

They had required fortitude to save the luckless recipient from wetting himself.

Ruling the school as its discipline, Master Craven had devised a ferocious tennis racket handle with a huge piece of tyre inner tube attached, to use for his floggings.

"Three strokes, trousers down and bend."

For the drawn-out process of beating, the thick rubber shaped like a huge tongue, took advantage of the whole buttock; shamefully exposed with only grey saggy y-fronts as protection. The almost pointed end to his fearsome flagellum flicked at the finish of its down stroke. A delayed second cut more painful than the first but not as hard as the third, had left a fig-like welt, increasing with each full-bloodied swing persisted for days.

The man's gruesome heave, the swish through

the air, the landing plop, the simultaneous cry, followed by the piercing scream; echoed throughout the first floor of a junior school, housed deliberately close by in nineteen fifty-three to witness the blind executions.

Rather than teach, this thug had admitted in the article, his 'dream' had been to be a Solo Tenor.

Hindsight therefore had been successful in its struggle to abrogate an operatic and sadistic Pantomime.

"Evil old bastard."

Left with a deeply rooted hatred of rigid dogma, after an education riddled with similar incidents, the thrust of Thomas's book idea would be to question the objectivity of entrenched opinion; to underline the rather obvious truth, that words were biased by their author's point of view.

Recognising, how 'Roman' his collective storytelling label might sound, he had been unable to find a better equivalent.

"Never insult your readership boys."

Inspired by his English teacher, Nobby' Clerk, a far kinder man; rather than the 'downer' of violence, Thomas chose other maxims to rage against.

"Massage it.'

Before teaching English boys in this religious

denominational school, Nobby was a 'whispered about' Anglican bishop; defrocked, because he might have done a little too much schoolboy massaging.

"In Xanadu did Kubla Khan,
His stately pleasure dome decree."

Tall and erudite, he had worn the best clothes, and the most exquisite scent, young Thomas had ever smelt on a man.

To 'massage', intellectually, was a concept, like many suggested by his cultured instructor, well beyond a working-class schoolboy's limited view.

Exceptionally, after one precious school assembly poetry reading, he had received twenty three out of twenty-five points for his performance of mud stoked tug stacks, a life affirming prize.

Interrupting, the regularity of the staple clicking at his desk, Chelsea fans outside had been over-stimulated by too many gratuitous lunch-time pints. Migrating in large numbers passed his stained-glass front door, when he turned his head obliquely to the noise, they were visible through his open living room door. Semi-transparent sides to a portal designed by him were in heavy tribute to Mondrian. Distorted through brilliant-red chrome-yellow and permanent-blue stained rectangles, the crowds filtered more prettily than on the surveillance camera on the main 'drag'. Front shutters in the room were shut in anticipation of the scrimmage, so his desk light had been on.

"We are the championsssssssssss."

Transposed' on a good day, 'copied' on a bad one, Thomas's proposed an addition to his writing method inspired by the movie maker Michael Haneke, a director beloved by Cannes film festival.

Contrary to the maxim 'the camera never lies', film mechanics work, totally by deceit as any aficionado 'in the dark art would testify. Utilising the inability of the human eye to register anything of a duration shorter than one fifteenth of a second, the film camera photographs its images in excess of this speed; projects them at a similar rate giving the continuous lie of movement.

However impartial the author might think his words, Thomas hoped to reflect in his writing how he saw things. When people talk out their experiences on multiple occasions, time will mould reality to form the story; adjusting facts a little to make them palatable; to like the one before not the original.

Auteur, Haneke, makes his characters turn, occasionally, to the screen to show an awareness of the deceitful process.

To reveal him filming the story, so not as to 'suspend disbelief' entirely.

Deliberately, he interrupts the automatic assumptions a watcher makes, to emphasise the need to look carefully.

Perhaps to see other truths.

"Hidden."

"Jesus did you liked that film pater?"

"We didn't understand a minute".

"'You're going to hell, sis, with that blasphemous tongue."

"He says Jesus all the time."

"But he's catholic."

"A fucking ex catholic"

Based around his accumulation of interesting snippets, seeming to contradict conventional beliefs, Thomas had hoped to draw an audience in a comparable way to the German.

"You can never give up Christ Av."

"Like skin colour?"

"Or being a Jew."

"He was Jewish?"

Thomas knew Haneke's actress mother was a Catholic; his father a protestant; but had no evidence of any Jewish blood.

"Don't think so. "

"He's German.?"

Though a hard worker, Thomas the commercial film director came to accept he would not be remembered by posterity for his film work; though he believed he had had ability and had won international prizes for his directing, including curiously an Emmi he had never received.

But film making would never include him in the pantheon of great Artists.

"They aren't films father".

"Just commercials."

To help swallow this hurtful and unsavoury truth, the writer came to the realisation that he had shared his fate with many working creatives, much cleverer than he.

In fact, with all of them.

The mediocre, he surmised, were ninety-nine-point nine percent of all those who were 'called"; Numbered in their millions; even discounting the amateur weekend water colourists.

Experiencing the fluctuations in the flow of ideas, as any creative would endure during any career, the writer had awoken on most recent mornings, with the faith in his second-string talent rekindled.

Despite this morning's gloom.

Understanding denial was an issue between the

sometimes sentimental middle-aged non-fiction writer, he would admit, but only ever to himself, it was well into a third decade before he had abandoned a secret childhood belief in winning his England cricket colours.

Even with poor eyesight and exceedingly left-sided ball hitting talents,

"We are the championssssssssss."

"Chelsea. Chelsea. Chelsea."

Gutturally, in endless small groups, the crowds hustling past his front door anticipated the success of their team of millionaires in the regular Saturday rite; a routine so inviolate, it was unaffected by the ever-increasing ransom needed for match tickets.

By comparison, watching football, when Thomas was a child was a more sedentary affair; forehead resting on cold curve-ended steel scaffold barriers, with no hint in the interest of health and safety.

"He didn't see a banana till he was ten you know?"

"Not a banana sis; an orange.

"Oh ok"

Indeed, Thomas had been lucky, if he had had the threepence left over from a silver entrance shilling to buy a wax-coated cup fitted with a very thin straw, half-filled with weak orange water. Nevertheless, he had made it last to half-time.

"Who ate all the bananas?

"Rich people sis"

"Ah, the rich people."

"Chelsea. Chelsea. Chelsea."

Born at home within a mile of his current one, Thomas had witnessed the transformation of his neighbourhood from post-war poverty to the present self-interested community of rich consumers; living in the large semis, where once coal had been delivered weekly in sacks, through manholes into basement by a man with his horse and cart.

Shifting, uneasily, in a comfortable office chair to accompany his computer purchase, he reminded himself, that he was no longer poor.

Needs expanded, smaller families surrounded his house, with mostly newly minted mothers. Attractive women, for sure, with fully made-up anxious faces, just visible above the steering wheel of oversized cars not built for the smaller streets but mud and country pursuits. Their tiny urban paratroopers strapped in the back prepared for an encounter at play school, dressed in designer camouflage in tanks of a new middle-class driving route he had trolled with his sisters in a pram second-hand' a decade before it had been handed down.

Invaluable, on trips to Bishops Park, the indestructible stand up and beg, had been the one he was blown out of by the exhaust blast of a war bomb. It could hold both his small sisters, sometimes even with a small friend, the week's drop-off 'bag-wash', a football never blown up hard enough, lemonade, the grease-poof wrapped egg, salad cream sandwiches, a strawberry jam Swiss roll, with still enough room for Grandma Maher's cat. The spiteful marmalade stray had always managed to jump aboard uninvited, to spend hours tracking, they knew not what, in the substantial privet hedges by the paddling pool. Bushes housing, they already understood, a pervert on occasions, recognised even in those innocent times.

"Work Thomas"

Sparked by a last rush passed his door, it peaked and converted to a gentler rumble of manufactured thunder as match time approached.

Saturday afternoon reminiscing was not helpful to the would-be storyteller.

A lifelong town dweller had tried to resist the new City customs, but they had fissured into his grown-up consciousness. Instinctively, it would be hours before he could even attempt an escape from the football invasion. If he had moved his car, he would never be able to re-park it in a two-mile radius of the house before eight o'clock in the evening; even with his precious resident's permit.

Dylan was playing softly in the background; 'man

in a long black cloak'.

Some things changed with time but always remained the same.

From funds saved over the years, to finance his special endeavour, the writer had treated himself to the new super-computer, supposing it would help him in his new writing task.

Currently, it sat on the desk in front of him, glaring, threateningly back.

According to son-in-law Ben, when the boy first laid his eyes on the thing, his set-up would have been out of date the moment Thomas gave over his credit card number.

"In five years, there will be nothing but laptops mobiles and tablets."

His daughter, Av, was the first of his girls to couple; still incredibly young.

'Mr Super-intelligent' had been discovered on her gap-year travels in Thailand.

'Dad', unfortunately, was not a huge fan but grew to admire him.

A massive vulnerability in all things close, which he had sought to hide, clearly a daughter would do everything to protect the love of her love. Thomas as he got to know him would like to have been closer but with the bad start, something he fell short of. Lovesick, after travelling together through 'Ossie', and the lad had trailed her back to London and won her heart. Sure, he was 'tall and pretty', 'knew plenty of stuff,' with 'loads of degrees,' but unfortunately, even before he reached his majority, the boy pontificated 'something rotten'.

Enacted, quite lawfully, because a grudging father had asked his lawyer to check on it; the matter had been concluded under a willow tree in a muddy field at Glastonbury with both partners dressed in long white robes and boots.
Green Tory Wellington's,' to boot.
A 'travelling' drum-playing Anglican parson had recited the marriage vows in Saxon English from an internet print-out, without him or any of the other family members present.
Save, of course, for her shadow and sister, Em.
His youngest was the official 'chilled' chief bridesmaid, which required her to be kitted out as the 'Golly Green Giant', in green body paint, G-string, loincloth, florescent green shock wig and two illuminated and blinking emerald nipple tassels.
Proof of this was the computer copy of their wedding photos, sourced from several mobile telephone cameras and given in exchange for a later day bounty.

Lacking the bouquet accorded by legend, the bride had ripped off her sister's green loincloth as a replacement leaving her in fragile lace panties.
Rolling it into a ball, the bridal floral substitute was launched, traditionally, over her shoulders into a muddy coven of libidinous and intoxicated wolves. They had fought to claim it, so his other, green, still single daughter.
Again, several telephone cameras amply covered

the episode.

Though her blinking tassels disappeared luckily the mud by this time had secured her modestly.

"She can look after herself daddy."

"God, were you really such an innocent, when you were young?"

Truthfully, Thomas was continually, surprised at how much of family life had passed him by in those early years, when he had travelled so much. He had lived long patches of time abroad, when they would come to visit often, but had never stayed with him again on a permanent basis.

Abruptly, despite Thomas's continuing furious thumb pressure, the reassuring sound of the tiny stapler suddenly ended as it ran out of staples.

"Damn."

With his palm edge, he speedily discarded the pile of useless bent metal from an otherwise spotless desktop into a large racing-green Venetian ashtray at his feet.

Having, cautiously, pulled the dish out from under the desk with his trademark red-socked feet, a determined ex-smoker returned it to its place in the same way. The expensive, carved piece of Venini was already full to overflowing with the debris of other anxious moments. When thinking creatively, Thomas liked to tare single sheets of discarded paper, particularly junk mail, into tiny squares of confetti; to end their life in the ashtray.

Remembering the wasted staples, without reloading, he returned to his clicking with a much less satisfying result.

Highly sensitive to the glaring blank screen mocking his literary presumptions, he lobbed the stapler in the direction of his huge soft sofa, where it landed with barely a thud.

Impulsively, unable to out-stare his illuminated tormentor, he half-raised himself on the armrests of his typing chair and bent forward toward the screen. Pressing his nose hard against it, he held the uncomfortable pose for much longer than was prudent, searching like a vexed child for the origins of the digital image. Half-blinded by the fierceness of the light in close-up, peering through the reading part of his trifocals, he was able to submerge himself in a pointillist world of blue, red, black and green dots. Happily, he was no longer capable of reading the bothersome page he typed onto the empty electronic page, no less daunting than its virgin paper counterpart. After seconds of this visual tripping, when the strain on his eyes became too painful, he flopped back down onto his seat.

After his move back, the offending page again became legible.

Simultaneously, like a yawing giant, a huge, disappointed gasp at a missed chance, reverberated from the far-off football stadium, while a last straggling group rushed past his house to the melee.

Distantly, he heard himself moaning and turned up the music to cover any further crowd noise.

"We are the champions".

CHAPTER NINE

Any character choice, for the fledgling author, would never have been entirely imaginary, believing as he had, that good fiction had needed to form reality.

Kicking off the piece on the downbeat, the thought of giving his painter a disability might have been the reason for a grump that had felt too real.

So, that had been rejected.

"Too tedious to deal with."
Not a style decision then, simple distaste.

Likewise, he had dumped the Theatre thought of Sam as a woman, always the director's impulsive first bad idea, after a bad script read-through.

Anyway, clever wordy children would never have allowed the access.

"This has to be written through woman's eyes Pater."

"But don't ever suppose you can write like one."

"Any pretty face can turn you."

"Mother says you've never learnt a thing about us."

"Mother....mother? Is that a rich relative of mine

to sis?"
"

"Mater.

She who birthed us".

"Ah yes, hers I know."

The female approach would have looked like offloading male deficiencies.
Maybe the concession was to amalgamate.
Use the tricky real talk of his daughters without naming them.

Recklessly, have the guts to ask their permission upfront.

"Like Pinter?"

"Pinteresque"

Avi had enjoyed this idea enormously.
More amused than anything he had done in ages.
Almost cheered it.

"Didn't realise you had such wisdom,"

"Daddy dearest."

"But change our names."

"Or we sue."

"What is our pay, by the way."

"Everlasting life."

The eruption this caused, then had needed his several promises.
Of shoes,
Of ball gowns for a 'certain Booker' in the wrong fiction category, in order to quell the hurt.
Shocked his comeback, would have inflicted real pain, it had never, ever, been meant to.
It was an attempt, a clumsy attempt to enter their byzantine world.
Henceforward, now they knew, such thievery would need to be more devious.
Receipt of patronage was enjoyed enormously,
They had allowed him to give them cash.
Rejection of it was the first prized exemplar of independence in an extensive armoury.

Understanding pessimistic sequencing was at risk of disengaging with readership before the tale had begun, the amateur poker player, cocksure with an unbeatable hand, had hung on to hole' aces.
Even paid up with a special stack of fivers, when they caught him copying.

Despite the extensive female wit, Chapter One was 'tacky',
No other way to describe it.

The provenance of his first male protagonist already beginning to irk him.

Quite obviously the character was his painter chum, Donald.

Whatever oblique route, Thomas had believed he was treading, the facts he had presented were clear; left perfect tracks away from juicy misshapen fruits fallen way too close to the home tree.

Skipping, through the first few pages, his imagined artist would have been immediately identifiable by anyone.

"Or god forbid, the man himself."

On a second review of his opening, the brand-new novelist saw only capriciousness, where he had hoped to dazzle.

Maudling Sam was way too attentive to a writer's attempt to be original.

More alarming, the actual and the imagined had become so muddled in Thomas's mind as to be almost indistinguishable. Making it hard to believe, events described in Sam's fictional studio had not already happened in his.

Worst of all, as the artist grew with each re-reading, so too had the awareness of the deceitfulness of an author, too cowardly, to ask permission to reference his one-time friend.

Ready to ditch the feckless painter he had loaded on himself; Thomas could no longer hide the vitriol seeping almost unnoticed from his vengeful soul.

He tried to move on.

Veni vidi vicci

To consider the next option in his outline.

Things were no better here.
The précis had called for Sam to disappear overnight, leaving his wife not knowing where he had gone. Going for even a single night would have been something the fractious artist, would never have done. He was way too dependent.

Contradicting the intention to write only what was real, the idea was simply utterly fake.

Given a friendship that if nothing else was long-standing, Thomas's view of the extensive body of Donald's artwork was entirely negative and he had always tried to hide it. Never confronting the fact head-on.

He thought his paintings were without merit.

"Period."

Not a casual viewpoint but a cold professional one; drawn after a careful review with the artist of all his exhibited paintings, a few years previous.

Nothing he saw in the proceeding years had changed this view.

"He can't paint".

Brutally, he saw it was the point of including him into the book.

Buddies while at the Art school, two loners grew

close in the hothouse of freedom in those first years away from parental control. Student Thomas had a great deal of fondness for the blundering, untidy, only child who was always with dirty paint-stained nails but generous with his floor space when he had needed an overnight stay.

Having taken up their friendship a few years back at a school reunion, though Donald could still charm, what once was the endearing foibles of a young art student flowered into a monumental adult ego. It had allowed little to grow in its overhang.

Within a few meetings the reunited friendship developed into a huge distaste.

At least on Thomas's part.

They had continued to socialise as neighbours only because of the painter's wife Alice.

At first, Thomas had tried to find a few pluses in Donald's paintings; to hide his true opinion of the stuff. Soon he had avoided the discussions altogether.

The work saw as hackneyed even childish whilst trying to grapple with the themes of love, life and death. Several huge canvases he was shown were beautifully stretched, primed, meticulously stacked, carefully made with obviously expensive oil paint, and laid on a perfect ground. They would have outlasted many an old master canvas if some charitable people were not to burn the rubbish first.

Thomas was amazed, then and now, that a person so thoroughly steeped in the history of art could convince himself he was so great a talent. Had spent his whole life painting.

Admitting his bias, he saw the man had done many other things with his life but still could think of no more appropriate way to explain a wasted one.

"He can't even draw.
Least I can draw".

Guessing his own fascination was with this terrible denial.

In inurement to the obvious, he recognised the keenness of a deadly thrust directed at a hurtful spot in his own nemesis.

Besides the sudden and rude flashes of humanity, Donald's strength rested in loud, cruel opinions, often disregarding context and always argued, angrily, no matter how docile the prey.

With an extensive, background reading and a photographic memory, he could recall details to silence most adversaries with bullying certainty.

"Poor Alice"

Completely, contradicting the portrait of an erasable fascist, who needed to win every argument, whatever the cost, Donald could not function for more than half a day without the support of his wife.

Much to her own disgust, she was more a mother to him than a lover. He had overheard her admit it when he stayed with them overnight on trips from France.

So, Donald would never have disappeared overnight; making it entirely implausible for Sam to either.

Releasing him from the agony of decision-making, Thomas's phone rang.

Quite coincidentally, it was the real Alice calling.

Instantly, full of guilt and he was on the defensive.

She seemed on edge.

"That music is awfully loud Thomas."

He reached out and zapped down the DVD with his remote.

"Sorry."

"He's gone, Thomas."

"What?"

"Disappeared."

"Disappeared?"

"Wasn't here, when I came home last night."

"Really?"

"I called the police, and they laughed."

"Laughed?"

"Men do it all the time evidently…. disappear."

"Not Donald."

"All the time."

Though it fitted everything he was researching about missing persons, ashamedly, Thomas could hardly believe what he was hearing.

"Where could he have gone?"

"I have no idea."

Still, a remarkably attractive woman, if a little intense, he felt sorry she had lumbered herself with Donald. Both he and the painter's wife were half-marathon runners; she with an engaging, high-legged, bouncy running stride from her dancing days, he with much more of a shuffle.
They would sometimes cross on their early morning routes.
When on longer jaunts, both liked to make it to the river in Bishop's Park; common ground given by the church and nestling into the shadow of the Fulham football ground the other stadium in the area.

"Minimum 48 hours before you can make someone a missing person.

"Is he with you?"

"Me?"

Thomas was shocked.
Became more monosyllabic.

"Me?"

"Yes. You are his closest friend."

"Me?"
"He would go to you,"

Thomas was dumbstruck.

His best friend?
Me?

Well in a way his eldest friend from college.
There was a ring on the doorbell on the other end
of the phone line.

"Sorry have to call you later the police are here
again."
Almost immediately, the phone clicked dead.

His best friend?

It left Thomas breathing heavily.
"Where has the bugger gone?

Had he found a mistress?"

The idea was an intriguing one.

Turning to look out through his undressed French doors to the garden, Thomas was startled to see the darkened garden. Only a moment before it seemed there had been full sunlight.

Feeling a momentary wave of sympathy for the real husband lost out in the descending darkness and he tried to settle his wayfaring hands in his lap.

With absolutely no evidence to support his claim, save his imagining, he turned the lost husband into an adulterer.

"Sam."

An involved writer was already back on his computer.

CHAPTER TEN

The pollen count was high.
But not that high, she had offered later and certainly had had a point.

Sam had been sniffing, since breakfast time, in those early days of summer, had he not taken precautions, he would likely find himself stuck in a puffer, all the way through the flying plant sperm season. When wheezing through these bouts of asthma, the painter's simpering regressive state had made his wife's life a purgatory. Conventional medication had helped a little, but Alice was determined to do something else about it this year. On the advice of a fellow sufferer with a similarly affected partner, she had prepared herself with a powerful, hopefully effective remedy, bought on the internet.
The pills were the size of animal medication and carried a warning they caused drowsiness.

" You say you have the constitution of a horse. God knows what's in them, but Jenny's Adam took them last year and he had no side effects.

Sam held no fear of such things.

"Yes dear."

With little more of independent knowledge drug taking than at college, where you were never sure what was in pills the potency was mostly diluted.

"Take after eating but absolutely no alcohol".

On the back of the unopened see-through plastic container, with blue, hard-to-read instructions, she read the dosage; determining he should take it after supper, when he had finished his days' work and could afford to be a little dopey.
On the kitchen table next to his covered supper plate, laid with a cold chicken breast and potato salad, she had left him the packet of twelve tablets.
With her dream of a second home in Italy one day, she was off to an evening class to learn some Italian. So, she could not have dispensed the pills herself.

"One pill only."

She set out each detail of her preparation, carefully, but with the regular degree of vexation.

"Yes dear."

He always took the medicine she had ordered; but not immediately, like a disobedient child, delaying his mid-morning milk allocation to wallow in the brief attention.

"Maximum dose is two in twenty-four hours.
Just one.
Do you hear me."

"Yes dear."

Curiously though, unconsciously maybe,
certainly vicariously, while fully understanding
the danger, she gambled and left him the whole
box of pills.

"And on no account drink alcohol."

"Yes dear. I mean no dear."

" For a moment her strained expression,
showed more alarm, as she recalled something
else.

"And do not forget that Girl is coming
tonight."

A fan from his lecturing tour was insistent on
visiting his studio that evening.

He would have to deal with her himself.

"Damn it, I'm not his mother."

It was a thought verbalised on other
occasions, which he had not reacted well to.

After some noisy crashing about, he had
sulked for days about it.

"Yes dear."

Sam's triptych was going so well, visitors
were not welcome.

Half-attentive to whom the 'she' might be he
decided to play his visitor 'by ear."

At eight, the front doorbell had rung.
Later, both parties would agree upon this.
Under deposition by his lawyer.

Sam remembered taking a second pill, two
hours after the first one,
which would have made it just before he went
to answer the door.

"I was still sniffing, and they didn't seem to be
working."

He remembered because he had just poured
himself a second large, after-supper brandy.

"Professor Smith?"

At the front door, glass in hand, he was
bowled over by the gorgeous creature standing
on his doorstep. From her strong, breathless,
country twang, it was evident the girl came all
the way from the large state of Texas.

"Professor Smith?"

Additional unearned academic colours accepted so readily in the States were not a comfortable cloak, back home in Fulham.

"Mister is fine here mam.

'I'm Sam."

He stood for moments gaping at a stranger.

Other students, always women, who had heard him on his American lecture tour, often called up, when they were in London just to say 'hi'. His professorial presence usually stirred the bosoms of less, spectacular-looking, Americans, mostly older ladies of the dream.

"Am I expected?" the girl asked.

Of course, she was expected.
Just not by him.

"Come in, come in."

"I was expecting to see his wife." the American girl had said she said later.

With no one to verify it, Alice was at her class till ten with Mr Angotti.
And she was right about the potency of the

pills.

"Very convenient" the American girl had said later.

Hereafter, opinions would differ considerably about what went on.

"Could still function though; as always." was Sam's reflective response.

Slightly small beautifully, proportioned, a most definitely natural redhead, the girl tripped into his home on delicate rose-coloured high heels, dressed in a rust red chemise with her long main unfurled and prancing in her wake.

"The dress is for you and Degas."

"The dress is for Degas," she said later, she had said.

Her corsage played tribute to the French master's painting of "woman having her hair brushed"; a picture seeming to have been dashed off in a few inspired moments with God-like skills a hundred years before.

Pronouncing "Degas" in a perfect guttural French, worthy of the intimacy of the woman in the red picture had captured, the incendiary remark stoked his pot to the boil.

The graduate from Houston had attended one of Sam's 'inspired' lectures on the picture; demonstrating the notion that when unconscious brush strokes were made, like those of a calligraphic Japanese art, they came straight from the soul.

On her first trip to Europe, she had visited the picture at the National; after spending an afternoon shopping in Camden Market, she came to pay impulsive, overdone homage to the address offered thoughtlessly in America.

Slow to focus on the context of her startling costume, Sam was unable to keep his eyes off the crimson swirl, the swishing auburn wriggle that made its dangerous passage into his den.
Moments later they were alone in his large studio; with the door secured.

"Why did you lock the door?"

Finally, a clever student was aware of the danger she had put herself in.

She had expected to see his wife as well, her lawyer explained many, many times later.

"It's always locked."

Truly, no one ever came into Sam's locked studio, casually.

He thought he had explained the situation to her.

"Could you unlock it please?"

Slowed by the pills and the brandy, Sam made no move.
Sure, he had stared a little.

"She was gorgeous."

"Please don't assault me."

Again, he had thought it "tongue in cheek".
The way a woman sometimes would, when they had wanted something else.
Saying no, meaning yes.

"Then he grabbed me," she said later.

" Ah, well Yes," he agreed he had put his arm around her.
But a reassuring arm.

Maybe the move was a little more awkward than had been intended.

"You pushed me," she said.

And later,
Again, and again.

Undoubtedly, she had wobbled.

"On those silly high heels."

And yes, he had grasped at her to stop her from falling.

Anyway, they both lost balance and ended up on the floor together.

"He was all over me smelling of liquor," she said.
Very conscious of their closeness yes, he had kissed her.
She had seemed to want it.

"I bit him, very hard."

Only much, much later were the police called.
By Alice, who was beside herself, when she had seen his lip.

CHAPTER ELEVEN

After a difficult start, Sam's character had become a lascivious distraction.

Fault lines so conducive, the subsequent hours of writing him had sped by, hinting at becoming more profligate later. This oddball, having a sexual side gave him dimension; rescued him from becoming a carbon of the person that Thomas had begun to despise.

Conjecturing on what a wife would have made of her man turning predatory, was more of a brainteaser.

Where all day he had been fluent, this proposition turned him to lumber.

Then his girls had arrived.
With a thermos.

A prop guaranteed by previous assignations that the visit not to exceed fifteen minutes; whatever their problem.

"So, he won't ramble."

"Coffee"

Setting nervous fingers, a shredding again was the back page of an M&S wine catalogue.

Additional book dialogue regarding the origin of ideas, drifted in as they chatted.

"Was influenced by the style of brushwork. "

"He copied it?"

On a previous trip to the National Gallery, daughters had been shocked, when they had found out about Matisse and his small perfidy with 'Women combing girl's hair by Degas.
They were still grousing about it.
As if their father had been to blame.
The daily presence of the actual picture in his own home must have played some part in making his Red Room of 1908.

"Thought the whole point to it was being original Daddy?"

"Shit even I can copy."

"And you are no Van Gough, are you sister dearest? "

Em, at the time was studying the history of art.
Emphasizing her vowels in a way appropriate to an undergraduate was not to the liking of a streetwise sibling.

"Oooohhh oooh Van goooooofff. Why not Van Goff?'

"He was Dutch. And don't say shit in front of daddy."

"Then how come he lived in Paris?"

"Had a rich brother."

"Lucky boy. Will you support me in Paris, when you find your rich husband; sister dearest?'

"No"

"Let you cut off my ear?"

"No."

"Why bitch?"

"Because you can't paint."

"But I can copy."

Other painters, famously 'sharing' at that period had been the youthful Pablo Picasso and an older George Braque.

"More nicking here me thinks."

Both girls had united to vilify identical contemporary canvasses.

"Brown, ugly and a bit stupid."

"Like alphabetic scotch broth."

" Very Marketable?"

Conjoined for a few years, the two Cubist painters had instituted a claim to the parentage of today's art in the public's consciousness, while there had been many other founding fathers to Modern art.

And of course, Picasso had stolen from Matisse, throughout his career.

"How can you share having an idea?"

"You both can't have it.

"Doesn't make sense. Bye Pater must shop".

Beverages hardly touched, two sisters, sounding like twins but were not, were gone.

Whatever its derivation, unquestionably, the 'Red Room' was a major work of the twentieth century.
A cross-over picture all but abstracted.
Contrarily, Donald, so Sam, would always deny it with the usual deadly bluster, refusing any value whatsoever in anything but total realism.

"I don't do abstraction."

He would see such a painting, a primitive representation of a woman in a red room.
Irritated suddenly with himself for his wasteful tic, Thomas expressed the shiny coloured chards on his lap into the fine art glass bowl.
"Confetti"

Musing on the attractiveness of the handmade abundance slipping through his fingers, he pondered its commercial potential, flashing on his days as an altar boy.

" Plight thee my troth".

Dressed in the black cassock and white laundry-starched cota, with a D-shaped bust line more suitable to pregnant women than to his once skinny frame, he would sweep up the wretched pastel-coloured flakes after weddings. A difficult chore in the wind but it made money, once a whole ten-shilling note from an usher.

Shamefully, an illation then made him smile. Stealing a man's identity could be considered a victimless crime if the secret of his inspiration lived only in the mind of its inventor.
Thomas would never tell.
Yet here he was writing it in a book.

"In thought word and deed."

The credo of his cold-hearted Catholic teachers maintained the act of thinking evil, itself was sinful.
Decades after he had abandoned religion, visits to his childish psyche were primed full of guilt.
Never properly forgotten.

"Hedonist"

Bolstering his spirits, he collectively renamed his crimes.

Good humour inched back in.

Worryingly, the only conclusion to his sometime-friend's vanishing act, was he had been involved in an accident. The guy would just never go on a walkabout.

Excepting, the pleasantries batted between friends and their wives, Thomas possessed no great background on Donald's attractive partner. Other than what his partial eyes had supplied over the years.

Certainly, she was difficult and no great self-promoter.

And quite obviously Donald had worshipped her.

Plainly, could not do without her.

"But what had she seen in him?"

He knew she had spent the first five years of their marriage getting a master's degree. Quite a whiz with computer problems, friends would go to her for help if there was a problem or an app needed installing. It had spun into a small, money-making investment.

Additionally, she had her mother's money to fall back on.

Sometimes, conscious of her unusual, but striking attraction, Alice was a generation younger than her bellicose husband. Because of delicate features, long limbs unfathomable brown eyes and caramel toffee-coloured skin, Donald loved to kid her she was his Gauguin native girl; delighting in some back-door bigotry. She would invariably become sullen with his jibes, in public at least. Never voiced anger, choosing to remain silent and enigmatic about her roots.

Besides their jogging, she and Thomas shared a love of Art glass; discovered shoeless in his front room, on recognising his Murano art glass bowl used for his paper detritus. She had explained she owned a set of late Galle vases, given to her, or so she said by her mother. For a reason he could never fathom, he had not believed the provenance when he had been shown them. Uncomfortable with her explanation, she had avoided further discussion on the subject. Each of the three pieces had been the real thing, and pricey. Thomas's taste in glass was more the post-war Modernists. When living in New York, he had collected Higgins Bros. studio ware, crude by non-enthusiasts. On viewing his small collection, Alice had been excited by it. Shortly afterwards, she had started to collect similar pieces for herself. One expensive hanging ceiling light, again with her mother as provenance, he would have 'died for'.

Either way, he was flattered but had tried hard not to read anything into it.

Over time he had felt himself becoming more protective of her, vis a via the obstreperous husband.

Though ignorant of her exact ancestry, he would

111

like to have included some of her evident Asian blood into his written wife. Hopefully, he could do this after the choice of a new name. Another work in progress.

Sam's wife still existed on the borrowed tag Alice, without her permission.

His first choice had been Heather. In the permissive Age of Aquarius and Free Love, the gorgeous petite, but promiscuous Indian drama student had been his first-ever lover. To the sombre timbre of Leonard Cohen, Thomas delivered his innocence 'to that perfect body with his perfect mind', early one Sunday morning in her cousin's double bed in a cottage at Harrow on the Hill. It took him a couple of goes to get the hang of it after a few limp juveniles worries he might have been homosexual. After the loss of his virginity, he was anxious to repeat the experience; for a lifetime thereafter, wherever and whenever it was possible. Latterly, with women he never should have gone near.

The act of lovemaking had killed all the deeply buried religious roots. Such a pleasurable and satisfying encounter could never have been sinful. It had been redemptive. Sent to earth by an over-discerning God, he most certainly could not continue as a free sex-hating Catholic. The turning point came with Heather, styled to a ruling class that her accountant father had never belonged, neither in his native India nor in his hometown of West Ealing. Her deep sonorous projectile lacked a volume control.

112

With one year of actor training, she had determined to conquer the world. Incomprehensibly, for a Thespian career, sadly gone nowhere, she had traded her name for not something delightful, evocative of her loveliness; but to something entirely forgettable, even derisory; in much less correct times.

'Sammy Fleming'
Sammy could never be the replacement for Alice, not yet renamed.

Obliquely, Thomas had also begun toying with the idea of doing a painting of the real Alice.

As yet, he had not approached the idea full-on. He had felt somewhere, it was not the thing to ask her.

Categorically, the writer would never fall into the trap he had with Sam,

Making his fictional wife a copy of the real thing.

Besides the professional pride entailed regarding originality, or the lack thereof.

CHAPTER TWELVE

"You want to paint me, Sam?".

Rules can apply, when reproducing a face.
But cultures hardly ever agree on them.
Ancient Egyptian method invented a
mathematical process, usable in face studies.
Its results look nothing like ancient African
reproduced faces, made instinctively, and
encouraged by the sensibility of Picaso.
Joyously we can all indulge these extremes to
worship.

Studies tell us facial perfection can be divided
according to ancient right into six rectangles in
the ratio two by three. The upper horizontal
division would be the top of the head, to third
eye height. The middle section the base of the
nose, eyes as the mid-level. The lower section
ending with the chin, mouth at its centre. A mid
vertical nose line dissecting all three.

Following a series of experiments, modern
researchers had sought the most attractive
length and width ratios between modern facial
features. Each woman's face had been
compared to her own. Features not changing,
just the distance between them.
The perfect distance between eyes and mouth

114

was just over a third.

Thirty percent, by the length of her face, from hairline to chin.

Width wise, the space between pupils just under half, forty six percent ear to ear.

These Anthropometry studies have been included in plastic surgery planning.
A suite of measurements of about 30 in total,
Attempting to characterize the range of variability.

By consensus, the modern portrait process had been best executed in front of the subject.

Up to his death the most important twenty first century British painter, Lucian Freud, had refused to work on a picture, when not in the direct presence of his sitter.

Francis Bacon, our previous centuries best English oil paint worker had similar instincts.

Or so he had claimed.

Results of his genius and the truth of his words on his personal picture making process, have been more recently questioned.

The ability to mimic human reality has been the way most observers will distinguish talent.

It's difficult, if not impossible to assess abstraction, universally.

Most agree when judging portraiture, likeness simply was not sufficient.

The viewer needs to be taken deep into an expression of the essential person.

Not just given a flattering view of the features. Sam had considered this over time; including it in his pictures when it had been relevant to him.

CHAPTER THIRTEEN

The real Alice, Thomas understood had an unusual look.

Only in some lights would you think her definitively attractive.

Though she had no trouble finding partners.

She had loved the male physiognomy, especially in gay men.

Odd-looking effeminate was her type.

Bisexuality is her turn-on.

"Straight" Thomas had decided, either look would be important if her selection had not been included in his picture, when he chose to paint her.

One photo, among a group of her pictures by him, she had found absolutely her.

It could be classed as scary.

The kind of self-image that had gone for creepy, but not intentionally.

However, the pose and the picture had passed her approval.

He had decided to use it.

Thomas had thought it odd but had marked it.

Certainly, he had not understood it, could not even guess it, unlikely truth.

CHAPTER FOURTEEN

"When I first started, what was very, very important to me was dealing with the nature of the process. So, what I had done was I'd written a verb list: to roll, to fold, to cut, to dangle, to twist...and I just worked out pieces in relation to the verb list physically in a space.

Now, what happens when you do that is you don't become involved with the psychology of what you're making, nor do you become involved with the afterimage of what it's going to look like.

Basically, it gives you a way of proceeding with material in relation to body movement. In relation to making, that divorces from any notion of metaphor, any notion of easy imagery."

RICHARD Serra

Humming with inevitability, the sculptor's words demystified his process.

This morning, slow metallic monsters outside Thomas's front bay window, looked like the rusty red-brown Serra's sculptures. Defiant cutters on the Council sweeping machines, had blades set ravenously low at the kerb side, to scour indented cobbled pitches, spinning discarded greens into a mixed street salad, with over-ripe plums, bruised melons and a few rotting apples. Its copious grey condiment contained a thousand cigarette butts, topped by a used adult nappy; jettisoned during a busy day selling freshness to the great Fulham public.

Recently the cover all healthy, had been added to raps by younger parchment-faces doing the barrow boy. Since childhood these exaggerated cockney cries for attention had felt intrusive to Thomas; wasteful exhaust gas to complete with the number twenty-eight bus on its major London Transport route for the time in memorium. With such a distaste for the sounds of marketing, he wondered once again how he had spent half his adult life filming commercials.

"I want to do a picture about Serra like a Rothko".

The machines slowly progressed into the middle distance.

An idea had flown in the care of the hated council.

Appreciation of the work was not admitted by a grudging daughter, who hated Serra.

"They look like bits of tankers to me that someone forgot to spray."

"And dangerous."

Unpainted, red-oxidised steel worked the themes of material weight load scale and texture intuiting themes.

"It is a widely accepted notion among painters that it does not matter what one paints as long as it is well painted. This is the essence of academia. There is no such thing as a good painting about nothing."

"Mark Rothko."

Thomas admired Rothko's modern soft-edged finish.

Much less his utterances.

Skills involved in constructing a three-dimensional piece, he felt ranked higher than the abilities needed to paint a picture.

"Pater lies you know Em.

Rothko was a drunk and you know how he hates drunks."

"Oops... can you tell I have a hangover?"

"No babe you look your normal green to me."

Following three early morning miles running, with no Zulieka sightings, and the consequent empty letter catcher, Thomas had set an ambitious agenda for himself; made even more so, when Em had popped in.

Recently turned vegan, she was enroute to the fruit market for a big shop.

"Why three canvases Pops?"

"It's a painting about a sculpture darling."

She smirked.

Planning to explore the ideological differences between the American sculptor and his alcoholic countryman painter, Thomas wanted to contrast their process, putting each in the lesser medium. Carefully for two weeks, he had collected all the materials needed to start the elaborate new painted work.

"The 'brides' chair'"

Since Rothko's process insisted a picture must have a subject, Thomas had wanted an ancient well-known analogy for his visual comparison.

Making a list of objectives, according to Sera's way of working, the Pythagorean theorem with its planetary diagram registered itself top of the page.

"The area of the square on the hypotenuse will equal the sum of the areas of the squares on the other two sides."

Properly translated as a winged insect, and nothing to do with marriage, the familiar geometric construct was named by a miss-translation of the Greek.

"Pythagoras again?"

"Yes, darling.

"Two smaller canvases exactly matching the area of the larger one."

After due consideration, with index finger crossing an unpainted pout, pointing skyward to assist the thought process, she noted the impressive aggregate.

"Very clever. One plus one equals one, right?

"Thank you, sweetness."

The previous evening, he had made up the three special-order stretchers after covering the entire front room and the furnishings with dust sheets.

Stretching and stapling the cotton duct to the stretchers, he had laid the virgin canvases onto the protected floor, applying two coats of white primer, sealing in the innocence.

By morning all three painting surfaces were dried and ready for painting.

"What's happened to the flash computer?"

"I'm giving the novel a day's rest."

Not intuiting a connection before and her distaste for them, tensions surfaced in an exaggerated, kabuki grimace.

"The scary Serras? "

The sculptor's recent one-man show in London,

Thomas had visited recently with both daughters a regular family chore without hubby in tow.

They had seen a curving set of Sera's gigantic steel plates set parallel in an eye-shaped ground-plan. Two massive sheets of metal seemed to lean in for support of each other but without ever touching; combining to make a terrifying blind walkthrough.

"That's original. Assassinating your visitors to a one-man show."

"Are we covered".

With the catastrophic threat of collapse, apparently nearby, some paternal handholding had been needed to see Avi to the end of it.

Sister Em had grabbed at his other free hand to supply the tag.

"I need a fag?"

"Not in front of him babe."

The interior of the Mayan pyramid at Palenque had induced a similar shaking in Thomas when the writer made it down through sloping walls and stone steps to King Pascal's tomb at Palenque where he had shot an American Commercial.

Reusing the much-used personal simile would not have been reassuring to either anxious daughter.

Both unusually displaying girlish fears; he had kept his mouth shut.

"Reversing his process. Like the thick heavy squares hanging on the walls."

"A sculpture pretending to be a painting."

"Exactly.

He was using primary red and cadmium yellow and mixing them to keep things simple.

"I read somewhere that colours are related to feelings.

What does yellow make you feel?"

It was a question Thomas had not asked himself before

Momently upsettingly, it felt highly relevant to what he was doing.

"You know I don't know. Coffee?"

"No catch you later pater.

The street cleaning finished; the artist was totally alone.
Left to work out for himself another imponderable about colour.

"What emotion was associated with the colour yellow?"

CHAPTER FIFTEEN

"That Ego is so impenetrable. Those lighthouses at two lights Cape Elizabeth are self-portraits; it was pitiful to see all the poor dead birds that had run into them on a dark night.

I know just how they felt."

Josephine Hopper 1946

Careful to lick her mascara brush and then push upwards with the curl, Alice was riding on top of a half-empty bus on her way to the Italian class. Thankful for some privacy and a little elbow room, she was putting on a 'full face' for the first time since a similar journey the previous week. It took most of the forty minutes to perfect the satisfying paint job. The current craze in the media for photos of women without the disguise added a charge to the ceremony as she 'layered it on'. The dichotomy consistently provoked her peevishness. Why women the world over who enjoyed the process and its effect, ever had needed such a pretence in the first place? As redundant as silk ties on men, it was never about those other strange creatures; ridiculing themself, if they were caught using anything but the minimum splash of after shave.

Minutes after her preparation had finished, she was off the bus and on her walk to the top story of an Edwardian school building. Catching her own view in a passing convenience store window was mostly a gratifying astonishment. Sometimes, when she chose the wrong foundation, she looked like a white-faced witch in the impossible-to-dodge reflections on life. Truthfully after 'all the nonsense' with the Texan girl, Sam's wife was having much more trouble with her own appearance. Luckily, for his well-being, and, the girl's, the 'red-haired hussy' had been refused legal aid. Diminishing the taste for any further revenge by not putting full trust in a difficult daughter, her parents would not risk their hard-earned dollars to buy English justice. Accordingly, she had been recalled home early from her studies.

Which had evidently put her in a huge funk.

Alice's idea to cool angry emails aplenty had been to send the family a small watercolour made by Sam, based loosely on the ubiquitous Degas picture.

A clever female diversion, it had helped to re-establish good Anglo-American relations.

A week after receiving the picture, a gushing acceptance of the apology by the girl arrived written on her father's headed paper; together with a promise to call on Sam during next year's summer school. A rendezvous never to be completed, if a nearly Italian bilingual-painters-wife had anything to say in the matter.

Thomas's lusting had relieved Alice's now permanent guilt a little, that she never had had his child. She just could never have imagined herself as the mother of his offspring.

Such a conception had crept in, to seem inconceivable.

It would have been far too disruptive.

It took her days after their infrequent intercourse to get herself straight.

If intimacy with him was so disruptive, what would a child do to their situation?

The distance standoff at current levels suited her fine.

Aware she had needed a husband was frustrating, she could never predict his actions.

Lately, admitted to with more conscience, the weekly schoolgirl flush on her cheeks had not been achieved by just her soft carmen, blusher. Other retribution for her sinning spouse, had been to herself out loud. But not this one. During the special attention paid to her in class at the review of homework time, not quite covered by the sweet, but unrecognised foreign deodorant, the man-scent of an admirer of her graphic work was the absolute highlight of her week.

Swarthy, besuited Mr. Angotti, with his teasing musk, was as moistening as the rosemary mint and pork crackling' of a favourite Sunday roast.

Perversely and prompted by two deceased American painters he had loved, Alice had taken another, partnership leap, vowing adamantly to Sam, that she would no longer sit for him when he needed a life model to paint.

Though certain of its good sense, Alice compiled not much of an excuse.

Other than saying she was too old.

Unwittingly, Sam himself had been the instigator of his punishment, when he had bought home an illustrated biography, of Edward Hopper. While he had flipped the pictures avariciously, she was more curious and had digested the words, cover to cover.

Its story had caused massive additional, tension, between her and her husband.

In the book about the life of his idol, the famous artist appeared to her mind to have been a bully; generally speaking, a withholding and unpleasant character.

She had hated with a familiar hatred.

Details of the Hopper marriage reflected badly on the things Alice had to put up with over the years in her own situation with a painter. Unlike in the famous twosome, Sam had never hit her. Though she would have admitted to coming close to throwing a punch at him on more than one occasion. A life begun in the bliss of youth with a total belief in Sam's talent, her feelings had dissolved over time; into contempt then to a distant discomfort, whenever she was required to back up his work in company.

The relationship of a truly, great, painter, Hopper, and his spouse was far more complex than the easy truth that they had slipped into.

Perhaps that was because he could paint.

Intelligently, sensing from her comments what

the problem might be, Sam had tried to explain himself to Alice on several occasions only, increasing her aggravation.

In the Hopper's physical domestic battles, which appeared constant, Jo Hopper gave as good as she got. An artist herself with good ideas, by her own account, she had inferior brush skills. So, she had decided to live entirely for the relationship with her more talented husband and his painting, but not completely in his shadow. After marrying him at forty-one, they shared back-to-back studios in their apartment, overlooking Washington Square; with a mirror between his side and two street windows. She was a constant presence always in his view, a diary tracking every picture he made. So much so that she became an important part of his success, considering his paintings their children, her own as caste off waifs.

Arguably, she and her critique were co-authors to his strange and brilliant ethos.

Extraordinarily, and quite contrary to Alice's wilful stance, Jo Hopper had refused her husband ever to take a life model other than herself. She saw it as a marital duty to sit for him even nude, when he needed it. Even in the later part of her life, when her body had grown much older. Perhaps seeing her place in posterity, her 'period' curves and uncomfortable solo poses with far-off stares were known intimately to the millions some of whom worship his pictures. With its empty spaces and leaving many unanswered questions on his own, Sam had been one.

Though her physical passion waned to nothing, Sam had asked Alice to sit for him again and again. Not only unwilling to pose, but she was also hostile to him using anyone else; predaceous of a husband, much like Jo Hopper, she had been fearful another woman might steal what had belonged to her.
Till death do them part.

Portraiture, sourced by ancient roots, has been intuitively to reproduce a likeness. By defining the facial features precisely in the moment, we try to capture the image timelessly.
Few pictures painted vibrate as strongly as Rembrandt's self-portrait, sitting before a mysterious faded circle, aching its heart out at Kenwood.
Equally, incapable of erasure after one viewing, rear lustful views of the beauties Marie-Louise O'Murphy de Boisfaily and Venus in the mirror; by Boucher and Velasque respectively, additionally follow into the mind space where it desires.
Bacon and Leonardo, among many hugely transformative artists, use male nudes, presumably to produce comparative uplift.
Conscious of this, Art trained Alice had come up with an idea for her husband to continue his

work. Having believed so strongly in his talent in their early years, she pondered ways to work and maybe redeem himself. Painting from a photograph had felt safer and for her an acceptable resolution.

Though this had been against conventional Kant, Sam had half wondered about it himself.

But never had tried. Too anxious to go out and buy a magazine including such unclothed treats. Alice rightly pointed out to him, with alarming honesty, the avalanche of porn on the internet made no such search on the top shelve necessary.

Just the press of a keypad.

After a few salacious but permitted hours by himself on his computer with his studio door locked he found a site which showed a gallery of nude pictures, assuring the world all the girls on it were over eighteen. Taking the internet on trust and marking one picture as a clear favourite, he downloaded it onto his printer in the corner of his studio. The girl was slim and very young-looking, but he had no idea where the picture originated or her real age. As he needed to pay nothing, he did not much care.

The painting Sam intended was of a domestic house from the outside, much as Hopper might have done, a brick wall with a window through which the young woman would sit naked looking out Her expression was to be unsurprised but not unaware of her state.

The frame and the outside wall would be parallel to the picture frame but would not run out before either of the edges of the picture.

Eager to begin he attacked the task with endeavour and practically finished the young form in a week. Alas before temporarily sketching in the brick rendering which he found much more problematic. He laboured to make the brick realistic and had not succeeded.

Unusually, one morning after a silent breakfast and sensing from his aggressive mood that something was amiss, Alice noticed Sam had left the studio door unlocked while visiting the downstairs toilet. Seizing the opportunity, she had barged into his sacred workspace to check what he was up to.

Instantly, on seeing the picture and in a tumble of emotions she saw what he had so obviously missed.

Fearing something awful had happened in his private space, Sam rushed back in on hearing her anguished scream.

Entirely naked in both the painting and the photo and it was possible to see her growing pubic hair and breasts at the stage identified as 'puffy'; when the aureole was almost as large as the not fully formed mammaries.

The girl was underage.

Instantly, ragingly Alice contended he was copying a child.

His immediate defence was the site had proclaimed it used only eighteen-year-olds.

Even he realised his argument was on badly made foundations.

After a blistering row, his cuff on the ear, at her deep penetrating bite on his arm, almost to the bone, moved them up to the level of Jo and Edward Hopper.

Alice had stormed from the studio; forbidden ever to enter it again.

Near paraplegic with anger, Sam's skills despite working from a photograph had been remarkable.
 It was the best nude, bar none he had ever painted. He was loathed to destroy it.

After tempers cooled, Alice offered him a devious suggestion as a truce flag.
Maybe he could dress her.
Paint on a bra and tiny panties.
Thinking it was worth a try; his task was facilitated more easily than he thought possible and had not destroyed the painting's validity.

Headily Alice was invited back in again for a viewing.
Alas, after one look at the picture she gave off a derisory, hurtful laugh.
Agreeing he was no longer prosecutable; she also savaged his painted brick wall as Mickey Mouse Hopper.
Again, she was excluded for his holy of

holies, for all eternity.

CHAPTER SIXTEEN

Weeks before, at his large French farm table protected by his drawing board, with set square ruler and sharp pencil, onto a pin-down sheet of A4 regular white cartridge paper, Thomas had measured out the scaled Marquette for his triptych.

He wanted to decide the actual sizes of canvases according to the formula.

…. the hypotenuse was equal to the sum of the area of the other two sides.

He was enjoying the surgery slicing up the paper along the edge of his metal ruler with his box cutter; a Stanley knife well-loved aid in England but considered a weapon in America. Curious to see what would happen, when the ancient two-dimensional form was made with flat Serra planes, he reasoned the three painted squares totalling exactly equal areas.

Would it balance visually in an abstract painting?

The little Marquette was rapidly assembled with balsa cement.

It produced no surprises.

So simple, it gave little information about scale.

So, he needed to calculate his own relative proportions.

Later in the week, the finished stretches had arrived to be covered with painters' linen, rather than in heavy steel.

He would employ a paint finish to them, stopping before the edge and parallel to its sides just like Rothko.

It was so simple a notion on paper that it looked like a 'home run.

A simile ingrained, much to his daughter's distaste from his time in the US.

The erected triptych would be too tall for his large upstairs studio, so he put the pieces together, much less conveniently, in his downstairs living room with a higher ceiling.

During the restoration of his old family home, he had removed the Edwardian dividing partition doors from his two ground-floor rooms. Joining them into one big space, keeping the well-crafted window shutters on the lofty front bay windows.

He had liked to write at the garden end and away from the road.

"What would Nanny have said?"

In his Mother's Day, before America, and his purchase of the second house in what was presently his second-floor workspace, there had been three bedrooms. They had been always assigned to the grandchildren when they had come to stay. Each room had its mattresses and was a space, to sleep in of their own choosing. Slumber time was often spread between all three. It had become the kingdom for his growing daughters and their cousins. At the times of greatest thrills, the number of sleeping little bodies could grow to eight or nine.

"You have destroyed our birthright".

"Usurped is the technical word."

Consequently, its conversion to his studio had brought a deluge of complaints.

He indulged it as a healthy expulsion of a poison; dreading a build-up might affect their love for him because he had once left them.

From an early age, they had understood his sensitivity to the reproach and milked it.

"Abandoning your children again?

"I think some sort of large financial retribution is called for."

"Yea Money talks"

Since their twenty-first birthdays, both girls owned their own small flats in East London.

Not bought by him but with money put aside by his ex-wife's thrifty parents.

"Daughters don't get alimony."

"They should."

Nevertheless, he was required to promise they could use his en-suite bedroom on the first floor, whenever they visited; regulating him to one of the two single bedrooms one floor above.

"Give you a taste of being homeless Pater."

By covering his desk and shifting the pieces of furniture, other than his massive and incredibly comfortable sofa, the rest of his large living space could be used as an improvised studio.

Careful to cover this precious, overstuffed couch in double plastic and cloth covers, Thomas was even more 'anal' about the wood floor.

"Walnut is for cake and apple and endive salad Pops. Not floors'

Inspired by a visit in his early twenties to a Dordogne château, though with nothing like such a large width of board, his polished floor was walnut and pride.

"And cricket bats?"

"No that's willow dummy?"

"Wind in the…?"

"Yes, as in weeping."

The wood was given to him by a friend in the trade who had no use for the special offcuts.

Before laying by a specialist carpenter, Thomas had supervised their milling, grooving and watched over their installation.

Cautiously, over two weeks, he had lacquered the timber himself; let it dry slowly; and then lightly hand-sanded the five thick coats of clear varnish.

Save for the last one.

The glorious finish he had achieved, made the heavily striated amber-and-dark brown grain look like pouring molasses into golden brown syrup.

"It's like a fucking ice rink Av."

"Don't say "fucking" in front of Dad, Em".

"Feels nice though; take off your heels."
'Fucking hell it does"

CHAPTER SEVENTEEN

Walnut was a "soft" hardwood, more suitable to furniture making than flooring, and sustained a few dimples from high heels at its unveiling drink's party. The wine flowing easily at the pleasant inaugural Sunday lunch, when he had first noticed the effect; he barred 'heels' unilaterally thereafter from the room.

Propitiously, his directive continued to polish and sustained the brilliant surface with the unusual side effect of bringing a quicker break-down of social inhibitions during his parties; as pairs of unadorned female feet massaged their way, adventurously across the surface.

To make the ancient diagram of his triptych, Thomas would use the three canvasses connected.

The largest would be secured at the base, the two others slanted left and right at the top in the air and the void between them would make up the triangle.

He laid them all out, face down on the dust sheets and joined them toe to toe at the back with metal plates of slightly less width than the stretcher.

It took time to assemble.

When finished it was a meaty piece.

With the rough flannelette covering on the shiny wood surface slipping, it was a struggle to turn it back over to begin work on the side face up.

From the perimeter on his knees, he began to

work with a three-inch home decorator brush.

Dipping into a kitchen bowl to paint mixed to the consistency of pancake mix, he determined not to go to the edge of the canvas; so, left the colour in irregular rectangles.

First, he painted the smallest of the square's cadmium red.

The colour of passion.

Thomas understood every mark made on a picture was related to its edges.

Like on a graph, each dub or splash took a position, which could be identified by a vertical and a horizontal coordinate, a concept used by digital preproduction.

Additional marks referenced every following mark.

Drifting off on repetitive hand motions he thought about Sam, almost as a living breathing, human.

Then he thought of painter Donald

With some shame.

What was the colour of shame?

Cowardice was yellow.

Envy green.

Rage was purple.

But Shame; shame, it had no colour.

Not black?

Though mood could sometimes be black.

Despair was black also.

Fear was white.
And Pure was white.
But then neither black nor white were colours.

Black was the absence of light.
Yet white light was a composite of all colours of the spectrum.
A scientific explanation as to why the Impressionists worshipped it.
They banished black from their palates.

But shame; shame he could not colour.

Finishing the first canvas, he stood up to inspect it lying flat out on the floor in front of him.
He had painted the red rectangle on the square with an irregular white ground frame around it.
he had stopped himself from increasing its volume to make it perfectly symmetrical.

Like a Rothko

Moving around the work he started the next size canvas up.
From a second large mixing bowl of cadmium yellow and a new brush, he began to paint again.
Hopefully, this square too would end up a bit irregular, yet he did nothing deliberate to make it so.

Recalling each psychological Chakras had its own colour, related to a different part of the body, and he began another wonder, what yellow would have been to them.

After a five-minute break found the answer in a book of his ex-wife in his library.

Evidently, yellow was related to the solar plexus, situated below the ribs; a group of organs comprising the liver, spleen, pancreas, stomach and small intestine.

On the psycho-spiritual level, this area is related to self-worth; how we felt about ourselves and how we feel others perceive us; in the Chakras of personality, ego, intellect, and self-confidence.

So, like cowardice, yellow would be the colour of shame.

Finishing off this second canvas more quickly he was happy to see his yellow square was even less square-like than the red.

After combining, exactly, similar amounts of the red and yellow pigments in his largest mixing bowl using his first brush he made orange and with it painted the largest canvas.

When the whole process was finished, he repeated it; each surface had two full coats of paint.

Well on schedule and his work was finished before noon.

But he was not ready yet to assess his work, feeling as if something had been neglected.

After lunch, a brief siesta and with the acrylic

paint dry to the touch, he lifted his unwieldy structure upright feeling apprehensive.

He had seldom completed a large work with such speed.

Once he viewed it upright, he knew the hard work might begin.

It took considerable effort to manoeuvre the thing up and lean it against the side wall for a proper viewing. When vertical it almost touched the ten-foot ceiling height.

Half-squinting his eyes with his glasses off, he wanted to see the work not in close first but from the other side of the room,

He wanted to have a full view at the proper distance.

He had learnt over the years to review his work when eyes were focused at infinity.

The usual depression hit as he stared at it for the first time.

It had felt unfinished.

Black exists.
The thought struck him,
Then, inspiration.
He would like to have some black in his work.
He liked the impulse; it made him feel more creative.

Coal was black.

Black carbon, when left for a few million more years would itself turn into diamond.

When cut and illuminated, it was the most beautiful of all purveyors of light.

And the depths to which our spirits could sink was very dark.

Excitedly, he mixed the red and blue to achieve the colour in a spare bowl wanting to keep all the other colours uncontaminated.

Recklessly, he filled his large brush, included as an afterthought.

He had never dreamed he would use it.

With several abandoned arm-sweeps, he graphically joined three canvases with his strokes.

Dynamically, swooping circles and careless drips on the painting, up close were satisfyingly, chaotic. Elated, he added further dripping dark lines to the very centre of the other three canvases to increase their directionality. Unable to get to the upper parts of the high canvases, after a speedy trip to the kitchen he taped the brush to his kitchen broom with masking tape to achieve his arm extension. Though anxious not to splash the living room wall, the higher marks on the canvas felt satisfyingly, uncontrolled.

Then suddenly, it was all done.

The final crazy dash had lasted thirty minutes at the most.

Turning his back on the three-part picture, careful

not to touch any of the covered furniture with messy hands, after laying down his broom with the brush over the bowl he picked up a paper towel to clean his hands.

He strode to the other side of the room to take his first proper look at the image.

Full of expectancy and pushing his glasses firmly into place from his forehead which left only a small black fingerprint as he turned, alas the effect of the painting was not the balance of floating forms he had thought it would be.

"JESUS"

Indeed, like a de-brained doll and Christ was exactly what Thomas had painted, albeit in figurative abstraction.

A menstruating, Vampire nun on angle dust, wearing last night's sucked-out undies.

Instantly, he interpreted the canvases as a lopsided top half of Christ hanging from the cross.

The voided triangle between them circled in black, looked to all the world to him like the thorn-crowned head hanging between crucified stubby arms and body of our supposed saviour.

Carefully applied flat colour had absolutely no power at all to override his last rash descriptive gestures.

At this point, there was no denying that the ex-commercial film director had blinked.

After ten minutes of studying the monster, he had created, without any regret, the black barely dry, he disassembled the picture again, into its three separate parts.
Moving them to the spare room along with his other disappointments forgotten, and he would paint over the canvases at a later date so as to remove any lingering demons; so not to disturb his sleep next time the kids came to stay.

It had not taken him much longer to get rid of the plastic, wash the brushes and the painting gear, return his room to the pristine writing den.

Finally, after an entirely wasted day, he sat back down with his back to the smaller double-glazed backdoor. With a second intense care, he scanned the removed dust sheets and his large floor area for any lingering signs of splashed paint or signs of disarray.

Because he had been so careful, he found none.

"Christ that's better."

CHAPTER EIGHTEEN

Unsettled by the disappointment, Thomas was ready to shut down for the evening; to beach himself in front of the television in his ergo-dynamic writing chair, to wallow in the distant reality of cable news.

Preferred viewing would have been from the over-stuffed sofa, but aware his

special place would have him snoring in minutes, he was not settled enough for sleep.

Besides, he needed to eat and think.

Instructions from his offspring had him snack nowhere near the pale expensive upholstery. He checked around the room again for paint with a shudder but found none.

"Do nothing on it that will stain".

"We check you know."

"And if we find any marks, we divorce you.'

Remembering a stale grain loaf in the bread bin from Sunday lunch, he decided to help his debilitated ego with a culinary favourite, a ready-made fondue from Sainsbury's in its plastic pouch.

With deadly-sharp chromed kitchen scissors, a recent gift from his girls, more surgical than domestic, he snipped open the top of the sealed vacuum top, pushed its contents into the saucepan lasciviously. Encouraging a simper every time he used the sharp cutters, they had been tagged "lest we forget", on a Christmas label in September, still in the Harrod's green retail plastic bag.

His staccato remembrance was of their mother's wedding anniversary. The thoughtful 'necessity' was given him after any mention of her became forbidden territory for twelve months.

It had been a minimal gripe to have caused the split. At the site of the tightly fitted peach suit and matching hat, she wore in another school mates wedding photo.

"Ah, the pink, sugar plumb fairy"

"All you ever do is bitch about her."

'That's it, no more weddings. You're banned'.

Not relishing a scene, the girls thought it best he did not attend a forthcoming festivity,
though insistent he send a present.

"You know how she made you laugh at Primary school Daddy".

The scissors had been a guilty thank you for the gift, after he spent too much on it.

"Not a word about our mother till your next anniversary"

Squeezing out the pale inners of the wrapping in one lump, to heat to the molten creamy delight, which never appeared scolding but always was, looked sexual. Suspicious of the intoxicating punch-like waft escaping the recipe, indicated it might contain alcohol, as most certainly its Swiss cousins had. Resisting a check on the list of ingredients, lest a bona fide non-drinker was forced to stop eating the delicious cheesy lava, he satisfied his conscience, multiple times, with the logic that boiling it would drive off the alcohol.

To put down the scalding, iron saucepan, improvised as his fondue dish, he grabbed at a metal coaster for his desktop surface. Over the years the dark-brown mahogany-faced top to his asymmetric kidney-shaped desk had seemed impervious to all his spilling and mopping up.

Even with the mistake of the chlorine cleaning liquid, he had tried to protect it.

Manoeuvring passed the keyboard to between stationed supper plate traffic, he had parked the hot pot by the plate of symmetrically diced bread and a large glass of grapefruit juice.

"Perfect"

'He eats off it when no one's around."

"Really. Can't be hygienic."

"Can you divorce a father Em."

"Nor sure....

"They do in America".

Almost comfortable again after the stressful day, Thomas clicked on cable TV and immediately muted it; wanting just the background fuzz, while he checked his emails.

Salivating on an aroma veering toward the sexually feminine, he twisted a hard whole wheat cube speared onto his long fork into the molten delight, while with his other hand, he checked with his mouse the front page of BBC internet news. Careful, not to splash or drip anything on his writing machine, he popped a transitional wedge of bread and slippery hot cheese into his mouth; after it, speedily, spiked another, then another.

Savouring the blinding flavour rush, strong as nicotine on lighting up the first cigarette of the day, when he had smoked, every flavourful hit would diminish exponentially; increasing the pickup speed, till it became reactive.

Flashing its way into his consciousness, at the bottom of his monitor screen, an email had arrived in the inbox.

Suspect, after he mechanically clicked it up, it was from an unknown source with an attachment. Likely junk mail, or worse. He was about to trash it, when he noticed its heading.

Alice?

The lady had said she would call back; but that was a day ago.

Since then, he had heard nothing.

Still anxious from the wasted day and the huge failure of his project, Thomas was reluctant to go chase after more bad news.

Vacillating for several dangerous seconds, in the end, he had opened the message, trusting his expensive firewall would protect if it turned out not well.

There was the lovely lady.

Well, she, or someone who looked like her in an old black and white photo attachment.

Curiously, there was no note of explanation.
He double checked.
Other than the heading, there was no text.

On closer inspection the photo looked as if was from wartime Fulham, so it could not have been Alice. A gas mask and satchel were laying on the bench where the woman was sitting, in a place, he knew well, since it was on his short cut to the station.

'Lily road pond'

At a speed too fast to assist healthy digestion, he saw that the fondu was nearly gone.

He was sure the picture had not been doctored.

Less in number these days, the sturdy wooden oak benches, inscribed on the top of their back rail to lost loved ones were his turning marker on many early morning runs.

Evidently these seats had been in place just after the war.

"Why had he been sent it?"

Trying the address for return mail, it was returned, instantly, as "undeliverable".

The new fiction writer was absorbed in a mystery.

He studied the photo, looking for other clues.

The woman was dressed, as they all had dressed, when rationing was still a major factor in life, just like his mother. She had worn a floral headscarf tied like Mrs Mop, with an additional Robin Hood felt hat, sans the feather.
The long black woollen coat looked threadbare.
Matched with 'period' heels, they would ever find fashion again, except with Mini Mouse.

"It had to be Alice's relative.
Maybe the mother she talks about".

Studying the picture, scrapping the remnants at the bottom of his pot with a spoon he was satisfied he had eaten everything not secured there by the heat. He put the empty glass into it with the bread plate ready for transport to the kitchen.
Engorged, he was ready to belch.
He wanted to know what this picture might mean, picked up the phone and called Alice.

Remembering the missing Donald, only as the dial tones began, he would check on him also.

She answered almost before his rings, appearing to have been waiting with her hand on the receiver.
She sounded stand-offish, when she heard his voice.

He concluded, inaccurately, she was waiting for someone else to call.

"There's no news of Donald, Thomas.
I'm going quietly out of my mind.
I called the police".

"What do they say?"

"They are very hopeful.'

"Right."

"In their experience, they come home he said."

Right."

"Or make contact; the detective said."

"Right." "

"Mostly sooner than later."

Wondering in another pause, if there was a more believable way to register his feelings, his concern for the man was not overwhelming.

She had seemed too upset to notice.

"OK. Right."

"In spite of saying they wouldn't, they've done a hospital check.'

"I'm so sorry."

His sentiment sounded, horribly hollow.

"But nothing."

"Right."

Sensing a break in her flow, Thomas slipped in his own question.
Hoping to sound more concerned.

"Listen, don't know if it might be relevant but I've had this email."

It went quiet on the other end of the line.

Thomas could not hear her breathing.

"You there Alice?"

"Yes."

"OK?"

"I have to stay here in case he comes back."

Thomas offered no argument.

But why would he?
Of course, she had to stay home and wait.

"Sure"

Shockingly, she, then reversed herself.

"OK no. I'll come over right now, just need to change."

Such a lightening shift stunned the fiction writer to silence.
Forbidding any further query, she hung up without another word, leaving him to puzzle for several confused minutes, the receiver still in his hand.

"The email?"

When the sediment began to settle after replacing the phone, Thomas found he was more curious; dangerously delighted by her contrary decision to visit.

"She's married Thomas.

And you are supposed to be a friend."

Truthfully, he had felt no huge concern for the

man.

Growing ever more excited, he left the email up on the screen for discussion later.

Sensing an unnamed complicity, he felt elevated.

Scar tissue from other intoxications, even at this early stage, held him to his chair.

Reflectively, holding onto the dinner crockery and pan he looked around his special room for familiar reassurance.

Registering the back-web to his thoughts, his heart was racing, noticeably,

Top of his cheeks burnt red.

"Careful. "

Close by on the grey wallpapered wall next to his desk was a small late Diebenkorn that he loved, painted on a cigar box. Bought on a whim when he had first moved to New York; the reason, a huge discount it had fallen into his price range.

Over the years it was becoming too expensive insurance wise to keep in the house.

The piece was both representative and abstract art which he found reassuring, changing its apparent sensibility according to his mood.

On present viewing it veered toward the figurative.

Thomas saw the woman in it against the sunset on her Californian seaside veranda.

Other times the colours would bleed as easily as

the eye changed focus into almost abstraction.

The American who had painted it was one of the few out of the hordes to follow the efforts of Matisse, to try the match between the reality and nonfigurative.

This simple little picture was an honest conjunction denied to many.

It typified Thomas's taste for other artists and mini pictures.

Careful buying and selling over the years needed him to double the house locks and reinforce the front door because of the insurance.

Latterly an alarm system was installed for which he had needed to sell an early Caulfield litho.

The statistic, which never ceased to perplex and disturb the collector, Van Gough hardly sold a paining in his life; except to Theo; the brother who had kept him.

Currently Vincents paintings were exchanged for prices higher than all others.

Since their houses were close neighbours, Alice's arrival was imminent.

Still Thomas was leaden legged. Unable to stir himself.

The dark-grey-green-mottled living room wallpaper acted as a terrific background for the small paintings in the collection. Made up of a few works by him and others much more famous, it had begun, when he was eleven with a self-framed drawing of a 'red' Indian in full feathered headdress.

Framed in a cheap mount work with sanded glass edges the image was copied from an Eagle comic; a publication the great Norman Foster cited as an influence on his future visions; like the Gerkin.

Often the smell of fresh printing inks evoked this purchase of the second edition of the children's paper from his grandpa's newsagents; pieces of folded coloured paper that would have been worth big money had he preserved them.

"Alice."

Released suddenly from his lethargy, remembering her visit, he was up fluffing the sofa cushions with Pavlovian intensity, on his way to the kitchen with his pots.

"Did he have time to fill the ice bucket on the drinks tray?"

Deciding positively, he would slice some lemon for the gin and tonic.

It was what she had liked to drink; a long one with loads of tonic.

Never more than one all evening.

Never drank wine with dinner.

"Already he knew all this."

In his grey steel and slate kitchen extension, preparing his lemon and his nibbles, the tired but horny writer conceded his caddish preparations were aimed at seduction.

it took the familiar rusty 'ballerina' chimes on his doorbell, to shock some sense into him.

Screaming, internally, to be cautious his knees wobbled in anticipation as he dragged himself down the corridor to his reinforced front door, sensing her rather than seeing though dusk light the diffuse red, blue and clear stained glass.

In pretence at nonchalance, with nervous eyelids half-shut, he slipped with the catch on the door.

It flew open.

She had passed him in a trice.

Knowing the routine, her coat was off and already tossed at the hat stand as she kicked away her shoes.

Without pause she was into his living room and onto the sofa with her feet curled up under her.

Left breathless in the hallway, enveloped in cloud of her exotic bouquet with a lung full of her pheromones, his engaged engine was ticking over on pure adrenaline.

Always admiring of her scent but thinking it too forward to simply ask er its name, on his last trip to his second home in France, he had spent an hour of his afternoon on his stopover in a Paris at a perfumery trying to identify the fragrance.

Drawing a blank, he half-admitted even then, it lacked the personal chemistry to finish off the elixir.

All this before the cock had crowed even once.

Gliding into his own living room, in a second go at

being effete, his heart palpitated a few extra bumps, when he took in what she was wearing.

No, anticipatory widow threads these.

Trying to use, toned shapely bear arm, to cover up lovely-unmasked creamy shoulders and an uplifted bosom, made the sight of her ensconced on his sofa, ever more captivating.

Fully made up, perhaps for the opera, clearly done at a time before the agreed allowance for a clothes change, she was dressed in a short fitted red evening gown.

Dior, he had guessed.

Not used to the revealing cut that struggled to retain her sensuous curves, her unmasked skin glowed luminously; like a baby's, exposed for the first time to the light.

After a positively defiant frown, she smiled, cautiously, at him.

"Well?"

After months of unwanted celibacy, faced with such a banquet, starved hormones tore between them.

Dropping all pretence, a writer's critical antennae, he gawked on at the painter's wife.

Thoroughly confused by the aberrant outfit, her husband lost out there somewhere in the wilderness, Thomas would have done well to have been more circumspect about other things. To have remembered his own careful lighting plan, with strategically placed large, grey-shaded table lamps to diffuse the luminance that lit her satin skin, irresistibly, against his dark green, grey walls.

Learnt from years of photographing women to sell things with their beauty, all he could manage was to marvel at how the ageing process seemed to have passed her by.
Certain her appearance was by no means accidental, would not have changed one single struggling breath; or to have lowered his over-heated red blush by a single degree.

"Pravda. Never got to wear it with him."

Over the years, diligent use of a good hairdresser, a cosmetic consultant, diet, regular running, exercise, everyday application of skin and rejuvenating creams, coupled with her indigenous, Asian ingénue, all were factors in creating an apparent unblemished perfection.

Without children, she had had the time and her own money to indulge herself.

The youthful looking Alice was thirty-nine, evidently, a very dangerous age for a woman like her.

"He thought it was too revealing."

Never, leading the seduction, a shaken Thomas sunk down next to her on his overstuffed sofa.

"Said I looked like a whore."

Even under normal circumstances, once a body was placed on this large soft piece of furniture, it was hard to get up from.

"I like dressing up just to cheer myself up.

Drawn into his own Venus trap, Thomas lingered too long over what was meant to look a brotherly greeting on her cheek.
She turned her head, wordlessly, to present her lips, ferocious black eyes, wide open.

"Well now I can be."

Urgently, after several milli seconds of inaction, her lids closed. She greased his with livid, carmen ones. Joining mouths rudely searched for an opening for the prize of a confusion of wrestling tongues. Sampling a sweet after-taste, the definitive sickly aroma of alcohol, was mixed with an undercurrent of tobacco, Thomas's passion was somewhat diluted.
But not by much.
Though curious about how many drinks she had downed, as a non-smoker, he was surprised at discovering what else was done covertly.

"Oh Thomas."
Other signals ought to have bought him back a little to his senses.
Partially; at least.
Then she was all over him again.

"Oh Thomas."

Folding into each other, searching for novel places to delve with their progressive tongues, he felt the warm firm exercised torso, the womanly softness of her breasts against his chest.

"Oh Thomas."

Too quickly, he became excited; to his immense shame, like an adolescent schoolboy, he was already close to messing into his fresh underpants.

Following the unmistakable cadence of a fast zip opening, she pulled away from him with a shimmy, yanked down the top of her dress to reveal not large, but pert breasts, while exposing engorged, dark-brown erect nipples with definite spherical shape. Pulling his head toward her using both her hands, she carefully, guided his slobbering embouchement, first to the right one, then to the left; each for a few delicious seconds. For an unrepeatable moment of absolute bliss, reaching under the fluffy petticoats, he discovered she was without pats. Pulling out his ravaging hand they grinded. Throwing back her head she let out a huge and continuous howl; a release sounding both climatic and painful; but, surely, could not have been both.

Suffice to say the elongated invocation to an unknown deity sent Thomas right over the top. Oblivious to his predicament, and clearly against her own needs, with the assurance of drill sergeant, Alice ordered everything to a halt too late for the

164

inadvertent spill.

"Enough"

The next moment, with no difficulty at all, and the poise of a trained triathlon athlete at transition, she was up off the sofa, tugging at her dress while pushing her breasts back into the little wire reinforced carriages from whence, boisterous infants had alighted.

"I'm sorry Thomas but I just had too, but I must go.
I just can't sleep with you on the first night.
Then I would be a whore."

Leaving no time for the red-faced writer to even insinuate about the sticky mess in his pants, she grabbed both his hands and pulled him up laughing.
Scooping up her shoes and coat blissfully, as she went, she dragged him after her to the front door, turning, when she reached it to give him a final sloppy kiss on the mouth.

"I'll call you."

With that she was gone.

Thomas stood frozen stupefied seconds behind, his mind on delay.

He watched her coat less skipping into her shoes as she ran happily away down his path, carefree to any expose to other watchful eyes in the deserted street.

"JESUS

Taking a few more stationary moments to adjust, she disappeared from view.

Eventually he closed the door.

Instinctively double locking it.

He turned on the alarm for the night, despite the early hour.
He had not known why.

Licking the last taste of her from his lips, he walked back into his living room, beginning to see the funny side.

"Wallow adulterer"

Though short and sharp, it had been undeniable fun.

She had really tasted so formidable.

Reeking of her smells and with the additional mess in his pants, he really needed a bath.

Wanting to savour her intimacy a while longer, he moved to the garden window, lifting the hand she had baptised to his nose.

He was not a bad person he had argued; merely, human.

Then another justification dawned.
Maybe, he had feelings for this woman.
She was so willing; she might even return them.
Unfortunately, though, she was married to that loser.

CHAPTER NINETEEN

To the echoing cacophony of fast running- water, set among indulgent, grey-smoked mirrors of an otherwise entirely slate-tiled bathroom, all too soon, guilt had consumed a dirty scribe's heavily-compromised soul.

He nudged his way to the free-standing tub.

"She's married, Thomas. married..."

Swiftly overboard with recriminations, he wondered, when it had ever been important to see umpteen unflattering angles of his less-than-perfect torso. Recalling, that he had redesigned the space himself with the builder, he tried to shift the blame to a man obsessed with its future resale.

"Everyone wants three bathrooms."

"No, they don't."

Distracted, he forgot to test his bath water. Finding it way too hot, only once he was standing in it, then acting on a foolhardy masochistic impulse, a blasphemer decided he 'should' take his punishment.

"Marymotheroffuckingjesus.'

Granted the operation of the mixer was a puzzle to him in perpetuity, submerged to his knees in scolding water, the word smith heard the reverberation of his distant screams, in an acoustic usually greatly flattering to his bass-baritone.

In purgatory even after he had scrambled out of the tub, to save himself permanent scarring, the extreme pain began to subside. For once able to gauge the direction of the cold lever correctly, after he determined with considerable fortitude to resume his ritualistic cleansing. Temperature back to manageable proportions, he backed into the bath to avoid the reflections. Sinking, thankfully into obscurity, pleasant still steaming water around his calves was not felt. Debilitated by excess, he could find no less brutal an adjective, than the utterly appropriate one for the only disgrace really to have mattered to him. Looking down at himself, seeing it turning his lower half bright red, intensified the tideline between the bath water and pale body. Again, deep in his psyche, he flushed redder at the woefully over-excited performance.

"The angle of incidence is equal to the angle of refraction."

Open to any distraction, he speculated on the distortion, caused by it in his bathwater.

It led to pictures by Pierre Bonnard who had painted his wife, submerged like this up to her neck in the bath. Seemingly, equally vulnerable and defenceless in the pictures, it must have been inspired by the same visual effect. Appearing as a muse in hundreds of her husband's works, the wife had a reputation for rashness. Though no great beauty, she was in competition with a better-looking mistress, who had committed suicide, when Bonnard would not leave his marriage. Marthe would spend much of her time submerged in her bath. Then it was the only treatment for tuberculosis, which eventually would kill her. Making the tenuous leap to Thomas's new love tie-up, though to his knowledge she had no life-threatening problem, Alice's impulsive behaviour was discomforting. The visualisation of her naked in his bath presented no such problem.

Clearly, when she wanted something, she could be formidable.

Apparently, she had wanted Thomas.

It was a novel and pleasing perspective.

Rationalising his misgivings, he understood he was quite incapable of stopping this dangerous affair before it had got started.

A late arrival at the 'Impressionists' sun-lit altar, Bonnard had given his allegiance to the early masters in his search to recreate the luminous energy to light his beloved. Black pigments had been excluded from their palates. The consequence of this simple genius was to produce some of the most astonishing pictures of that age; some would say of all ages.

It was not a concept, in stricter Thomas's view, then or now to guarantee masterpieces, turning some of the studio-painted sunsets of a foggy, dirty London town by an accomplished painter, into pictures fit for chocolate box tops.

Washing himself speedily as the pain subsided, the pink painter -climbed out of the bath, startled once more by the triplets who had shared his dismount.

Defensively, towelling his body dry with his back to them, he draped himself in his long black Chinese robe, anticipating a childishly, early, night.

Spontaneously, he heaved a huge sigh of relief.

The bath had done its job.

Infelicitously, the anticipated release was a fraction ahead of his luck, in an exceptional passage of a full life. On his painless way to the kitchen for a night drink, he made one last check of his emails and found another had flipped into his inbox. Enlivened even more by any change of focus, again without any concern for the risk, he opened the message.

It had not disappointed.

"Alice"

Again, it was a photo of the woman who had looked a lot like her.

A picture seemingly taken earlier than the first one.

She was dressed in black knickerbockers; at a seaside spot that seemed very much like under the supports of the West peer at Brighton before it had been burnt.

Like the first missive, there was no text.

Leaning across his desk puzzled, he ordered a print from his laser printer.

Noting his shaky hand, he decided to seek the familiar comforter in the front room to contemplate his next step before bed.

"Must be her mother. But why to me?"

Settling into his sofa, he discovered it had lost none of the pungent reminders of his lustful battle, worrying, when next his daughters would visit for an inspection. Within moments of him leaning back into the heavily upholstered comforter, he fell fast asleep, engulfed again in her musk.

Two hours later, from no outward disturbance, he sat bolt upright on the sofa.

His face was clouded with the despair of an unarmed man fleeing a bullet.

Struggling to extract his body from the upholstery, which would not push back to help, eventually he freed himself and hurried back to the computer, the crumpled email still secured in his fiercely clenched claw. Urgently, he needed to document the remaining phosphorescent shards of a dream before its projection was stripped from his aroused unconscious. He believed it might hold the code to the story he had a need to tell. Not wanting to know where the dream would fit into the diorama of his misplaced images, he cut himself loose, into the viscous flow of spontaneity, the whispers of a radical inner voice.

Two hours later though it was very late, he returned to his pale fragrant sofa and sank into its comfort to read aloud his efforts in the final writing phase he had taught himself to conduct.

CHAPTER TWENTY

"Congregated over several billion years in the expected eleven to one ratio of our cosmos, an almost unimaginable aggregation of hydrogen and helium atoms had formed into a soft-edged dodecahedron. Created by massive attracting energy into a constant mass about the size of our moon, it had surrounded itself with a homogeneous inert shield, to secure its internal reactions. An invisible electron jellyfish, in a far space well beyond our galaxy, the unique attraction of polarities travelled as the watcher to the universe, entirely independent of any other life source. Having solved the need to replenish, its intelligence was self-contained and eternally in the present. Amorphous, and a relatively small miracle of mass, compared to the rest of the universe, it owned an infinite bank of data and knowledge.

To it, our highly complex human DNA sequences would have been, merely, an afterthought; such had been the brilliance of its imperishable memory store. Calculating, infinitely knowing, its purpose was to observe with no master to explain its findings.

Yet it was none of these things because these were human attributes.

This was a thinking machine with not one speck of an 'us' in it.

Coincidentally, with similar electronic particles, its streaming multitudes never derived from our world and the sun but from the energies existing beyond our universe at the Big Bang.

It had all the things needed to reproduce us in abundance, without end.

Assuming supremacy over animals as we have because they cannot reason like us, put plants, who cannot think at all, one step below them, and then hierarchically, this calculating mass would be well above our own.

It could only be viewed by we humans as supernatural.

Because it had not designed its own beginning, it could not be sighted at the highest level.

It was not a God, but one step below.

It lacked any lust for power like Adam because it had already owned it.

With the capacity to reproduce and remain constant, it had been he, she, and all the degrees between.

Lacking a brother Able and there had been no need for an Eve.

It had reproduced itself.

With an eternity to decipher us, it learnt the secrets of our creation accidentally, for the domain in which it operated, as random as Brownian movement.

Intercepting a way to understand us and our world was not by the transmissions of our hopeful wireless or ultra-sonic wave motions but by the vibrations of single thought.

The timbre registered at the creation of a new

creative idea.

Only then had we become evident.

Maybe, when Rembrandt painted on his canvas the face of an old lady who would there after never die while her oil painting could be viewed. Or maybe when Cezanne realised the French landscape, he had studied religiously could be manipulated to fit into his painted message which would resonate with most men. Already knowing the secrets of creation and how it will be destroyed it saw the truth of life after death."

CHAPTER TWENTY ONE

Moments, into the consummate flush of a huge success, Thomas's triple back flip was as effortless as a Chinese Olympic high diver, into a turgid aquamarine lagoon of triteness. Instantly, the disappointed reader had recognised his blundering, which would be seen as such by others. Head bowed and swinging negatively like a well sprung door without its doorstop, his monologue had been silenced before it had begun. Each silver-plated truth, inscribed for 'revelation', polished nearly down to its copper, was held in the two-page print out of his once of solid wake-up convictions and torn to shreds.

Frankly, wandering around any ideas, which considered Art magical or made it out to be sacred, had to be destroyed.

Correctness might come later.

When good work had been worked through

But never at the beginning; till scourged of clawing ego, the forerunner to all trash.

Ingrained twists from a polluted upbringing, drew his unwelcome smile,

They had encouraged a skilful about face in Catholic.

"One thousand hail Mary's boy or I strap you".

Taking sudden heart from an article, he

remembered he had read somewhere, the weekend supplements such let-downs were not unknown to his new trade.

Authors, involved in similar hunts often slipped after they had drawn blood from a new kill.

Over time good ideas would reinstate themselves. Such extreme mood swing, years before would have been reason to self- medicating with alcohol. To increase the regularity of gloom. Since then, he had tried to earn other ways to find peace.

Remain at one level.

Staying with the discomfort, trying to outlast it. Seeing how long he had been at his current task, a stimulant other than an alcoholic one seemed appropriate.

"Coffee"

Jumping up at the healthier alternative with surprising vigour, the spring returned to a notably more pliant psyche.

Clicked on Leonard reverberated.

"Its three in the morning ...I'm writing a letter".

Spryly, he bounced to the kitchen, despite the hour, to manage a coffee and to hum; light-heartedly play acting for his psyche.

"Jane came by with a lock of your hair, said your favourite blue raincoat was torn at the shoulder.... "

Continuing, a comforting, well-leant- task, he separated the pots aluminium half's, skilfully, emptying in the cone for fresh grounds. Refilling the bottom with water, he joined them and put them on the gas ring.

Hands set at the top right quadrant of the violet neon wall clock, he guessed it would be some time before he was able to sleep, with or without caffeine.

Soon he was disobediently back on his sofa, with his brewed mug of black tranquilliser, a clean t-towel on his lap in case of spillage, and a taffeta mat for the side table.

Lacking companionship and any real discussion opponent, he sat sipping and mused on, talking more than usual to himself out loud.

A lapsed Catholic was familiar with dialogues to an imagined being.

Religious images from the past were always accessible.

Once conjured up by black-cloaked clerics; mostly ruddy-faced Irishmen and women, a few, admittedly, had been clever and charismatic.

'Father, forgive me.'

Drilling the fear of a 'God' into an unwary child, by making them converse with the supernatural, as a real man, was how the death-cult sustained itself over the centuries. Under constant threat of an eternity in the flames of hell, his betters demanded total obedience to the imaginary voices. Encouraged at a sophisticated level with the words of the evil genius avoider, Thomas Aguaenus.

Christ as a man did not fit the general perception,
So the Theologian invented the Christian concept of
the Trinity.

Three gods for the price of one.

Avoidance is so profound and duplicated that,
has been argued to present times.

A theological reply was ever available to a clever
child.

Common sense reasoning regarding clever thoughts
was not seen as an asset.

Canning fiercely, and imbedding submissiveness
with discrete violence were added to weekly
confessions of even the smallest impure.

Child abuse is at the lowest order.

If there were no sins available, you invented them.

'It has been 47 years since my last confession,
and these are my sins'.

"How long child?"

"47 years"

"47 child?"

"Yes, father ...47".

"And last night I nearly fucked a married woman".

"Tell me about it, child."

"Certainly not, you dirty old man."

Realising he was too wasted to be talking sensibly, even to himself, Thomas finished his coffee.

Sleep was hardly ever affected by his favourite brew and bed seemed a safer option.

Properly, rested, he might become a better person.

Deciding, in lieu of redemption, he would spend what was left of the night amongst her adulterous smells soon he was snoring on the sofa.

Lamentably, after barely a few minutes sunk deep into the soft curves of the upholstery, under the spare Glastonbury shed by an offspring, a very late phone call came in. Received groggily on the extension sitting on the sofa table, he made an instant not altogether surprising guess.

"Alice?"

Having sublimated her thorny problems to a lower empty drawer, he was aware of those concerns again by the tightening of the muscles in his abdomen.

Not troubling to announce herself, she was, breathlessly, ahead of his game.

Soft tones gave no room to express alarm at the late hour.

"Still no news, Thomas."

Attention diverted so effectively toward the wife, guiltily, Thomas was reminded of the spouse.

"Really?"

"Afraid so, darling."

This was the first time; she would use the endearment toward her conquest.

"Really?"

Resonating with the terrifying tinkle of exclusivity, at the 'get-go' he had hated it.
Anticipating, how badly the world would judge him for his behaviour toward a distressed friend's wife if she had been overheard addressing him so familiarly, he learnt quickly it had advantages.

"Let's meet tomorrow if you're free."

"Why on earth would he not be free for her?

"Not at your place DARLING.
I'm still not ready to do it there so where?"

Sinfully complicit with an acquired sexual directness, she added the second sensational embellishment. A toke on a strong drug to which he would become addicted.

"Somewhere special, darling."

On hearing the darling, a third time he had shivered.

So, tempting in its implications, he was too of a man not to relish it.

"Well, we could go to the Tate Alice."

This odd and slightly dangerous choice of meeting places, perfectly, reflected Thomas's state of mind. Thoughtlessness about being recognised was disguised by weariness.

"At the Modern?"

"Yes. In front of the big Rothko's."
For her part, he could not have made a better choice.

"Say eleven o'clock?"

"Bit later."

"Eleven thirty?"

Her squeak over the phone, agreeing to so romantic an assignation, reminded him of the earlier one which had caused his tumult.

"Wonderful, Wonderful, Wonderful, darling."

There was the word again; quietly, transformed.
In minutes this woman had him panting in anticipation, as she hung up the phone.

CHAPTER TWENTY TWO

Numbed with apprehension and lack of sleep, Thomas found himself in the chapel-like gallery housing the Rothko's at Tate Modern, barely minutes late. Staring transfixed ahead, Alice was sitting on the bench, in front of the two massive black and maroon canvases; masterpieces to be numbered in the pantheon capable of communicating sublimely, if there ever had been such a category. Captured by the well-documented phenomenon he had read about; the pictures seem to have brought her to tears.

Formed as part of a group, the paintings were commissioned by Seagram for their exclusive Four Seasons restaurant in New York but withdrawn by the artist after his first visit there. Overwhelmed by the owner's bourgeois pretensions, he gave back the deposit, saying he had intended to make the plebeian dinners thoroughly uncomfortable anyway.

Caught with older fears chilling up and down his spine, the writer had been inexplicably wary of approaching Alice. Listening to a dissenting inner voice for as long as he dared, he had put off the reunion.

The elegant dark-toned apparition was costumed in black heels, clinging black Lycra trousers and a short black bolero jacket. Against the majesty of the works in the deliberately dimmed light ordered by their creator, she looked fragile; more elusive than ever. A modern-day princess locked in the bramble against a storybook tower.

Displaying a near-perfect form to his bigoted eyes, he could think of nothing else than ravaging her.

Sliding onto the streamlined upholstered leather seat, looking like it was designed for more private living rooms, he offered her a fresh tissue; pocketed at home; a handy pack anticipating an adventurous day of inadvertent spills.

"It makes other people cry too. He said it was meant to."

Turning to look directly at him, Alice gave no hint of surprise but was delighted to see him.

"I know darling I know."

It seemed an ice age since he had heard the endearment.

"Donald explained."

Not so the reminder of a husband.

"I was crying for myself."

Baffled by her admission, Thomas struggled to rationalise.

He could not see the reason for her upset. Other than his own ineptitude,

So, he had apologised.

"Sorry"

"Don't be silly".

Taking the paper handkerchief, she dabbed it carefully under well-made-up eyes.

Quickly, the tears, though not her concern, disappeared.

"You needn't have waited so long to come over."

Unhappy she had caught him, reaching surreptitiously across for the comfort of her hand, once it was in his, it stayed.

"Thomas, I feel as if I'm being followed."

Totally, in her world again, he had not taken note of a single other gallery visitor.

"Followed?"

Gradual awareness after yesterday's private fumbling, that other people might be interested in his closeness to a married woman, Thomas understood, this had not been an ideal choice for their meeting.

"Maybe it's the police."

Attempting, to smother his alarm, Thomas turned to look where she had half-pointed.

Struggling with a walk-around-info phone, a swarthy Italian with a necklace of three cameras was trying to follow the TV guidebook in the gloom through dark sunglasses.

"Him"

Looking an unlikely spy, an obviously harried 'papa', was immediately joined by three long-legged adolescent girls, all with long-flowing dark-curly hair, streaked violently with blonde as if with a paintbrush. Dressed in identical tight bell bottoms, each was in different layered tops, revealing thin tanned bellies. Simultaneously, they had each asked a different question in raucous Italian; stage-whispering to be respectful to the penetrable silence; but carrying across the gallery for everyone to hear.

"That family?"

Pouting, at his tone, Alice looked ashamedly away.

"Let's get out of here."

Seeing the sense of being somewhere else, he nodded acquiescence.

"Thank you, darling. Where too?"

A perplexed 'darling' needed more time to settle.

"How about the British Museum?"

Unused, to reading her delayed responses, he took her surprised expression as a no.

Was way too speedy with a follow-up.

"Well, there is this place called the Westbury.'

To balance the indiscrete hand in hand around London town with someone else's woman, he had earlier searched for a hotel on the internet, central and accessible to the Museum.

"We could have coffee there."

Behind a nod of oriental submissiveness, Alice agreed. Left in the no-man's land of British uncertainty, with her seeming lack of enthusiasm, Thomas became unsure. But had established the option.

"Then the British Museum it is."

On their way out, with hands discretely disentangled, they had passed the group of 'suspect' tourists. A fourth, equally languid but older long-haired Botticelli angel, filling a shapelier grown-up version of her children's pantaloons, re-joined the group, quelling the pubescent fray with a fierce maternal glare. To loud murmuring sulks, cameras were re-hung around younger, slimmer necks, with crinkled tresses shaken haughtily. Now with a full view of them, Thomas could see only two of the almost identical gangling adolescents were female;

the third was a tall, beautiful boy. A shock to make him gasp.

Alice's glance at him was stern. To compensate, she then had leaned in closer for protection.

Just as soon as they were outside, they were quickly into a cab.

Mrs Donald Grey willingly turned down her danger finder to almost nothing.

Protected from prying eyes by 'celebrity' smoked windows, the cab interior mixed the smell of expensive new leather with her exotic essences. Choosing a submissive, more seductive guise, she earnestly sought protection from an expected paramour.

"Are you OK darling?"

Nuzzling into his shoulder, she carried a full tank of worries but chose not to share them.

Weary from lack of sleep, Thomas's insecurities broke the surface.

Maybe someone had seen them.

Had he been more aware, earlier, it would probably have made no difference. He would have found it hard to believe anyone would have been interested in following across town. An understandable conclusion. But an entirely, erroneous one. Centre black circles at the heart of her thoughtful brown eyes, set impenetrably at infinity, he had needed reassurance. Homing in onto the perfect black dots for nostrils, incredulous at the perfection of so symmetrical features, he dared to reach out and touch. Stunning in close-up perfect

Japanese, English rose porcelain hid emotion flawlessly. In moments like this, Thomas had not a clue what she was thinking.

"There is no way to find the mind's construction in the face."

Slow, even hostile, her turning gaze fazed him. She smiled, curiously, at which point they moved closer to communicate urgent needs. Through soft lips and eager fingertips, resorting to share reassurance, thus, a brand-new coupling had slipped, effortlessly, into co-dependency.

CHAPTER TWENTY THREE

Red baseball cap, reverentially in hand, adolescent skinny sideburns seemingly longer than the day before, Benji pretended to study the Rothko's with his mouth open, as he had at school when confronted by teachers of his ignorance. With no hint of what the huge areas of colour canvas represented, to him they had been the fear of being tufted out for not paying to look at them. Earlier, discovering the English woman he knew had spelled trouble. Providently, with depleted funds because of the previous mess, he had been relieved to have no entrance fee to pay, so could pocket the tenner issued for travel and admission. Warily, he had carried his legitimate train pass to travel uptown as a backup; issued by the school, though not designated for these rarefied spaces in the city. His mother had encouraged both boys to visit galleries, but her gifts had not been handed down to a very efficient left-side wing forward who loved football.

Stripped of street assurance, in an official-looking building, after slipping over an occasional tube barrier, he thought himself an obvious interloper. He wanted out. Under orders to keep tracking the promise had been a payday from scary hard men, who had never seemed to lack cash. His elder sibling had taken the blame for losing the precious supplement, but they had increased the number of trackers without experience; insulting to him; who had perfected his tracking skills after home games with likeminded pals, following Blues fans to ring their doors bells and run, in the dead hour before tea. They never caught him.

Checking the right street number in Fulham early morning, and picking up his tail, he had ended up all this way up at the Tate Modern an hour later; well out of his depth.

He had to keep the others informed on the telephone. Almost live.

No one in several multi-formulated texts back and forth had calculated on Alice but had buzzed about her the whole journey. Changing to orange socks had left home but not gone to work as they had surmised; quite unaware of the dangerous Arab caravan following. Benji had guided the trail of six followers of Islam to the next Museum. More comfortable alone and on the move, the hirsute youngster had continued to stay close to the love-sick novices; overhearing their cabs destination and keeping the rest of the party informed. They had forwarded ahead to London Bridge station. Mouthwatering anticipation of the food stall he had passed in the foyer, the others were quickly there by London Transport and Shanks's Pony. Abruptly without warning but welcomely, he was released by the men he had feared.

"Go home"

Freedom felt intoxicating. It tasted like a hot dog with extra mustard, on the other side of the bridge.

Skipping jubilantly, with the remaining expenses in his pocket, he leapt onto the curving space-age footbridge across the Thames, free to a victorious heel kick at the top, he jogged spiritedly to home.

Treacherously relaxed, the study in stealth then was himself surprised like a novice. His personal space was invaded without him getting a 'whiff' of the interception. The pathway forward over the splendid "swaying" structure was blocked by three 'hoodies. Speedily, advancing on him they crowded him to the ship-like glass steel barrier guarding the water. Though alarmed, Benji's immediate thought was a 'stop and search' courtesy of the 'terrorist branch'.

Smelling heavily of mint, the biggest of the mountain men was in his face giving him no 'wriggle room'. He knew never to call out. You just had to take it, for fear of implicating others.

Selflessly, remembering the mobile in his hand full of incriminating family details, he needed to be free. He raised both hands in a fake surrender; continuing the action skyward he was able to lob the phone over his shoulder toward the Thames. With comical absurdity, the mobile seemed to hang in the air forever, Showing the efficiency of a good slip fielder, the big man's arm shot out and grabbed it.

"Silly move Benji baby.
That's what we were looking for."

The boy's capture gained an audience. Everyone sensing trouble immediately avoided it.

Stunned that the man knew him by his nickname, he was immobilised by a single thick hand completely encasing his skinny neck. Benji watched his precious mobile pocketed,

192

"What was the address of red socks street boy?

Terrified but instantly understanding the question, it was answered quickly with a splutter.

No reason to be loyal to the Englishman who was causing them so much trouble.

"Tournay Road.'
"Number?"
"46'"
"You'd better not be lying."

A small packet the size of a Malteser box was pushed into his trouser pocket.

"Post it through his letter box.
Don't dare open it.
Or we'll post you.
You have twenty-five minutes.
it's primed, so get moving".
After spiting depreciatively over the rail, the big man turned to two black-clad associates, nodded for them and moved off.

"Paki's."

Departing as quickly as they had appeared, the trio turned like a well-marshalled platoon, pushing through the tourists into a trot, leaving Benji breathless and close to tears.

Another awful event to explain to his brother

without his precious phone.

Not stationary with anticipation, he speeds to Fulham, no longer with a way to communicate.

He had to meet his mother on an errand today at Earls Court, to chaperone her to a doctor's appointment as well. If he uploaded his package, the address was close enough to the station not to have to change the arraignment.

Which he could not make by phone anyway, for obvious reasons.

So, he ran.

CHAPTER TWENTY FOUR

Unmuzzled for three centuries, fighting its noisy way through the daily din of London traffic, an ancient church bell double chimed, half past the slowly progressing hour. Finally, prospective lovers had agreed on a game plan. Already passed first, second and third bases, they had careened head-down towards the catcher and home; incredibly, concluding without ever discussing a hotel room. In case the other might find the talk of sharing a bed somehow offensive.

Thus, into a grey city afternoon, the prospect of relief still unrequited, a valorous Thomas had been leading a children's nursery rhyme. Purposefully, hand in hand with his doxy.

"Oranges and lemons,
Say the bells of St Clements.
You owe me five farthings,
Say the bells of St Martins."

"My mother used to sing that Thomas."

Twixt and between lingering kisses in the ceiling-high encrypted- walls of Mesopotamian hieroglyphics, fitted impossibly into an internal Museum gallery, the writer in his anxiety had decided to explore the surrounding streets of old London City. If his delightful, near forty-year-old companion had learnt nothing about the whiles of men, long as a quiet wedded partner, she

understood they had feted off a good listener.
Absorbed in his own self-scripted lecture tour, they
were as far along as the law courts.

"How much is five farthings Thomas?"

"' Fourth' of a silver penny."

"It's a quarter?"

Still unexplored, had been the email pictures.
There had not been a single mention of them.
Sensing the time for adult action, Alice decided to
act.

"I was brought up in Boston by my mother. Till I
was eight."

The coin rolled along the groove and dropped into
the slot dispensing good sense.
Hearing the other bells that had been ringing for
some considerable time, one perfect peel had finally
resonated with Thomas.

"I'm talking way too much aren't I."

Pathways, which Dick Whittington had believed

paved with gold, suddenly had become lustrous.

"Let's find somewhere shall we darling."

"Turn again, turn again, Lord Mayor of

London."

"Are you sure?

Handing off an advancing City black lamp standard with the enamelled red and white George cross, a diligent full back shove saved him from some bad bruising.

With a gaff and hardly a break in her twirl, Alice had turned wickedly schoolgirlish, a rapid switch to become more customary by day's end.

The inevitable was agreed to in the small hotel he had researched,

Pricey enough for the experience not to have been as tacky as it was.

Taxing to the place, almost in silence, in an older cab with the leather aroma less prominent, unsurprisingly gave no competition to the arousal of her enticing essence spiking the air; anticipation of the start of a first downhill of the season on the daring red slopes, with a Christmas roast promised to follow.

Prematurely almost dark in London wintertime, they had completed the short journey in a blink.

The Westbury was a building, he must have walked past a thousand times on his way to the museum, but its name never had registered before.

Certainly, he had never thought of staying there.

"It looks fine darling. I won't be staying the night. I must be home for his calls."

For Thomas, there had been no calculation of the afterwards or anything else.

No consideration of Donald or his absence.

Only of her and his lusting.

There was still a vacant room.

Several in fact.

Thomas would do the paying while Alice had visited the lobby toilet.

"I need to change my shoes."

Suddenly the occasion became whimsical.

Like many anxious new lovers, he had never been able to book into a hotel with a woman who was not his wife, without remembering the Graduate.

"How will sir be paying?"

Imitating the afternoon street-ringers, words rang around the lobby, like calls to the gallows.

"How will you pay me?
says the bells of Old Bailey".

If he used a credit card, he would have to surrender a name.

"Cash"

With a derisory scowl, but accepting the

198

announcement without comment, the man behind the desk, abruptly, abandoned his keyboard, reaching for a scruffy signing in book from under the counter.

"Cash? Mister, eh?"

'I do not know says the great bell of Bow.'

Often affected in times of crisis by the vagaries of a loose tongue, Thomas used the first name in his absent brain, which happened to be his prospective lover's.

"GRAY."

The stranger could hardly hide his derision at such a limp lie.

"With an E or an A"

"G. R. A. Y"

Thank you, Mr. Gray."

Thereby, his cover became as inviolate as marriage vows.

Without any form of baggage, beside Alice's fashionably large handbag, suburban urges made for more discomfort; eliciting excuses that were not needed.

'We've missed our flight."

Dressed in a maroon and grey striped waistcoat, the young man had a badge pinned to it reading 'night manager'. In a good hotel it would have been enamel, not the shiny printed card he wore.

"Next flight's not till the morning."

Needing to demonstrate, whatever it might look like, that Thomas had not just picked up the gorgeous creature on his arm from around the corner in Berwick Street, he clumped on.

"We hate sleeping at airports."

Turning to face Thomas, the young receptionist looked him straight in the eye.
Plainly, he was not swallowing a word of this fable.

"I'll need to see some sort of ID."

"Ah yes."

Panicked, Thomas stumbled again for the driving licence in his wallet pocket which he could not use.
In a mild sweat, loathing to supply any of his own credentials, unless it had become an absolute necessity, he skipped through to the back. Among business cards, he spied Donald's elaborately embossed one, with a note made on the back for a cab number. Since Thomas was about to steal the

man's wife for the night, after ripping off his character in his novel, why not go the whole hog and have his identity too?

God forbid his girls ever found out about these Machiavellian machinations.

"And we'll need some sort of deposit for bar and phone calls.
Say twenty pounds?"

Sensing the manager's tone was becoming appeasing, the hotel seemed to provide little in extras to explain such a charge. Thomas twigged the money was not for phone calls but the usual grubby gratuity for not putting a client on the electronic register.
The night manager nodded at him, identifying a bad set of Dickensian teeth too early in life.

"Twenty?"

"Yes twenty"

To his endless shame, a completely unscrupulous seducer then placed a friend's business card on the counter; together with the room fee, plus the additional twenty-pound note.
Without so much as a blink, the manager colluded; and became his bosom friend.
Quickly, writing Donald's name from the card into the tired old book, he swivelled it one hundred eighty degrees for Thomas to sign, which he did illegibly

with the proffered biro. The pen returned, the card was pushed back, and the book snapped shut, to be returned instantly to the dark cubby hole. The room rent money was swept into a cash drawer below the counter leaving a single twenty on the countertop. So, its previous guardian knew it would have a safe home, watchfully, like a conjurer at the start of a trick, showing he had concealed no hidden doves, the manager extracted a thin, personal wallet pompously from inside his uniform waistcoat pocket. Carefully, he placed the note in its centre folds, snapped it shut, and smoothly returned it to the pocket.

"You can settle any additional bar balance in the morning."

At this point Thomas's darkly designer-clad passion emerged from the hotel reception bathroom; a good five inches taller. She had exchanged walking shoes for dangerous black heels. Having repaired make-up and painted her lips with a shiny fire-warning red, she came fluttering her adoring black lashes for only him. Sashaying across the lobby, baring no resemblance to mature Mrs Robinson, she looked svelte and ready for work, like a tall extravagant Oriental ingénue from a deviant Tokyo sex movie. With the Jimmy Cho's had arrived a dangerous other person.

"Everything all right darling?"

Too familiarly, the over-impressed receptionist

answered for him.

"Yes, thank you, Mrs. Gray. Now we are legal. Sorry about your delayed flight,"

Momentarily, time slowed again at the surprise peal of her real name.

"Pardon"

When she caught sight of her husband's gaudy calling card, still in her prospective lover's hand, she shivered, distinctly. With the mercurial speed of an experienced teller, she readjusted her story with divine inspiration, putting together what Thomas was propagating.
Turning theatrically, she gave her shoulder with the bag its full prominence.

"Airplanes are such a bore."

Her once shy affront radiated vampish.
Then delving expertly into her bag, she embellished further.
Pulling out a legal British passport to massive silent applause.

"Aren't they Donald darling?"

Flashing the documents without relinquishing it, she substantiated her family connection.

Clearly, she was having fun.

"We are going back to Hong Kong."

That final detail the home city in the fanciful web, sold everything to an impressionable young man.

"Hong Kong Mrs Grey. Wow"

Naughty goings on in that city of the night to his proprietary eyes, were in a universe unto itself; where rich wives, posing as hookers, were trivia.

"I'm Maurice by the way."
Thomas recognised a strong Australian accent.
 The boy also was in the first stages of growing a slightly ginger goatee, which he stroked, copiously.

Let me show you up to your room."

Cramped into the ancient, embarrassingly slow lift, it would not have been large enough for three people carrying baggage.
The tight space was shrouded in Alice's reapplied perfume.

**Here comes a candle to light you to bed.
Chip chop chip chop.**

Spilling out of the scrapping doors into the second-floor corridor the young man stepped forward a few paces to open their room; close enough to the Victorian transporter to be heard inside every time it had operated. Happily, that had not been often.

With the expert slash of a plastic key, the new door flew open.

"226. It's just been redecorated."

Though there were two more floors above them Thomas could not believe there had been twenty-six rooms in the whole hotel.

Presented with the room card, lovers were ushered into the clean but unspectacular room.

And yes, it had smelt heavily of emulsion paint from walls in shades matching his uniform maroon.

Here comes a chopper.
to chop off your head

"Goodnight Mr. and Mrs. Grey"

The newly, refurbished door was slammed with soft finality sealing in the scented DIY air.

The old man's dead

At last, they were alone.
Thomas had needed to apologise.

"So sorry about involving Donald."

"Doesn't matter, darling."
Stunned, initially, Alice had been delighted by the inadvertent make-believe of a borrowed husband.

"The perfect disguise."

Knowing nothing of Thomas' writing on Sam, prudence could only wonder if she would have been so forgiving of his literary thefts.

Fatefully, taking command, she then locked the door from the inside,
Other difficult concerns were for the future.
Effortlessly, gates holding back the flood all day subsided, and tensions sluiced them effortlessly open.

"Alice."

"Thomas."

"Darling."

Driving forward, raging unstoppable waters again threatened mutual satisfaction.
Dropping her large handbag where she had stood, without any pretence of deference, Alice needed to be released from her clothing, which had become tight and cumbersome. Ripping open her black, multi-buttoned top without first getting rid of it fully, revealed a wide-open breach to perfection, unsupported breasts and long pert brown nipples joyfully to attention like a stalking cat. She grabbed his hands to massage the twin trophies of consensual fornication. Tiny but lethal perfect manicured digits, free to roam, needed live flesh to manipulate. Skilfully, she was inside his shirt.

Expressing their desires in grunts and groans, he delved lower attacking her stretch pants. Eventually, they were down and off, together with a flimsy expensive pair of see-through panties.

A perfect female human torso he saw marked by a surgery scar at the point where the Roman spear had found water, not Jesus's blood.

"Don't look at that kidney surgery stare at my pussy".

Don't worry darling, I can never have children."

Chip chop chip chop.
Chip chop chip chop.

Careless of any medical risk, her panting drove him greedily,
His pants were down, he was on and in her.
Screams Rose too primeval. Unfortunately, with such thrilling accompaniment, after all the stress of the day, his first time inside her, she was so tight he came. Far, far, too quickly.

Old man's dead

Even more world-ending, immediately in those blissful moments between paradise, the climb down back into the real world, but still half hard inside her, he was so exhausted he fell fast asleep.

Or passed out, whichever justification for his crime makes it more forgivable.

207

Either way, he was not on her level of consciousness for the next few hours.

Examine well yourselves in time to repent.
that you may not to eternal flames be sent.
And when St. Sepulchre's Bell in the morning tolls
The Lord above have mercy upon your soul.

CHAPTER TWENTY FIVE

Not deep and surgically irremediable, as Michael Jackson's post-concert Propanol into the afterlife had been, Thomas awoke with organs functioning and reeking of sex. To the furring coating inside of his mouth and temporary memory loss, an additional throbbing ached, resentfully in his abdomen.

For something, he could not immediately identify.

"Alice"

Cutting through the blur, he reached out for the novel security of her bodily reassurance; not needing to search further for the cause of his distress.

She had upped and left him.

"JESUS."

Sequent to the ignominious slide into the 'land of nod', bad-temperedly he realised, she would have discovered the family secret; the uncontrolled trumpeting of his clarion nose-horn.

A sound to first delight his girls on youthful stopovers, when he had cat-napped on the home sofa.

Generally, he had tried to hide the unconscious music-making.

At least at the start of an affair.

That disgrace alone could have been the one to have driven Alice away.

Let alone the pathetic display in the sack.
Despondency sloughed to a dangerous low.

In a hotel room without a wash bag, he
possessed no toothbrush to get rid of the disgusting
residue in his mouth. Needing to absolve himself, or
at least wash away some of his shame, he rolled off
the bed, remembering something he had seen in a
John Wayne movie. Stiff-jointed from all the walking,
he hobbled to the small bathroom, via the wet bar
for a miniature. Reluctant, to wash his hands
because they smelt so strongly of her, he
substituted two fingers for a toothbrush and covered
them with whiskey from the small bottle.

When finished, he gargled the remains without
swallowing.

Curiously it had performed the trick; leaving an
after-taste to a non-drinker that made the occasion
that more surreal.

Returning to the main room after showering, he
dried himself with the two minuscule hotel bath
towels. the after-burn of passion still lingering in her
personal perfume. Tossing aside the flannels he
surveyed the room, lit by a chrome yellow streetlight
which had turned the scene into a badly lit
lithograph. He saw his clothes, carefully folded and
put onto a side chair, imagining she had watched
over him while he had slept.

Laying back down again, he turned his head, to
catch sight of his wallet on the night table.

Three crisp new fifty-pound notes had been

tucked inside.

Clearly, her gift was towards the cost of the room.

He wondered why she would be carrying such large currency.

Despite his dumps, reviewing his efforts as a toy boy made him chortle.

In the background, ever since he had awoken, an annoying tinkle rattled.

A faint yellow light on the telephone blinking half-heartedly in the semi-darkness, like a dying battery had been its source. Rolling back across the bed, enthusiastically, he picked up the odd flat-shaped receiver to answer it.

"Sorry to wake you, Mr Grey, It's Maurice here. We've been trying to reach. Even came up and knocked on your door but you were dead to the world. There are several messages from your wife. She's at her mother's. She's sick she says."

Alice of course was dutifully keeping up the charade.

"Oh right."

Thomas was heady with delight.

"She's on the phone again now."

"Let me speak to her please."

"Shall I wake you?"

"Thanks."

An exhausted Thomas realised he could not face trudging across London at that time of night.
The phone changed tone.

"Alice?"

"Yes, darling."

Just the one word, in a courteous whisper, made everything perfect.

"Sorry. I dared not stay in case he came back.
Thank you darling it was so wonderful.
To have you inside me, I will always remember the first time."

A fickle male ego soared easily toward heaven.

"I was terrible."

"No. You were a wonderful lover. I came all over your cock."

Colourfully, Alice had found her dirty voice again.

Thomas was truly, deeply, relieved.

"I'd been up for two days writing, that's why I fell asleep."

'Don't worry darling. And all that walking. It was

very flattering for you to be so relaxed with me."

"Did I snore?"

Her giggle made it seem as if she were back in the room.

"Just a little. I slept for an hour too.
When will you get home? I want to fuck you again."
Yearning at full stretch on the bed and smelling her on his pillow, she had Thomas panting.
No longer with any need to hide his passion, he tried to be sensible.
Despite what she was saying, he understood there would be a cost for such behaviour.
With her, there was no knowing its form.

"I'm still absolutely shagged. I'll stay here the rest of the night."

"Let's meet tomorrow then. I hate not being with you."

"OK I'll call you from home in the morning."

"Night darling. I want you."

CHAPTER TWENTY SIX

Half sleeping, half-conscious, but shot awake in the darkness by fantasies of the loss of his own head, suddenly Thomas's windpipe was throttled by a stranger's hard biceps. Seized, from behind, terror was racked up by its soundless enactment. He was turned ferociously face down into the hotel bedding, images swirling uncontrollably of punishment in the kneeling position of someone else's marital property.

Coming to full consciousness, his head was locked in a painful stranglehold, his mouth sealed closed by wide industrial adhesive tape, tasting of cats, which forbade him to scream out. Held by two silent unseen hard bodies on either side, a third slipped a black-cloth bag over his head, tightening the tie around with a string looped in its hem. Suffocating and blinded, his arms were forced behind his back, wrists secured painfully to his ankles by plastic restraints. Trying to kick out in one final breath on earth, totally secured by the cruel preparations, he was then offered spoken redemption.

"There you go mister art professor."

Breaking the menacing silence, a mocking London Cockney accompanied a chorus of monosyllabic guffaws from two associates. Giving clear prior knowledge of him, enormously moderated the panic.

"Let's have a little chat, shall we Mr Maher".

Even constrained, life restarted.

From the weight and muscle size of the knee pressing into his back, the speaker must have been a large man of immense strength. At the easing of the throttling, defiance to total compliance registered in nanoseconds.

Grasping the trick of breathing through his nose under the heavy muslin, Thomas understood any questions posed by them would be purely rhetorical. Stretching his body against the constraints enabled him to take larger inhales of breath.

The air began to flow more easily.

Close to his ear, the distinctive crackle of a two-way radio, probably clipped to a breast pocket, overrode the noise.

"Sarge?"

"Don't answer that."

Suspect through an obvious shouted order, the banter hinted at police.

He believed he had done nothing to provoke.

Deducing, almost simultaneously, that Maurice must have let them into the room with a master Thomas recognised the friendlier Ozzie twang.

"Said they were a terrorist branch, Mr Gray. What was I supposed to do?"

Unhappily, for the night manager, only one accent was allowed in that room.

Suffering some kind of body blow, he let out a muffled scream.

"Shut your mouth sunshine, or we hood you too."

Attention turned back to Thomas, who fathomed straight away that the manager would be able to see faces. Hardly the tightest security.

Each of the three men machine-gunned questions, anxious to be away

"One of their little Muslim buddies is your sunshine.

The recently turned novelist had no idea what they were asking.

Searching frantically in his recent memory bank, the coffee-stained Guardian popped back to him. Then the young Pakistani he had beat to it on the train seat. Even at the time he had assumed him Muslim. Racing ahead of logic and trying to breathe, he wondered if these men had seen the event. Assuming him part of the group that they had a diagnosed terrorist.

To be treating him as they had, these could not be regular London bobbies.

"What are you doing for them?"

"You give them money or something?"

Unleashing no further chills, the interrogation ended as rapidly as it had begun; clearly, they had not wanted to linger.

"When you get home sunshine, we posted you a little present, so you'd remember us.
Just don't dip your fingers into this again.
Understand
You're not wanted.

Obviously, that was the message.
Dexterously, slicing his bindings with an obviously sharp knife, the leader turned quickly away and addressed the night manager.

"Remember; keep that shut or I'll slice you another one.
We were never here sunshine."

Having control of his limbs for Thomas was hugely uplifting.
Rather less melodramatically, one of the lieutenants quickly needed his hood back, presumably for future terrorising. After loosening the tie at his throat, rather delicately, he pulled it skilfully from Thomas's head, exposing him again to the day's energy.
Lazarus like, vision was restored.
Though not yet his ability to speak because of the tape.

Screwing up his eyes in the sudden rush of half-light, Thomas was able to focus on the backs of two black-clad attackers. They doubled out of the door pushing the manager before them.

Caught in the minimum clip the mind takes to register a picture, the writer saw for the first time the grinning square face of the ogre who had been punishing him; the fair hair, born of the same Irish nation as he. He vowed never to forget it.

Thomas could never have known it, but these were the three thick-necked thugs who had terrorised Benji. Completed like a depilatory waxing of sensitive area, pulling the tape gingerly from his own mouth, it took moments before he could breathe regularly through two openings.

The men were gone; Thomas sank back onto the bed.

Enjoying the excess of oxygen, holding his sore face, he felt the shakes arrive in an empty room.

Shuddering, he imagined what terror awaited at home.

About his kids and Alice,

An instant dilemma was whether to call the police.

The theatre of the Policeman assaulting him already draining his credulity and power, and he had the urge to lie down. Shivering, he laid back on the pillow that no longer held her smell, way, way, past the time to be out of there before the folly struck.

Without another moment's hesitation, reality struck; he was up, on the long route down via the stairs to freedom. Ensuring on the way his wallet, the wad secure in his pocket, he told himself he would call the law from home if he could think of a plausible way of doing it without implicating her. At ground level having regained all his angry instincts for self-preservation, Thomas was conscious of the assistance maintaining his 'incognito, as he headed for the front door, weary of passing reception. The duplicitous night manager back behind his flap, desperate to arouse somebody in his organisation was on the phone to lead his plight, interrupted his call to stop. Striding purposefully for the door, hands thrust into his trouser pockets, he felt Alice's four notes protrude from his wallet. Spontaneously, turning a full circle in the foyer without ever breaking stride, he headed for the desk, pulling them out without pause, to gift Alice's fifties, like a fast right wing passing a slow left back. Depositing the money accurately on a familiar spot on the counter, content, he continued his way. It was not a huge sum, but enough of a reward for the pain the man endured on his behalf. Completely, bemused by such deviousness, the young Ozzie replaced the handset in mid-sentence, already moving for the cash. Happy to accumulate further untaxable income, he whipped it up and secured it in the folds of his wallet while shouting after the escapee.

"I'll have to report it anyway Gray".

A phantom Mr Donald Grey had already high-tailed it to the anonymity of a big city.

With no urge for immediate need for vengeance, dissolving back into the unknown London millions, Thomas made his way to the tube; the simplest route home at that early time of the day, without

ordering another black cab.
He had needed time.

Outside the hotel's confines, an unambiguous hand-tremble indicated the arrival of after-effects.

Judging a fast-paced walk from the Museum to Piccadilly tube would help, had been right off track. Stepping back into the free world, reassuring at first, casual looks had then seemed to turn hostile. Content all the manager had was a wrong surname and a friend's old address, he could deal with that if needed. All he wanted was to talk to Alice.

That he dared not contemplate before he had discovered what they had planted.

Hugely reluctant, he would call if the package had looked in any way dangerous.

Surely these men had not been assassins. Had they been they would never have shown themselves so casually. Fearing alarming her about anything, until he knew the whole strange story; after all he was the victim here. Had done nothing illegal.

"Well, nothing criminal."

He cursed himself a second time for putting himself in such a position by flashing Donald's card.

Happily, the gold-on-black eyesore with a swirling seventies-type face and pretensions to grandeur was not inscribed with the artist's address. It had an old-style post resultant post office box number. He had used to hand the thing about everywhere in galleries as a contact for sales not ever wanting to reveal his home address.

Terrified though at how daughters would react,
Papa felt inclined never to tell them.
Any discussion of events would, inevitably have
led to explaining his new 'infatuation'.

Unable to shake off the paranoic effects of
entrapment, quixotically, his attention was diverted
to another extrapolative apparition. The imaginative,
beaten-up writer could find no other way to describe
the truly odd. Customarily, in strange though
dangerous it made him laugh.   Not on a Venice
canal like Donald Sutherland, with the sighting of a
youthful Julie Christie on a black velvet draped
funeral gondola, but where he had tramped along
the much less prosaic Oxford Street; riding an
ordinary London Transport double-decker; the hated
Routemaster, rumoured soon to be ditched.
Seated downstairs on its left side, behind the
driver, he saw or thought he saw, Sam.
Not Donald, His imagined twin, Sam.

"JESUS"

Dressed quite differently from Grey's normal artist
leather jacket and jeans, this person had on a
rumpled, Harris-tweed suit, in a style dear to country
folk, fashionably updated with huge pale-green
squares and a fine lemon-yellow line.
If this had not been his lover's husband, which,
clearly, it was not, then it was his double,
A twin surely comes down through the same
womb to haunt him.
A relative Thomas knew for certain Donald never

221

had had.

Astonished by such a sighting, an already shaken victim started sprinted impulsively with considerable latent energy, after the transport. Careless of any danger, he was desperate to look the man directly in the eye, to ensure himself that he was not dreaming. For several rash strides he had followed. Helpfully the driver picked up enough speed to lose its stalker.

Baffled and exasperated, feeling as if he had missed the last transport to paradise, Thomas gave up the chase to catch huge, drafts of breath and sit on the pavement. Collapsing at the kerbside, he had aroused little interest from an injured public. After all, they had experienced everything halfway down Regent Street; including a trooper's horse killed by a terrorist bomb.

Minutes later he was up, off to home, calmer and purposeful without exchanging words of his chilling ordeal with another human.

CHAPTER TWENTY SEVEN

Twilight had given way to dawn.

Confined again on reaching the tube station in an oncoming bustle of pushing bodies, the occasional elbow thrown in to discern humanity, Thomas would travel against the regular city work traffic in simple wonder of the mind's acceptance.

In such a crush, picking up a coffee was an option, thoughtlessly taken up.

The morning Guardian was another instinctive absurdity.

Breakfast and the news would travel clumsily with him, as far as Fulham Broadway.

"Sorry."

"Sorry."

Entering with the thrusting crowd into a middle compartment, carrying his small take-out tray, the writer fought to protect it with his free arm; never remembering this sort of crush on the morning New York subway, where he had picked up the take-out habit.

Grabbing for stability, one-handed, onto the yellow plastic-coated pole, he was happy to share the new-world conversion of a familiar old support with double-handed grabs of two petite Japanese students; instantly wondering about parents if they would ever have permitted travel alone at this time of the day unchaperoned in Tokyo.

"Sorry."

Swaying, dangerously fast without upsetting his coffee, along claustrophobic steel-encased mole holes, Thomas was forced to make blushingly close contact with fragrances from the east, exotic morning oils and peppermint mouthwash. The two fashionably bespectacled girls, linked in his mind to news reports of uniformed guards pushing too many people into crowded subway trains. Efficient London Transport seemed to have caught up, close to out packing them in the movement of human flesh. Searching for a metaphor, other than sardines from another purgatory he had recently experienced he found no better, slices of seaweed too specific.

Considering the multitude of closed-down stares surrounding him; there were travellers who would experience this torture every day of the week.

The image of the blonde thug who had imprisoned him momentarily invaded.

Through primary colours, the post-modern curves of updated tube-train windows, gorged by demonic keychain scratching by angry young people the train popped from its burrow into daylight on a tube route he knew well.

Curiously, an eternity ago this had been a leg of the journey home from Grammar school.

Often, he had made the same search for dramas in the London backyards reversing onto the electrified rail line; musing on the exploits of the folks observed every day by several thousand tube-travellers.

Once a reassuring landmark, this morning, assisted by quirky perception, which sometimes lagged real time by as much as a decade, the houses were row upon row of boring terraces.

Another unsettling change in a morning full of them.

Offering a diversion at dado height in the compartment's ad space, an alternative view was proffered in the form of a poem.

Placed above regular head view, it exploited the exceptional tube space and the collective abhorrence to eye contact with strangers.

An aversion, perfectly expressed by the diminutive, downward-looking heads with silky raven mains he was being so careful not to spill his coffee over.

The advertisement was filled with numerous words and more complex ideas than he would, generally, have expected in a sales pitch.

Directly miss-rhyming of 'lain' and 'name' in the first two lines was a curiosity that had caught his attention.

Laid out so it ran concurrently, in a four -line stanzas on several of the horizontal panels, the hand-written eulogy was in a careful script; intended to represent its author's if it was not actually theirs.

Without, immediately, understanding what he was reading, the story-maker became absorbed in another writer's tale of horror.

Honour

Seared turkey-brown to where she had lain,
raw memory looped the girl with no name.
in redeeming swells, too devious
for our thoughtless, tourist-prying.

Brothers, turning from their bloody task,
had had the time to ask.
why the uninvited English had fled,
so pious in their tepid self-absolution.

In truth, fear had eaten us all,
half-drunk from meddling in that awful maul
as a sister slurped twice in family sperm,
minutes to her final desperation.

Body buried, but for an abundant oh-so
private down,
popping rocks had cracked the non-virginal
crown,
its corkscrew tresses defiled so recently.
Alas by forbidden hands, still living.

Dusted to a furry package, leaking into the
dying sun.
her un-braided beauty would not be undone,
Encouraging thoughts, too inexpressible, too
inexcusable
for such an everlasting wrapping.

Time, forgetfulness, even analgesic fun,
help sustain our leases issued just for one,

**allowing thoughts and rationalisation
to quarrel with awful recognition.**

**What unspeakable thirst must this be,
for men, never to be named, parent by me,
smothering what's everlasting to die in
shame:
A daughter savaged by a father; in some
god's name."**

Travelling through an unscheduled station without
stopping, the train slowed passed a platform where
a giggle of fidget schoolgirls had congregated.
Startlingly, to encounter them so early in the
morning, and barely into their teens, they all were
heavily but skilfully made up, which considerably
overstated their ages. Having achieved a very
tolerable but fake sophistication, it managed to
increase their impossibly pert childlike perfection.

Thomas could not even guess at the purpose of
this clustering cuddle of young flamingos whose
comparison to what he was reading was so
poignant.

Hair waxed in tight curls to their skulls, swept
back into small tails, to display huge, hopped,
earrings, these children were dressed in a street
uniform of micro-denim skirts, sleeveless t-shirts,
and flip flops. Clothes for the beach rather than a
spring morning in London town. Copied from pink
teen magazines and worn for no other purpose than
they were identical to each other, they made leggy
birds in the same freezing flock. A group not daring

227

to show the cold, in case revealing the weakness they were pecked to death by fiercer, more precocious 'sisters.

Disappearing from his view, and Thomas suspected the fragile doll-like beauty of the children would perish quickly before they reach a majority; like budding young cat- walk models, in just a season.

Indicated in by an informative flash which married its content, evidently, the poem was the winning e-entry in a competition. To bring awareness to the epidemic of honour killing, spreading through parts of south London like Ealing with a large English Asian population.

"Winner. Ahmed Khan. Dentist?"

What Thomas had been through was nothing in comparison to this savagery.

Perversely, it helped towards recovery.

Looking down suddenly to his black trainers, he saw his celebratory orange socks really for the first time that morning and felt under dressed. Most every other article of clothing he owned, some of it very expensive tailoring, was coloured navy-blue, grey or black, even his underwear.

The only place where he would ever experiment with colour was with his socks.

This new purchase had been worn specially for Alice.

After all this theatre he had entirely forgotten he

was wearing them.

Dear Alice

Disingenuously, since he had been the one doing the sinning, Thomas was becoming increasingly aware of a feeling of grievance against her wronged and disappeared husband.

Recognising his reaction as cock-eyed, some sort of transference from his fear, he was curious to see if his night of passion had infected his creativity. It helped him to be anxious to get back to his computer, wondering if he could work out some of these contradictions.

More circumspectly, he wondered how the past night would influence his writing of the fictional Alice.

If writing about her might taint the wonderful raw experience.

Raw feelings, the novelist was starting to understand were difficult to fillet.

A tough passage through the word grinder before barbecuing for human consumption.

The train reached Earls Court, evidently everybody's change station.

After an interminable wait for the opening switch to start blinking yellow to release the rush of departing clients, the automatic doors slid open. Gallantly, relinquishing a clear exit path to them, Thomas received the departing bows from the petite, pole-hangers.

Moving solo again, still clutching his cold breakfast, he was on his way to the already-arrived

Wimbledon train he had spotted on the other side of the double platform. Swerving quickly passed a thin dark boy and his mother who were in his path he quickly was onto his train.

Disturbingly, on settling in his seat in a near-empty coach heading for the suburbs, the writer was reunited with a copy of the campaign poster on honour killings directly opposite him. Promptly changing compartment sides to look back out on the platform sides he chose to search for profundity in the station map with its green 'corporate' colour for the district line, rather than to read encouraging words about learning Spanish.

Inadvertently, Thomas had saved himself from the disturbing looks of two dark faces; one of whom he knew very well indeed.

The train pulled away from the station, he missed the pair still on the platform feet away.

""BENJAMIN""

Thomas had not gone unnoticed by Benji nor by his mother.

Cold wired evermore to colourful pedantry, the boy's circuit blew a fuse on seeing the man in florescent socks.

Her favourite son's forward motion, uncharacteristically, frozen, Mrs Patel had stopped too, flushing at the sight of her old schoolgirl crush; thankfully, her head veil saved the honour of a faithful and long-married Muslim. The once highly productive graphics student felt the bite of loss, touched with regret that she and her old mentor had said nothing to each other.

"Keep moving. We're late."

On the way to visit a specialist up town, her conformist husband had insisted on a male family companion for her; so, her third son was seconded.
With the congestion charge in force, they decided to travel on the tube.

"Did you know that man?"

She received no answer.

When together, she and her hardest fought-for babe spoke English.
Naturally, because it was a first language, although they were fluent in Urdu.

Never daring to lie to his powerful mother, presently Benji's lips were shut as tight as Thomas's had been by the duct tape.
Discovering, previously, they had been on the wrong platform, the couple were about to re-cross on the Victorian iron passenger bridge spanning the electronic rails to the other side.
Getting no response from her son she would let it rest; till later.
She sensed something important was troubling him.
Presently she had the worry of a medical test results to occupy her.

"You've gone pale Benjamin."

Again, she received no reply and was certain he had an upset.

Starting the climb up well-worn brass-edged stairs to cross to the proper platform, she hid an excited and heavily pumping heart.

Teacher and pupil had been on transient paths, crossed maybe once in a second lifetime, never to dissect again.

Old memories, flaming for a moment, like a struck match, would burn out as quickly.

Easing an undeniable sting.

Such events occur every hour of every day on the city transport system.

Unknown, and unrepeatable.

Alignment of treasured oddities to be experienced quietly in the moment, then forgotten.

Not to be captured immortally on the prying platform spy cameras, which so clearly had freaked out her youngest.

As if any such trifling coincidence was the business of anyone but his mother.

CHAPTER TWENTY EIGHT

Buoyed by the belief he would soon be talking to Alice, Thomas moved more spiritedly passed the infamous rubbish bin on his way out of home station. Forgoing the toss at three-point range because of the mess it would make if he missed, he had dunked in his cold untouched coffee at close range, followed by the cardboard breakfast tray. The unread newspaper was retained.

Subjugating, the fermenting promise of real evil, in order not to have to face questions about her, he had rejected the sensible course of action to call the police.

Even after reflection, he thought the thug who had assaulted him, might be one of their own. A flaky aberration acting independent of the law.

Passing outside into the sunshine, inhaling full breaths of the liberated morning breeze', it fizzed in the nostrils of an ex-drinker; like never forgotten champagne bubbles.

His mood was lightening.

There was a pleasing smoky layer to the bouquet much like on bonfire night.

Curious as to why his new amour appeared at his house smelling of cigarettes and drink, the writer promised himself before the day was over, he would share a glass of something non-alcoholic with her. To dig a little deeper.

Maybe cook for her before they retired to the sack.

233

Catching sight of a familiar red phone box outside the station, instinctively he checked the missing glazing in the tiny metal windows making up its sides. He noted for the millionth time a perfect truth learnt from his first-ever art school drawing lesson.

Form is defined by the spaces between things.

The iconic minuscule red room, accommodating two when not involved in a Guinness book record dare, housed the two push copper penny machines into the old black phone. Pressing the satisfyingly smooth silver 'A' buttons was to escape into heart-fluttering journeys to teenage bliss.

Wretchedly, any pleasing modern impulse to call from here was eradicated by the stink of urine. After rejuvenation by the Post Office with complex email-sending telephones, the innards were gutted a second time by the mindless disdain for progress.

Spiritual cousins assuredly to the men who assaulted him.

Distractingly, along the Fulham Road, heavy sirens whined bronchially.

A fire engine raced a police car.

Both scorched past him.

Seemingly in the aftermath of a huge party, the closer Thomas got to home, the more evident became the lingering smell of fireworks.

Greatly increasing tension, the explosive additive was soon everywhere in the air, to form a heavy, early morning fog, well before Guy Fawkes night.

Coming to an abrupt halt at the top of his road,

directly under the hated lamp post camera recording everything for posterity, another worst, scenario was enacted.

"They've bombed my house".

Through watery eyes and the haze, Thomas was able to make out many more than the two emergency service vehicles which had scurried past him.

Surrounding his house was a tumult, resembling the enactment of a Jacques Tatti script.

From left to right, giving no precedence for size, which was mostly huge, were many double-parked vehicles; a fire engine, a red heavy-lifting fire brigade crane, two mini-police cars, two squad cars, a large L.E.B. van, a local gas board vehicle, a vehicle from the local council, and finally a massive water tanker with enough supply to drown the whole street; clearly not trusting in their own stationary pipes. Fortunately, or not, because it was a Sunday, many part-time volunteers, extras if you will, were on hand to assist the emergency services in an Orange Government Alert. Ahead of dismal forecasts after several badly managed trials, the contentious leaders of the Borough of Fulham, known to him from his letter writing believed they had learnt a hard lesson. Following scathing almost-personal- media coverage, they had instigated rehearsal after rehearsal with a willing army of gullible recruits ready to prepare for the 'big one'.

Here was the result.

On this sunny Sunday morning, they were ready to fight any conflagration, terrorist invasion or urban revolt come what may; even a nuclear one.

Only the specialist anti-terrorist transportation was not present in the weighty caravan; the bomb-disposal wagon.

This secret 'populace-scaring' part of assembly had not hung around long once the house was checked for dangerous devices; a review to last exactly two minutes and proved wholly negative, bar the one burnt-out squib in the letterbox that had set off the alarm.

"That's him. That's him."

Unable to recall a more embarrassing moment in his life, Thomas flushed red; bright as the original, three-step, Technicolor primary; then bleached to a pale grey; worthy of the best Ektachrome black and white; all in a matter of strides during the brisk but endless perp walk towards his beloved house.

"That's him."

A small crowd of old locals and city invaders formed to watch sinful fun on a Sabbath.

It appeared everyone assembled had turned to hiss at him.

"Winnie's boy."

Since his return to the area, Thomas had exchanged polite, but distant greetings, when he passed the few old faces that were left. They would have known him and his parents; before he cut his links to the nearby local church a 'century' ago.

"Used to serve on the altar at St Thomas's".

Heads bent, but not dignified by old age, line faces recalled childhood impressions of a community, which carried a discreet but troubling vendetta against his father.

"Always very la-di-da. Never could stand him."

Disabled from the army during the war with a breakdown, then imprisoned in an asylum for six months as a 'Commie', Dad had been given the popular coevally, barbaric, electro-shock treatment. Afterwards, a broken man he was saved by the devotion and sheer wilfulness of his sturdy, but difficult spouse.
A Kelly who had married a Maher.

"An artist. That's why he wears those funny socks".

The accent was unmistakably a 'Johnny come lately' city wife.

"Layabout."

On one night in the blitz, after a heavy air raid, his father was returning from his civilian duties as a warden to their downstairs flat. It also comprised a cellar which the whole house sheltered in. Everyone was awake to greet him. Wearing just a rough short khaki army cast-off jacket over his 'civvies', on his head was a flying saucer-shaped, tin helmet. A second-hand gas mask in a canvas rucksack slung over his shoulder. Unforgeable apprehension consumed his gentle face.

Thomas felt as protected as his father had looked on that awful night.

How can he afford the house?"

"Been in his family since the war."

"Does he work?"

"No, he's a film director."

Screened to knee height by Thomas's low re-pointed front garden wall and hiding the green bin of the recycling, a quintet of uniformed officers heading the separate emergency services stood in his front garden. The initial spark of excitement having petered out in the only mildly polluted air, the leading actors in a still-being-written screen play were forced to find something to do, inspecting the few slabs of his expensive York paving as if a contact lens had been dropped.

Though he should not have been there, a sixth officer from the bomb squad was also in attendance, left behind by junior comrades in their rush to get away once the squid had stopped fizzing and before the press arrived.

Humiliated by so public an outing, the specialist bomb diffuser stood away from the other aristocrats. Chasing after his departing truck was not an option for the brave officer in his inflammable, canvas, camouflage protection, accessioned with a reinforced welder's helmet, lead shin-pads and chest protector, massive metal clad boots and gloves.

His silhouette resembled the inflated Michelin man as everyone never failed to point out.

Not wanting to expose their so secret vehicle a second time to the civilian glare, muddled 'high-ups' thinking acquired a second less obtrusive truck to be sent for him. The home base was in Aldershot. To save time, a re-assignment was with a barrow trader sorting his green goods in an adjacent market lock-up.

"Mr Maher?

Nearby, police underlings, wearing complete white paper coveralls and masks were preparing for the erection of an 'evidence' tent.

Delighted at seeing the owner arrived home, safe and sound, the lead Policeman tried to cover his relief with a professional grimace.

His manner, instantly, antagonised Thomas.

Attempting in a small way, to control the situation, the homeowner would not confirm his identity immediately; already nervous of the questions that was bound to follow about his absence.

"I don't want that covering my house."

The response caused rushed intakes of breath from the encroaching audience, which was numerous.

Sensing a little power to himself, Thomas repeated his words more forcefully.

"I don't want that shit covering my house."

Cued for a stand against excessive police power, a scruffy '89 Luton van-hire with a mechanical tailgate reversed around a currently government-restricted-market-corner continuing the impulsive Council overreach.

Unused to its cranky civilian gearbox, a fully certified tank Sargent sashayed backwards down the street till the over-revved van's rear end came in line with Thomas's house, where it braked abruptly. Two of the four soldiers in it jumped down from the back solemnly, taking over the heavy, helmet, gloves and waistcoat: holding out helping hands to moon-work their rotund commander onto a shaky platform. Normally used for the passage of vegetable boxes, neither service men dared make eye contact terrified the elevator's electric engine would be massively overloaded. Like a strangely, over-decorated, Eastern bride they levitated skyward to van floor level to other pairs of hands guiding him inside. The vulnerable, senior officer was unable to control his terrible indignation, one second longer. So close everyone could hear him,

Thomas too had to sympathise with his disposition.

"How could you forget me?"

The power of speech forsaking four experienced, soldiers likely to regain the rank of private before the next dawn bugle, not necessarily in this outfit, one mute brigade glove, knocked twice on the side of the vehicle to begin a retreat in the forward direction on a journey, officially, never to have existed.

"We are glad to see you safe and well Mr Maher."

Content to shred the embarrassing scene from his reality, as he would in his report; the terrorist officer in charge shifted his attention back to Thomas; ready to battle to the heart of the matter.

"No one blew you up then."

Obsequious humour seemed the favoured form of communication.

"Someone left you a present."

Again, the home-owning victim got aggravated.

"A present? A present? "

"Any ideas who your friend might be."

"A present?"

"A smoke bomb."

Thomas was relieved when he heard this; and surprised.

Everybody, it appeared was amazed so small a container, the size of a large beans means Heinz can, could make so much smoke.

Thomas had believed the thug was planning something more fearsome.

He was used to the smoke devices that prop men in America.

"A film smoke bomb?"

The thing ran without stopping for nearly half an hour filling the entire neighbourhood with smoke; till the Fire-brigade had arrived. While they had discussed what sort of foam to use, it had extinguished itself.

"Nothing more serious than that?"

Reluctantly, the whole watching group of officers nodded their agreement.

Thomas moved towards his front door to inspect the newly made scorch marks surrounding the rat-tat-tat where his elder sisters tied their skipping ropes when his head hardly reached above it.

But this much fuss was excessive.

"To bring out this lot?"

"We suspected it was a bomb."

Adrenalin from aggression helping to restore some personal power, Thomas waived his arms about; to make his point. Though, properly incredulous, he too was affected by a crowd.

"That's fucking ridiculous."

Uniformly in denial, the officers shifted feet uncomfortably, unhappy with his characterisation of a 'near faultless' operation.

"Mind your language. Sir."

"And now you want to put up your marquee to have a party."

Seeing little damage done, with a little luck, shame might stop its erection.

"That's way beyond overkill."

From the silence, it was clear the anti-terrorist officer was undecided about putting it up anyway.

"Well, sir. Must see about that.

Luckily, the paint blisters were high enough not to reach the lion head knocker; a fearsome summons; used only, occasionally; or whenever Avi came to call. Forever impatient with the decibels issuing from

243

the door chime, her repeated crashes on the brass jaws always signalled her arrival.

Because of his precious art collection, to back the stain glass, the insurance company stipulated clear toughened glass, so it survived the explosion; and their battering.

The only other thing really, to suffer damage was the lock which, given a lethal headache by the constabulary battering ram. In the absence of the owner and his keys, they had dared not leave it long before a search was conducted of the property. A carpenter and a locksmith appeared miraculously in the same white paper overalls and repaired the front door at speed. Replacing his lock, they had used the old core with a master, so he did not have to change keys.

A restless corps of officers shuffled.

"Hang on a second boys."

Via a second, more discrete earpiece, the officer was receiving other communication, which excited everyone.

"Yes Sir. The homeowner has arrived."

Spell bound; everyone held their breaths for the silent order.

When assimilated the embarrassment of professionals turned energetically to retreat.

"Pack it away boys."

Everything then moved into double quick time.

"Pronto."

A bomb scare turned speedily into a P.R. exit.

"Super says to get our asses out of here; wants to talk to you Maher."

In hardly a heartbeat, all the huge welcome home party became involved in a second Dunkirk without boats. The only permitted anxiety was to be out of there as quickly as humanly possible.

Fortuitously, for the health of rest of his décor, Thomas had ignored, the occasional tight fit of the larger modern envelopes in the letter catcher. The backs of any biggish package would foul up, stopped from dropping down fully into it. When posted the tube smoke bomb behaved several degrees off vertical, pointing skywards for easy ignition, difficult to get any further in or out. While resting diagonally against the metal mouth edge it held the letterbox jaws wide open; following the tiny pop of its delayed start up fuse became a masterpiece of unintended precision pyrotechnics. Smoke poured endlessly from the jaws of the opening, like a baby dragon after it had feasted on a forest of dead autumn leaves. Planted in letterbox the other way around the canister would have filled the house a dozen times over with soot and smoke.

But with a slight breeze running, Thomas's front door was the perfect street smoke machine; in moments the area surrounding his home filled with fog stayed that way for nearly an hour then disappeared in minutes.

Soon with little left to look at, the smells of the traditional roast, wafting from neighbourhood kitchens the smell of cordite diminished to nothing. Adding hints an imaginary gang of children might have been responsible for the 'firework', the police moved the tutting public from the end of the street.

Then themselves.

Excluded by a chance slip up, no attention had been focused by the Media on the display.

Most definitely, scripted to be active players, when the real Apocalypse went down, it was only a matter of time for that with so many citizens involved, before they found out about the overreaction to the smoke bomb.

Cut from the story by a flustered 999 receptionist at the switchboard, when news of the 'bomb threat' came in, inadvertently, she had categorised the emergency in an unfamiliar check sheet as a 'rehearsal; as it had been on several previous Sundays.

A simple enough mistake to make; but one, serendipitously, immobilising all local and National publicity making organisations from the orange alert.

Transfixed by the intense activity on her system automatically locating the services and personnel, she had not realised her error for half an hour. By the time she had corrected it, most everybody was home for a late Sunday lunch.

CHAPTER TWENTY NINE

Clearly comfortable with the exercise of her power, the sari-clad Indian dermatologist was reassuring to her Pakistani client; without any sign of the strain existing between their two countries. A specialist to her community she had quietly insisted there was nothing to worry about, as the biopsy of a small breast lump diagnosed a non-malignant piece of gristle. Eager to have the small protuberance checked out, female family and friends had mostly expressed less optimistic outcomes. Mrs Patel had been reassured, when the results of her previous trip to the private surgery had come from a doctor with the same name as her own. They had given her a Sunday appointment for the full results automatically because of her faith.

Encased in skin-thin transparent rubber gloves, the specialist's beautifully manicured, well-scrubbed hand had removed the growth under local anaesthetic, with a skilled scalpel-slice and the nip of a pair of tweezers. It took hardly a minute. According to the doctor's usual practice the neat wound was taped not sewn, to leave no unsightly stitch scars; for the occasions, when patients would wear a low-cut bra; a sometimes habit in marital privacy, of well-to-do Asian women. Aware of nature's gentle, spread, Paties body though womanly after three children was slim. The scalpel mark on a superb café au lait complexion had disappeared by the time Doctor and patient viewed it this morning like sisters.

Dressed, permanently these days traditionally, reminded by the doctor's thoughtfulness of a youthful passion for flimsy underwear and for a second time that morning she was stirred by aches of passed youth. Sadly, after a stricter up-bringing than hers, husband of the striking petite black-eyed cockney sparrow was uncomfortable around such finery. Saying nothing to him, she had relinquished the pleasure in the first month of their marriage.

Goodbyes between patient and a busy doctor were cordial but brief.

A satisfied patient paid her bill in the outer reception office; shared with three other Harley Street doctors. Hating to have any kind of debt, Mrs Patel handed over a ready-made-out check, signed by her husband. Solicitously, he had called ahead for the exact amount. This way of dealing with money would not shed any of its irksomeness over the years of marriage, but she reminded herself she was a good wife; he a shrewd manager. So, occasionally, at times like this, she would conform to the submissive role. Reluctantly.

With a smile so effortlessly insincere, that it could hardly have been more grandiose, the prim receptionist received the cheque as if it were an unwashed sanitary towel, which after disinfecting would be passed on to the poor and needy. Styled half a century before in knitted aubergine and pearls, the woman accessorised the Edwardian oak panelled office to perfection. Behind her head hung a signed, black-framed photo, presumably English looking partners, captured shaking hands with an informal Gordon Brown at a school tennis match. Unflatteringly, the once Prime minister was in short white shorts and a pair of grey socks. Never caring to hide her disdain for such snobbery, nor her angry raven eyes with a veil, Mrs Patel swivel on an expensive heel without a word; other than to her son who already knew their power.

"BINJIMIN lets go".

Exiting through the heavy frosted glass and mahogany portal of the gracious old English consulting rooms, in obvious dander, there was enough speed to her door slam to crash her emotions and the door frame to other startled patients, adding another small crack in the Edwardian wrinkled glass.

Crisply outside again she was her commanding self.

"BINJIMIN"

Most in the street community where the family lived for thirty years, called her youngest son Benji; for it seemed to sum up his luminous personality, perfectly.
But was never heard in her presence in a household she controlled.
Pati hated the diminutive.

A spirited but not spoilt son, even if he was the youngest, was called by his full name.

Admittedly, mostly by her in a raised pitch using only the single London 'I' for vowels.

An accent authenticated by living not under the shadow of the Bow Bell, but in Ealing.

She had loved this first name and hated it ever shorten.

"BINJIMIN"

Chosen as her first boys first name, she had nourished the idea of using it for a son, all the way through Comprehensive School to honour a nine-year-old Jewish school chum. A first ever crush was cemented in her psyche with a second backstage kiss, while performing her primary school's nativity play; playing Mary to his Joseph. Sadly, he had caught polio during a Christmas holiday and moved to the country. She never saw him again; but other friends told her he walked with a perpetual limp but had happily married with his own children.

"Yes Mum'

Unable, because of family practice, to name her first son as she wanted, her wish had become a reality with her third child.

"Home."

In a distant past, where everything was possible, she had done most things, while still wearing the veil, to be like her white, schoolgirl chums. Still skilled with the make-up brush, when she needed to be, she no longer pined for that recognition; was her own modern woman, a wife and mother in Islam.

In a coincidence that would sometimes happen in the crowded London Metropolis, not just in novels to tie up their stories, the once blushing thirteen-year-old Muslim girl had been well known to a younger Thomas Maher. He had been her visiting Art Lecturer; later to become her mentor.

"Pattie Patel."

Sharing a definite graphic skill seemed to have passed onto her eldest son, and Pattie was a youth prodigy. With the encouragement from her school and the grudging assistance of her bemused, but proud parents, she took A levels in art three years early; she was that good.

Desperate, at the time, to fit in with her Western school girl mates, she had had her second crush on her visiting teacher, which had helped spur on her efforts.

At home they all sang his praises to the heavens.

"Mr Maher"

After she had passed her exams with special mention, the crush had drifted to a memory; which had died a month later with her first wet kiss from a distant cousin; who lived in her street.

A distinctly chirpy personality, never afraid to tell

its own tale, she was never free after that of hunting males.

Soon one persistent, family-approved, suitor came calling; an older cousin from the North; a fine man whom she grew close to over the years. They had been married on her sixteenth birthday.

Allah forbade figurative depiction, and the piece of art remaining as a memorial to those special years was not made by her at all; but was a gift given by her father to Thomas in appreciation of his special efforts. A front piece from a Koran, which had been in the family for as long as anyone could remember. Believing it held mostly sentimental value, Thomas had liked the picture and framed it to join his collection. Because he spoke no Urdu, he had never checked its provenance; an unusual thing for him. One day he had promised himself he would check it out properly.

Given the esteem the family held him in, son Benjamin's actions would certainly not have been appreciated by his mother; when she found out all that he and his brother were up to.

Haplessly, as happens so often with a difficult talent to customise into marriage, her artwork was not kept up. For the early years of pregnancy, all that remained of it was a large portfolio.

Sadly, when searching through it in later years, one Christmas, she took all the precious work out and tearfully shredded it.

Sad at how much older Mr Maher had looked;

and how pale, she wondered how she could ever have felt attraction for so insipid looking an Englishman.

Only in lively eyes could she seen anything to excite.

Private, thoughts, to be shared with no one.
Not even a beloved husband.
A kind, caring man was limited, when talking about feelings.
Though he had grown to appreciate just how clever and independent a woman he had married.
Intelligence radically updated before sunset.

Passing back through Earl's court station on the correct train, so with no need to change platforms or trains, with a clean health account, she felt a lingering threat, still hanging over her morning.

"Do you have something to tell me?"

Her question was answered, negatively with a severe head shake, but without the denial.

"BINJIMIN"

Any mother worthy of the name would have noticed her youngest reaction, when he saw Thomas.

Added to obvious fears about the C.C.T.V cameras, there were issues that needed resolving.

"I want the truth."

It took her the train time between Earls Court to Ealing Broadway to draw it out in full.

CHAPTER THIRTY

The same day, an hour after the chaos, retaining only a pair of uniformed females from what had been a swarm, a personable lead police officer, wearing expensive 'civvies' arrived at Thomas's repaired front door.

"Morning sir. We have changed the lock."
He handed back Thomass bunch with the addition of two sets of new yales.

The astonishingly handsome man, with slightly lighter grey flecks in a well-groomed full head of hair, flashed his police wallet and a model smile of as identification, clearly a higher up, on a PR mission.

"I was in Brighton when they called. Fancy a burger. I'm starving. I'll pay."

Before hearing a reply, without time for a refusal, he good naturedly 'shushed' the pair off on a lunch errand. Young policewomen, who to Thomas had barely reached adolescence; another sign of his ageing had one been needed.

Save for his height, which was above average, the policeman could have doubled for the Portuguese Chelsea manager, who threw his medal to football fans that had been singing on Thomas's Street after a famous league victory.

Another leader to have forsaken the hair colourist to allow the grey to show, in the search of dignity in a high spiralling career.

"My name is Alan McPherson Mr Maher."

Cut for a boyish set of values, his carefully relaxed suit was tight modernist and two buttoned.
It had made the wearer look as if he were struggling with extended back muscles, tipping him continuously forward.

He was trying the informal route.

Disturbed by most forms of manly perfection, Thomas squinted perfunctorily at the man's credentials, discounting the anti-terrorist specialist by a Chief Superintendent.

"No thanks Inspector."

Noting excessive good manners, for further use in any written account of similar action, the writer could not envisage how he could work in the material.

"Lovely home you have sir."

Thomas waived behind him inside, the officer playing 'the good cop' followed.
The policeman took time to carefully evaluate the house ground plan.

He passed down the hallway, stopping to inspect

the living room from the door.
He said nothing; just cooed a little.
Not even a comment on the art collection.
But had looked at it long and hard.

Walking back into his beautiful kitchen, and
becoming more petulant by the second, Thomas
about faced to wait for his catch up.
Reversing the accepted order of interrogation, he
started to ask his own questions before the
policeman had got there.

"Do you know who did this Inspector?"

Pique slid up his calibrator to deliberate.

The Policeman though had seemed not to stiffen.
Unsurprisingly, no positive reply was forthcoming.

"That's chief superintendent Mr Maher.
Special branch,
But do call me Alan."

"OK Alan, sorry. I'm Thomas."

"Do you have any idea which pranking friend
might have posted this thing Thomas?"
Posed another time as a joke, the question
accepted, according to the Freudian notion that such
mirth was always disguised aggression.

"My friend?"

Attitude alone, and the specialist, had assured Thomas that the big guy had been a cop.

And they already knew it.

Perhaps a rogue element, in the self-admitted racist kinship.

"Shouldn't you be asking yourselves that question?"

The policeman was unmoved.

Had they been involved, of course it could not be confirmed.

The two pretty P. C.'s returned to break the standoff; with the make-shift lunch from the McDonald's on the corner.

He guessed their uniforms had got them to the front of the queue.

"She has the ap."

"Let's eat."

They had included Thomas in their order of burgers,

Believing all men eat meat.

Much a formality, he had refused.

"Pescetarian."

"Shall I go back get a fish sandwich?"

"No, no."

He had other plans for sustain himself; after they were gone.

"McPerson will eat two."

"Always does"

The women seemed casual enough with their boss.
Not afraid to shame him in front of an interrogation.

The beaming, perfect senior Policeman, elaborately counted out every spent penny, pocketing the tab before attacking his first burger.
Leaning back onto Thomas's solid green oak kitchen cabinets, all three interrogators munched away informally, while they studied their vegetarian victim with venal intensity.

"Please tell us all about it sir."

"Where were you?"

Under only this passive pressure, Thomas cracked, immediately.

"I spent the night with a woman I picked up."

Unhappily, having devised such a dashing tale a few moments before, it had made him blush.

"She left. I stayed."

Everyone nodded.
All could see the logic in that.
That it was total fabrication.

"Her name?"

More gallantly, Thomas was naming no names.
Not even made-up ones.

"You don't need to know that."

"'Afraid we do sir."

"What price did you pay her?"

Instantly, more uncomfortable with admitting he
had paid for sex; he would be admitting a crime.

"Got any mustard Thomas?"

Not wanting to open a second hostile front, he
directed the chief Inspector to a steel faced cabinet.

"Top shelf."

"Still sure you wouldn't like this burger?"

"No thanks. Not hungry."
Though he had been.

"There are nuggets?"

261

"Nothing with legs that walks."

Neither woman appeared restrained from speaking out. Part of a worked pattern.

"What was the hotel called?"

"I can't remember."
Even he had not believed himself.

"This is delicious by the way."

With the Dijon delicacy bought in Thomas's special village store in France, spread liberally on his second Big Mac, it was 'McPerson' the one less incorruptible.

"There will be police reports you know Thomas."

"Eventually we will find out."
Thomas began to reverse himself.

"Actually, it was called the Westbury."

The policewomen both looked eagerly to their commander.

"The Westbury?"

"The Westbury?"

Thomas sensed he had given top answer.

"Yes. The Westbury. You know it?"

The head man shook his head.
But undisguised female response had been hyper positive.

"And the lady friend?"

"She was not an old friend. I told you."

"I'm sure she was sir."

"So why don't you tell us her name?"

"She's married. I can't."

"Please Thomas you have to."
Supping through the ice from a straw, the exciting finish to two medium size diet cokes provided the background music to a long and awkward silence.

"We will be very discrete."

"If I've committed a crime, then charge me."

McPherson gestured to the more petite of the two W.P.C.'s.
She pulled out from a large flat black holdall an iPad already switched on.
The resourceful McPherson had had other more direct lines to inquire along.

"Ever seen him before?"

Thomas could not immediately recognise Benji.

It was a good picture but truthfully his Arsenal cap had been pulled down low.

Admiring, the good exterior grey paint job behind him in a second wider shot, was a semi much like his own. It took the deed holder several seconds to recognise his own house.

Deliberately or not, events came to a speedy conclusion with the next revealing query.

During another awkward silence, Thomas deduced the picture must have come from his least favourite spy cam.

Readily, he paused to consider what to say.

"Was it the boy from the train Thomas?"

"You know about the train?"

"Maybe.

"So, you know the guy who mugged me?"

Thomas's unbridled delight, instantly, exposed him to ridicule from both female interrogators.

"Mugged you?"

"Which assault was this, Thomas?"

"We have heard nothing about anyone mugging you."

A considerate McPherson stepped in to halt the savagery.

"We actually don't want to know either."

"Strictly not our business you understand?"

"Now, was it this boy Thomas?"

"Could have been."

"But in that cap, you can't see his face."

"OK we believe you."

"We'll keep an eye open for him."

Other mementos decisions had been taken without recourse to him.

"Not really much else we need to talk about."

The women's attention had already turned to clean-up.

"Let's wrap this up ladies."

Happily, that was the end of his police grilling. Thomas could hardly believe his luck.

Opportunely, at that moment, the top of the range mobile radios set on top of his polished steel kitchen surface, crackled to life.

"Stalking Charlie Victor."

The watchers were being watched.
Media had arrived via a scanner van.

"Looks like the football boys from down the road."

The TV crew were in extra, extra time; more accurately, after the final whistle, the showers, the celebratory champagne, lunch, and on the coach home.
Even so the energy in the room changed, entirely.
A street party threatened to break out all over again.

"They are nearing you Charlie victor".

McPherson was not happy.
Instantly, he strategized.

"Living room."

Apart from the slight scorch marks on the door outside, that could have been the start of a paint stripping, nothing in the street indicated the previous embarrassing upheaval.
Everyone moved out the kitchen.

"Maher. We might need you to front for us.
We don't want these guys starting to feed."

"Sure, but take off your shoes; it's a very precious

floor."

McPherson nodded his approval, without argument slipped off his expensive pair of black loafers and slipped into the front room. WPC's followed suit unzipping the sides of snazzy black walking boots from under the dark pants; so as not to damage his beloved walnut shine.

The windows in the room were shuttered during his absence, making it look mysterious in the half light. The gaps between the wooden edges made good spy holes and everyone positioned themselves to look outside, unobserved.

With its arm and vast scanning disc not yet raised, the black transmitting truck appeared at the top of his empty street. Darkened windows of a television crew, untrained for the task was its news gathering.

Back to his more usual depreciating self, it was clear the policeman had lost interest when confronted with replacements. To sustain in a day threatening to become wearisome; the chief inspector was as an art buff.

"This is quite a picture collection Thomas. Mustn't forget to reset your alarm before we leave."

There was just enough light to make out the pictures.

"Hope they are properly insured."

"Cost me a Hurst."

Laughing and continuing to enthuse in a whisper; the lacquered surface was working its magic on expensive, silk socked feet that began to lose patience with their boss.

"Diebenkorn was always my favourite his ability to swap between realism and abstraction very impressive. Remember lady on the veranda at the California beach?

"Yes, I do."

"Could never afford one of course; you are a lucky man."

Despite himself Thomas was pleased to be in the McPherson's learned good books.
Both female officers with no interest at all in Art talk hissed at their Chief to attend to business.
Nothing much was happening outside.

The van had reached the other end of the road.
Across the way a husband, satiated after lunch, still held a glass of red-wine glass, while peering out from behind his voile curtains. Two tiny children played through his legs. He was waiting for the afternoon match on Sky.

The unseen radio voice continued as commentary.

"They've stopped right in front of the house."

"You of course you know what that is Thomas. Is it real?

"Don't know."

Besides, it was in Urdu, the usually meticulous art historian knew little else about it.
The picture was the present from Benji's family.
It was old; but it had not been a period, or a culture Thomas knew much else about.
Other than he liked it.

"It's a page from the Koran, Thomas."

 "Yes?"

""When a woman in Islam sayeth, My Lord, surely, I vow to Thee, what is in my womb, to be devoted to Thy service; accept therefore from me, surely, Thou art the Hearing, the Knowing.""

"Wow"

Someone's radio squawked like a stray goose that had been trodden on.

"Turn off that, Jonesy".

Sorry guv"

With the home team on an away weekend, the skeleton crew, were billeted at the Chelsea stadium.
All three crew members were staring at the front door from their cab window.
No one ventured out to inspect it.

"Mind if I check it? We'll give you receipt."
Without waiting for a response, McPherson pocketed the blue framed piece straight off the wall.

"PC Jones, give him a chit."

"Yes guv."

Giving a glance in Thomas's direction, McPherson thought for a moment; then had changed his mind. His choice of mouthpiece to confront the nuisance was a revealing one.

"And Jonesie"

"Sir."

"Go talk to them."

'Yes Guv."

"And Johnsie.

'Yes Guv."

"Improvise."

Obviously, the class favourite, this was a strategic word.

"Yes Guv."

Pretty, short and busty but another who hardly reached the age to drink in a pub, or for that matter appear in a porno movie, in a moment she was swishing provocatively to the front door with boots on.

"HOLD"

Freezing her there, the land line sitting on Thomas's small Indian carved table started to buzz.

It had to be Alice.

Allowed to ring once more, McPherson scooped it up efficiently.
He offered Thomas the receiver, a hand cupped over the mouthpiece.

"Be brief."

For yet another time that day, all eyes were on Thomas.

"DARLING"

It was not Alice but Em.

She was calling from a trip to her in laws for Sunday catch up.

"Sorry but can we do this later?

"OK pater"

"Right in the middle of something."

"Remember the rules, daddy, no one younger than us.'

"I will sweetness."

"Call you back Tuesday."

"Love you. Bye."

Replacing the receiver delicately, quickly restarted the action.

Cute as 'moppet' and certainly younger than Thomas's youngest, P.C Jones zipped to outside his front door to confront the news camera pro-actively.
Transmitter to an ample bosom it picked up her improvisation.

"A gas explosion is what done it."

Astonishingly to Thomas, she was instantly believed.

"Rest mugged off ages ago."

Unfortunately for her career as an actress, no footage was rolled on a convincing Eliza Doolittle performance, other than the fixed council cam.

Initially interested in dallying a few minutes off the record, the males in the van also wanted to get back to watch the three o'clock game.

"Can't drink on duty can I lads?"

Doing their duty, perfunctorily, getting a polite, but giggly refusal, the big black van quickly disappeared.

McPherson broke his own rule about radio silence.

"Well done, Jonesie."

"Why, thank you Chief Inspector."

In character with suggestive, alluring tone, he allowed the minor flirtation.

When the news people, eventually, found out the truth about the smoke bomb, it was too late for them to do much about it. News of smoking letter boxes were on short 'leg-life' without pictures; especially when the police showed no interest at all in promoting it.

After calling the house alarm suppliers resetting the alarm, they made a speedy kitchen clear up.

They had been reluctant to get involved any further.

An attempt to talk about the big man bought shuffling feet.

Handling Thomas his card, McPherson was the last to slip out.

"Call me"

CHAPTER THIRTY ONE

We have eyes for two points to estimate distance from us.

Looking at an object, our vision makes small adjustments, continuously.

When driving, movement concentrated, the head looks forward onto the road.

Between blinks, self-focusing eyes adjust to light levels.

Most average eye focus will be around one hundred degrees.

We can see no more than this at one time, both eyes working in harness.

Within the angle, only a central of five to six degrees can fully focus.

The rest acts as the penumbra of our "out of focus".

Secondary simultaneous action will be noticed when something crosses our path.

Another car for instance from a side road.

The head must turn to bring the object to the centre if it wants to focus properly.

An entirely automatic process.

We can live without thinking about it.

Within the eye mechanics, lies the proof of our superior being.

No other animal can rationalise and abstract as we can.

Both hands arms outstretched in front, one eye closed, with the index finger close up and pointing, offer up the second index finger on the other hand, further away but in a line, directly in front to cover blocking its view.

Without head moving change eyes
The view of the finger will no longer be covered and appeared to have shifted.

Eyes spread across the head so will not view the same thing in the same way.

This ability shows us depth.

When two things of equal size i.e. our fingers get closer to the eye, they look far larger.

The brain knows they are the same but, automatically, sees them as different.

The eye, as a machine, sends wave messages to the brain via the retina.

For a few seconds this automatic function can be used to demonstrate a remarkable fact,
of which artists who copy reality will be aware.

Size can be compared one object to the other giving its dimension.

Take a well sharpened pencil and piece of white paper.

Fix it to a board or something to support it vertically.

With the picture plane of the paper up right and at right angles to the floor, choose an objective in the middle distance; say a vase sat on a table.

With the pencil held in hand and the arm fully outstretched at right angles to the floor,
measure the size against it; with one eye closed.

Compare the height of the vase with the same dimension on your pencil.

Mark the dimension on the paper,
You have defined the size your eye sees.

This was the miracle.

The human mind has assessed, then rationalised what has been seen.
Not the actual size but how it seems to you.
Turned to concrete distance.

No other creature with eyes can make this rationalisation.

It takes us above them.

Makes us God like.

A simple exercise known and forgotten by preparatory art classes the world over.

Certainly, it was how Sam would start his direct work with the life model.

CHAPTER THIRTY TWO

"There is no art to find the minds construction in the face."

Directly, the Police had left, the writer aimed straight for his desk phone, to try to contact Alice.

After saving his lover's good name, while her marriage contract remained elsewhere, he had felt urgently entitled. Though unable to express a needy, complex truth.

When writing the part of the wife to the Thane of Glamis, the Bard had been at his most sublime as a poet.

No question about it.

Reminding everyone, evermore, to be opaque when lying, to be convincing.

"To beguile the times, look like the times."

Perfectly, expressing these sentiments through the Scottish Queen, his spouse Grouch, who had not been named as such in the play. Lady Macbeth: on the first staging of the play, because the young person chosen to play her was ill, a man not a woman, which was customary, the Author had had to play the part himself.

Writing what he knew, the Bard was serving double time in the most duplicitous of human professions, second only to the world's oldest.

Even in those wondrous far-off times, for an actor

manager the show had had to go on.

Haplessly, with current cravings far less commendable, than salvaging anyone's good name, certainly not his own, our philanderer had been unable to reach his honey bunch for several minutes on the land line.
Recalling the concerned call to him at the hotel was from a mobile, Thomas realised, to his intense dismay, that he had never asked Alice for the number.

Nor had it been offered.

In the wait for a reply, the degree of artfulness seen, had not been recognised before.
Infrequent times she had called him had been on her mobile, never displaying=her calling number.

At first, for such an immense oversight, he had castigated only himself.

Remorselessly.

With concerns, also for her safety, he was sucked into the totally fact-less vacuum.

Desperate imaginings rapidly turned vapid.

Attempting to reach her afternoon long, with each try, a fiery physical stab had pierced his stomach, to be eliminated only with an answer to his call.
Which never came.

Building pressure in a steam line with a malfunctioning safety valve, his disability was known to the close wordy family.

"You've picked some real dogs, daddy."

In their mid-teens, while they had been staying with him in America, Avi and Em had discovered his weakness.
Encouraged whole heartedly by their mother, they had been amusing each other with it ever since.

"B.O.V.I.N.E."

At the time the younger sister was into spelling bees.

"Does that mean ape like?"

"No that's A.N.T.H.R.O.P.O.D.I.A.L".

Embarrassingly, the girls had run into their father at the Cineplex on East 19TH in the Village.

"Godzilla was playing."

On an afternoon tryst themselves, they 'had forgotten to tell him about, they were double dating two energetic twin brothers from the Ballet school chorus line: children of a friend.

"Godzilla."

Populous fare, they had never dreamed he would have been interested in seeing, was showing on the east side, well away from his apartment on his Westside Bank Street.

"MAGGIE MAY"

For years afterwards, a deliberately off-key rendition would rock shared households, if ever the subject of his romance needed retelling.
Or to juice up a boring family lunch.

"Where the fuck is she?"

By seven in the evening, Thomas had been unable to reach Alice. The seemingly deliberate refusal to pick up her landline, set a dyspeptic hot water geyser priming itself all afternoon, close to explosion.

Hyper-conscious of his plunges into the whirlpools of dependency with 'unavailable' women, Thomas was aware of the painful consequences of his obsessions.

Loud releases of frustration sounded scarily familiar.
While the blow torch flamed in his stomach, he wondered, if he was making the same mistake again.

"Maggie, Maggie May she took dad's breath

away."

Maggie was his tall and gorgeous student, but a highly questionable date.
Another who made it to his bed; but never when his children were staying.

"She'll never walk down Bank Street anymore."

Twisted and unhealthy as the short relationship had been, memories lingered long.
Were a warning for his present state of mind.
Not having realised it, he had become emotionally involved with the younger woman. He had sunken deep, needing much self-will to rid himself of real torment.
Gratuitously, he had written her out of his system with a short, rather vulgar story, published for an internet 'guinea' by an obscure writer's collective.
The only money, he ever had earned to date from his storytelling skills.

Way, cheaper than starting up in therapy again.

Because he could not find the logic in it, he was unable to calm himself further, by searching for a common-sense reason for Alice's silence.

More incomprehensibly, nor could he apply what he knew.

"I have to see her."

On the busy trail of freshly minted lovers, with first doubts over a newly acquired 'adored one', the urgent need for the 'face to face' was often a popular stratagem. Made in most cases, using massively wrong assumptions about the other partner, with large, non-verbalised expectations at a successful outcome, it hardly ever worked out. More usually it had had the opposite effect, often with tragic consequences.

Juliet et al.

But like Romeo, the multitudes and Thomas's need for action had been for right there and then.

He knew the contras because he had used the argument for the forceful impulse to know the exact location of a loved one was a major part in the success of the mobile phone business.

In spite the signs and all the work he had done on himself, he was reckless, far far too quickly.

Close to the speed of light.

In a vacuum 300,000 kilometres per second.

Pulling on jogging clothes, he began to act, without volition.

Like the first drink of wine after years of abstinence, it felt great; reinforcing his assumptions.

"Go for a run."

Slipping his feet into new perfect shop-threaded

trainers, he forewent all previous reluctance to break in the expensive highly structured 'runners'.

Deciding to jog across to the Grey's family house a mile or so from his home, it would take no time at all for a 'half-marathoner' in a virgin pair of racing red and white Nike's.

Callously, he had deduced, if the cuckold husband by any chance were home, Thomas's outfit would act as a disguise.

Feeling even more positive once outside, another mood rush was reconfirmed by air clear of the smell of cordite.

Sunday traffic bore no indication of the earlier conflagration.

Unfortunately, another metaphorical landmine had been primed and set.

An emotional bomb of real substance.

First, his new bouncy footwear set his mood in the wrong direction.

Lessening the normal tension release of the near sprint of the mile a half to her house, the new shoes squeaked ever so softly on every down tread. Understanding immediately Alice's high knee running style, she had advised him to buy shoes like her own.

On the first go around on her street, arrived at seemingly in a trice, he had missed his mistress's marital home because of a disguising sign erected in the front garden.

"Forty-eight?"

On another go around the street block, passing by the familiar house with newly vivacious steps, the confident writer received his comeuppance.

"Forty eight, right?"

The most incomprehensible surprise of a thrill-packed week.

Even after a massive intake of oxygen to feed his bloated brain, he was hardly, able to comprehend what he was witnessing.

"Forty-eight."

Outside her terraced house, much like his own, but not in such a 'good' street, an estate agent's For Sale' notice had been parked. Not just a panel to confirm the home was available for purchase, but one declaring in bold stapled on red printed letters, that it had been sold.

Running on the spot with the extra bounce the shoe packaging box had promised, Thomas attempted to collect his dizzy self; outside an empty, deserted property.

Eventually, the facts settled.

Neither of his friends, the disappeared painter, nor his devious wife, thought to say a word to him about their proposed house sale.

Thomas's reason spun into the first phase of a hot sloppy cycle, as he searched amongst the dirty washing for the last time he had visited their home. Discovering it had been five weeks before when he last saw Donald in the house, it was easily enough time in a local bull market for their property exchange to have been done and dusted.

To further confirm these incredible facts, he squeaked, half floated through the unlocked fence gate for a closer viewing. A security watch sticker was tagged to the inside of the stain glass front door panels. The deserted house was under professional protection.

"The bitch."

Choosing, instinctively and unusually, to blame her rather than him, Thomas, ultimately, had regained the capacity to curse.

His heart and his pride felt like they had been expertly skewered together through his anus onto a large discarded, rusty kebab stick.

"The fucking bitch."

Adding to the intensity of his shame, his next thought was to wonder, jealously, what their selling price might have been. Anything under 1.3 mill would have been a crime; however, speedily, they needed to move the deal.
"Two timing bitch."

Unable to drag himself up from the unfathomable depths of events, which he had no single suspicion, he peered into their front room, exposed by the street's lights. The Higgins was hanging the ceiling furniture in place, so eventually they would be back to pack it.

"You stooge Thomas."

On the striped Victorian floorboards, the telephone sat self-consciously in the middle.
Eerily, in the bleak half-light, as he scowled at the ugly, instrument with oversized dialling buttons, it began to ring.
Just audible through the single thickness glass panes in frames, not 'upgraded' to double glazing. disconnected.
Expectant that someone would come, answer, he waited; pondering who could be phoning at this time of the night, reassured that others besides himself must not have been informed of the move.
Till it stopped after a few rings abruptly, sending to even lower depths feeling more foolish than ever. If that were possible.

Eventually, a deflated punctured Abe Simpson balloon in the Macy's parade, dragged along on by strings by tiny people, turned and rolled itself towards home.

Anger and fear rising at a similar pace, they drove his legs in time to the soft 'duck imitations 'made with each long stride. Increasing rather than reducing his raging pulse, mantra un-conciliatory.

"Fuck her, fuck her, fuck her".

CHAPTER THIRTY TWO

Imagine a key.
Find the lock for it.
And the door it protects.
Then burn down the house it secures.

Yoko Ono

Often the sweet-smelling mouth exhaust was a forerunner to erratic action.

The ex-drinker might have been more alert to Alice's breath, on her visit to his house.

Sublimating concern to his needs; it was inevitable the obvious would return to haunt him.

Afterall, he had half a lifetime of warning.

Thirty years of sobriety.

How the Fellowship would have chuckled at the story of her disappearing house.

Cheered on when they had learnt that he bought a second home in a vineyard.

Like amiable monks, they had a great deal of satire.

Considering self-delusion everlastingly endemic, and worthy of the ridicule it was many times a laugh.

Members had applauded loudest, when you had remembered the day, you got sober.

An anniversary.

Even a one day one.

The most important; a first whole day without booze.

JUNE 4TH 1989

Having vowed to get healthy, all those years ago in America, with the help of meetings and an AA friend, Thomas had forsworn alcohol.

Bar the occasional rum Barba from Tesco's.

Split from his family, he had been unable to bear the awful morning depressions drink had caused. Out of the native culture, whose major social centres were the public House', he had recognised the blindness of his class to ingrained dependency.

No longer surrounded by colleagues who thought nothing of sharing a whole bottle of wine every lunchtime, Thomas had begun to appreciate his own pernicious habit.

"My name is Thomas I'm an alcoholic".

Oddly, this sentence, with its recitation, was the rock core of the organisation's ethos.

Why he in the end had moved away from the big book.

The rooms had demanded little else for the love, wisdom and endless free coffee; besides a dollar, if you had it. During meetings it was necessary to announce, at the start of speaking, a lifelong acceptance to your addiction, by sharing it with the congregation of recovering souls.

The sworn imperative needed you to be one.

He was not.

Thomas was never in his terms, or indeed theirs, an alcoholic.

Neither wet nor dry.

Truthfully, he had been a regular heavy drinker who on occasions, had binged.

Their spoken obligation had always silenced him at meetings.

Once they had helped put the idea of sobriety in his head, that he could stop, it had been as simple as that.

A bad mixer who had not needed the rest of their package.

A truly life changing choice, which he had never regretted nor ever went back on.

With a humility, learnt partly from them, he became more aware of his obsessions in full therapy. Consequent thirty years without drinking had proved him right in his assumption; he was not one of them. Fellow ex-drinkers would have laughed had he been allowed by his conscience to speak out. An occasional refrain heard in those redemptive rooms that also met with instant derision. Undoubtedly, he missed the comfort of their friendship; a quite unique experience; a spell cast by the group collectively was powerful; if not cultist. Hearing them tell with incredible skill of the extraordinary things they had experienced, when drunk, the listener was humbled, wishing his life half as full.

Contrarily, of course, these saintly folks were a herd of damaged people, ex-junkies and previous falling down drunks; a fact, when expressed by the sharer was rewarded by the evenings, most appreciative applause.

Thomas, fancifully, imagined these groups were like the early follows of charismatic people like John the Baptist. We have proof in contemporary writings he had existed. Unlike Christ whom we have no such physical evidence. A mountain of stories, but nothing a barrister would call evidence.

Strangely, numbers included few winos and homeless people for they would, mostly, be elsewhere pursuing their dangerous habit.

Just returned from his second long run of the day to punish his weak body, Thomas discarded his sweaty gear in the clothes basket and was about to take his third shower of the day.

His 'Dizziness' realised the tic like click in the air was from the computer.

Caught again by the ebbtide, he was off balance and dragged back on the draught.

"Alice?"

Naked again at his desk, he clicked up the email he saw in his email box, blinking hard enough to turn right.

Another picture of the woman, which emerged from the attachment looked exactly like the female he so dearly needed to contact; dressed in bathing costume from earlier times; a one piece from the sixties. An additional character was by her side wearing nothing at all but a pair of water wings and about the age Alice would have been if she had been a small boy. Sharing near-identical features the two just must have been mother and son. It could not have been a young Alice because the kid owned a small penis. The full length shot of the pair was snapped under a communal shower.

"This is so alcoholic".

The location of the square 'brownie" snap was the old Fulham Swimming Baths; a place he knew; intimately. On the North End market road and barely two streets along from his, it was a haunt of his schooldays. Reached through a resonating tiled entrance hallway, he had queued there since the beginning of time; behind indifferent grown-up's intent on hiring a hard white towel smelling of fresh laundry and buying minute bars of white soap with no scent at all.

His small threadbare towel from home, determined exclusively for swimming, was rolled up with a bathing costume inside, tucked up under his arm. He had to wait obediently to exchange three large hand-heated copper pennies, for the issue of a rubber wristband, crudely inked with a number. An additional paper ticket appeared by magic through an opening in the receptions chrome top counter; much like the pierced lid where the needle disappeared to do its stitching, in his mother's Singer sewing machine.

Once inside the baths, clothes were an encumbrance; to be pushed into key-less lockers,

Shivering, skinny post-war torsos naked save for the baggy water absorbent trunks, hung wet, and pendulous, like the skin under an old man's chin.

Vivid memories, a thousand times denser, and more meaningful than a digital facsimile.

Checking the earlier pictures again posed the question of whether he had known this woman who looked like Alice. Certainly, he was familiar with many people in the area, but he could not have known everyone who lived in Fulham.

Searching the new picture again he spied the extra thick band on the boy's wrist, unassailable provenance to the period, definitive as carbon dating. Without the rubber identification dangling from foot or an ankle, no one was ever allowed to swim by loud overly assertive attendants; whose gender, even with much clearer hindsight, was indeterminate. On a hot summer day when the pool was crowded, even, suitably manacled, the precious ident had to be surrendered at shrill sergeant major whistles, when a number and colour were called. Sometimes, after only twenty short minutes.

Swimming assists, like the child had been

wearing were forbidden; on a blacklist to include of one of his best gifts ever; a new pair of black 'flippers, worn lovingly as bedroom slippers for the whole of one Christmas morning. After barely a minute in the chlorinated winter paradise, where adult speech was at best distorted, these prized possessions were considered illegal on sight; and had met by the terrifying high-pitched barrage of whistles with half a dozen accusing fingers.

Segregated by gender, as strictly, as Southern American High school once was by race; the ancillary hot baths were used by locals without bathrooms; a place as exotic to a young Thomas as any Turkish baths of the future. Inside this tabernacle, the woman would not have been discriminated against with regard to her child because the boy was so tiny. Eyebrows most definitely would have been raised though at his lack of a bathing costume. Both bathers wore tell-tale rubber loops around their ankles so must have been swimming before they bathed which seem odd; but perhaps indicative of a protective mother wary of the infections a crowd carried.

Thomas conjectured on whom the photographer might have been.
Small brownie box cameras at earlier times were few but was getting nowhere with his quest.
He appreciated the email picture could not have been of Alice.
She would have been far, far too young.

Leaning back in his chair to ponder the riddle he looked down, shocked to see his uncovered manhood, correlating the distinct rank odour. Unsticking from his chair, he stood up to continue to the bathroom. Before going under the powerful shower stream, for the first time in ages, there was a ring on his front door chime. Temporally, to off pitch twangs of the barely recognisable Van Morrison classic, all critical sense in residence deserted him. Anxious to share his troubles, hopefully with a friend, Thomas could see no harm at least checking out his caller.

After one miserable thought, coincidence hastened several others.

Imprudently he made the short journey to the front bay window to look outside. Making sure to stay in the shadows, the naked ex-director peered through the bright slit between two dark edges of the shutters. To his surprise, not one, but two attractive uniformed young women were on his doorstep.

Both held small packages to deliver.

Duelling uniform hats registered the flattering benefits of the formal cut-down bowler, against the chic of the baseball cap. Talkative post woman Zulieka was deep in conversation with Policewoman Jane in starched white shirt, string tie and bullet proof vest. Skimming over what might still be a "spoken for' male, Thomas might have remembered the way his luck was running; that middle-aged men always look more impressive, clothed in something. Anything really.

Recklessly, happy to see them, with nothing available to shield him, he had grab at the multitasking Guardian, as he headed into the hallway, believing himself invisible behind his stained-glass door. On reaching it he opened it enough to cover his pride, to let in conversation.

"I'm in the bath.'

Poking out a pale winter arm, he went for one-handed, semaphoring to pass on the packages.

Catastrophically, though he had not realised his uncovered frame was wedged too close behind the opaque coloured, stained-glass panes, which made it more transparent than usual.

Transfixed, when, they had noticed the waving disembodied arm, both girls recognised humour in a situation, where some might have not.

Letting out stifled shrieks of pure joy, through cupped mouths, two servants of the crown advanced quickly down the final meter of his garden path, attempting to use their youthful, uniformed bodies to lessen the shameful viewing angle for the public.

Tardy with no reshuffle of his literary supplement, he was not cognisant of his terrible blunder until they were under his porch. As the awful realisation dawned, he gave a better rendition of receiving a punch than the Australian night manager. Beyond mortification, talking through the door jar like in a confessional, he could think of nothing to explain his shamefulness.

A well-trained dance combo, turned glances decently away, struggling with tears of mirth. PC Jones pushed her package behind the small divide between door frame and door. Zulieka followed suit with a hand addressed letter. Drying tears with a clean tissue from her trouser pocket Pc Jones tried to get serious.

"Chief says he needs this mess dead. It's your picture Mr Maher.

Says to tell you it's worth very. Not an original."

Postman Pat for once, had yet to express an opinion. In the shiver of sudden silence, all eyes averted, automatically, to the ground, and a full silent retreat was the only option.

CHAPTER THIRTY THREE

Slaving at his workstation the following evening, for most of the continuing night, Thomas had channelled his anxiety down keyboard fingers, attempting to blank the memory of events on the doorstep.

Perhaps in revenge, he completed the demise of his imagined painter.

"I killed Sam".

Fatigue, having slipped its heavy cape over aching shoulders, he headed into a quicksand of despair and stopped writing. His changes had not been made permanent, adding more uncertainty.

Staring for so long at his computer, its after image, had superimposed over the diorama of the back-lit garden beyond. Captive to the darkness through his French windows, 'Mr Kent" loomed haughtily; a well-preserved socialite in summer coat, attempting to hide its noticeably spreading girth with silver.

Changing his mind precipitously, he turned again to his computer and reinstated the original.

Thus, reversing a night's work, which stopped the clawing paranoia.

Abruptly, lesions of dawn, hinting at twilight, darted toward to full day.

Alas, the same vexing question restarted, like an unstoppable alarm on an absent motorist's car.

"Why Alice. Why?"

Not for the first time, he picked up the diversionary email photo of the sweet child, with a face which screamed of closeness to her.

A new physical bolt of terror rocked his brain.

A notion, so outrageous, he paused to exhale.

"Suppose this snap had been of Alice?
With a penis?"

Distressingly wearied, he had tried to head off the terrible consideration.

"Before she had a sex change?"

Once he had spoken the proposition it was a dried pea in a salt-pot.

There simply was no way to rattle it out.

Long-held acceptance of gay rights, dissolved into revulsion.

Shame became physical.

"Had he then, penetrated a man?"

His hour's tiring search on the internet had been needed to contain the flames.

Happily, Sexual Realignment Surgery, was no hidden secret.

Almost, breezily, retelling their experience as if it a first trip overseas, some of the men who underwent this life changing surgery, had used the worldwide web to share similar experiences in testimonials. Publishing well documented experience with hospital photos of their procedures at various stages of recovery. Nothing left to the imagination.

A prudish fiction writer was eminently shockable. Clearly behind the times.

Numbers having the operation, suggested a downgraded of paranoia, to an understanding.

Permission for the procedure, according to a Thai hospital website, was after two years dressing as a woman on doctor prescribed hormonal pills.

The prospective transsexual would then be screened by the surgeons before losing his penis.

In 2001 a specialist perfected a new procedure, using the entire genital sack and penis to construct the female organ. He was able to form a six-inch deep, functioning vagina, sensitive to sexual stimulus.

It was, visually, indistinguishable from the God made one.

Labia major, labia minor, clitoral hood, clitoris, urethra, vagina were created using the sensate pedicle method preserving the nerve and blood supply connections from parts of the penis glands with precise photographs of the results of the procedures.

Extraordinarily, the cost for such an operation

was about eight thousand British pounds.

Separate from the additional flight and hotel expenses.

A small number indeed, considering the magnitude of the surgery.

Nowhere near the financial commitment needed to buy a house.

No more than the cost of a new small car really.

The cost of becoming a woman.

Most surprisingly of all, the desperate, life-changing measure had not been undertaken by men who looked particularly feminine; as the writer would have presumed, like the gorgeous Lady boys of Bangkok. For the most part it was performed on physically 'ungifted' middle-aged men from the West. Men who had needed additional help from skilful surgeons to give their faces anything like a woman's streamlining, to match new genitalia.

Overwhelmingly, physical beauty was never an overriding issue in becoming a woman.

Rechecking his bias on a few pornographic sites, Thomas reassured himself of the beauty of the Asian men who had gone halfway on the transgenic journey; retaining penises and making themselves both male and female with the addition of breasts onto mostly, small, girlish frames.

Fascinated with just how people differentiated gender by just looking at the face, he was mesmerised by the perfection his search revealed.

Some female faces were of staggering beauty, again, more breath-taking even than the real thing.

Abruptly, the opening bars of the Marseillaise, the much-anticipated siren on his mobile, announced an incoming call.

A glance at his computer clock told him that it was approaching six am.

"Alice."

Auspiciously or not, automatically he was dead on the button.

It was the one beautiful feminine person, who could answer all his complex concerns.

If she had chosen to.

With absolute certainty.

At first, when he had clicked on her call, all he could hear through the crystal-clear digital fibre technology was her deep breathing. Close as if she was lying next to him on his pillow. Sounds so comforting they were unmistakable.

"Alice?"

Straining every dishonourable sinew, Thomas could not help but listen for the smallest hint of masculinity, in her breathing.

"Were have you been darling, I 've been worried sick. I've been going half out of my mind."

Still there were no words from her end of the line to confirm it was her.

"I went over to your house. Alice, it's been sold."

She would not acknowledge the sale.
Nor if she was hearing him down the phone line.

Her breathing though and intake of air were increasing.

"Alice?"

Many more tortuous seconds later with a heart-breaking sob, she broke the wordless regiment.

"I won't talk Thomas, while you are so angry with me."

Thomas hated himself for his next automatic release, the intensity of which shocked him.

"Where are you?"

Alas, his scream at her was another 'first.'

"I can't say."

Defiantly, she returned his violence with equal gusto.

"Please don't shout Thomas."

Effortlessly, his angry balloon was punctured.
With just one weary tone.

"But why darling. Why did you leave?"

Convinced he was hearing the voice of a woman; it was his turn to lose his words.

His 'darling' was instinctive, at a much lower volume.
He had hoped, appeasing.
Joyfully, he was unable to detect even the merest hint of masculinity in her gorgeous, husky, tones.

"I'm so sorry Thomas. Please don't shout it makes me shiver."

Compassion seemed, instantly, to have dried her tears.

"You have to trust me."

And he would.
Prostrate, flat as any Easter prelate, pleading his forgiveness, he would trust her.
He lost all need to scold; became her very own church mouse.

"What's going on Alice sweetheart?"

"I can't tell you yet Thomas. Please, please, trust me."

"I just got an email. Did you send it?"

The response to the question that needed to have been asked a century before, was quick and so sincere Thomas could not doubt its truth.

"What email? I did not send you any email."

Alas, the Rubik's cube would not twist so easily to a colour line up.
His puzzle was again in disarray.

"Please Thomas. Pick me up at the airport."

"The Airport?"

Angry lungs re-inflated.
Thomas lost all control; and flew to the ceiling.
Alice was accepting.
Even workmanlike.

Or work-woman-like

"Air India, the New York plane."

"NEW YORK?

"You are in New York?"

"Maybe."

Her tone again was hostile.

If she was in his one-time hometown, the five-hour time difference would have made it one in the morning; the earliest possible time for her to call him and hope to get a reply.

He reminded himself it was barely 30 hours since they had spoken in the hotel.

She could have flown herself there in that time frame.

To make any economic sense, she would have needed to have booked her flight in advance.

Again, adding penetratingly painful premeditation.

"Please don't shout."

He was not really cautioning her, but himself.

"It arrives in at six thirty am. Three days' time.
 the day after, the day after, tomorrow.
I must go. I miss you so much.
Please, please, be there Thomas."

The sound of his name singing in his ear, the phone went dead.

Had it been a public one, he would certainly have destroyed it.

But the hated instrument was Thomas's own pricey smart phone.

So, he clicked it off.

Slowly he laid it on his desk in front of him; his hand clearly shaking.

Never, could he remember a time when he felt so angry; or so out of himself.

"The day after, the day after, tomorrow."

Yet the intensity of it all was, hopelessly, addictive. Only a fool or a blind man would not see his passion for her. Instinctively or not, she had found the passage down into his volcanic core as others had. However difficult it might be to stay resolved; years of therapy insisted he maintain a more watchful brief; to edit his choices for forward action. Prone to obsessive women, it was only a very few short days since these connections with Alice were made; no history at all the way his therapist would have defined it.

But the time before he would see her again a few short days away seemed forever.

The day after, the day after, tomorrow.

Plainly, Thomas needed to construct a plan for himself.

Today was the sixth, Monday, tomorrow the seventh, Tuesday, the day after had been the eight,

Wednesday, so she must have meant Thursday the eighth.

Could he wait?

CHAPTER THIRTY FOUR

Grown accustomed to the vigil of his home, a stubborn campaigner's windows were still without curtains. After twenty-four consecutive hours with no proper sleep, his uncongenial body clock refused to shut down. Ultimately, it had needed two sleeping pills to fell him.

During the hours of disturbed slumber, he had imitated a childhood manoeuvre his daughters had terrified him with in their cots. Turning his whole body around under the bed covers, he had burrowed his way under to the other end of the bed; resurfacing into an awful wake up, wrapped like a mummy. Within inches of the television set, fighting to disentangle himself, it took several seconds to coordinate with gravity, after pulling out the remote embedded in his side.

One false click of this weapon, his un-submerged view became an inverted heavily made-up News doll from right-wing cable. Changed speedily to blaring of coronation horns, were quickly muted. The blockbuster movie revealed the updating of the God of Thunder to a hulking platinum-blonde, tall as a basketball player with a deadly looking hammer.

Exclusively twenty first century imagery was left for a time to course casually, through a consciousness already believing it had passed through the burial rites described in the Egyptian Book of the Dead.

A bedside copy was a recent crib for Sam's brief journey to the underworld.

"I am the goddess Sekhmet, and I take my seat by the side of Am t-ur the great wind of heaven.

I am the great Star-goddess Saah, who dwells among the Souls of Anu with the mdtft of biz".

The pre-burial ceremonial of opening of the Royal mouth man into the awakened state by priests in pre-dynastic times was by using a forked flint knife; later to be substituted by a small chisel named the Mdtft, the tool for before the journey to a 'better' life.

Another unthinking click of the remote, the image of the tanned woman reappeared.

Of indeterminate race, she continued her counselling of confusing facts; in a pleasing mellifluous accent, with influences disparate as Sidney, New York, and dear old Brummie.

Almost shamefully, more zings of pure-static zapped down from the heavens, leaving Thomas to ponder what terrible mischief he had done in a past life.

Absently, he had picked up the photo emails again, for no other reason than they were there, reading on the last line of this note, an address he had missed before. Scrambling clumsily out of bed he was awake and down to the computer before you could say mdtft.

"Buzet sur le Baise "

This was a château well known to him.
The town was his neighbours in the wine region near his French farmhouse.
But he knew no one there.

Or so he had thought.

Anxiously, rechecking the first email, the second address was not in it.
Punched by more uncertainty, how could he possibly have missed the address before.

He Googled the street.
Instantly three real estate listings came up.
Everyone in the world it appeared was selling their houses.

He discovered the actual address lower down on the page.
It was the local Buzet post.

"Oh fuck."

Not electronically stimulated, but of its own volition, with an abstract reasoning to sometimes turn a base instinct into communicating gold, a second deceiving prong of the fork lightning struck.
Inhaling, cosmic nose-dust from his planet Seera, Thomas remembered the last time he had visited the town.
It had been with Donald, With Alice and their friend

Jane.

He was floored.
He was bemused.

Buzet wine.
Red wine; red, red, wine.

Just a year ago, the Lawrences had been on a summer trip to Jane, who lived in France with a boyfriend; relatively close-by.

They had visited Thomas in Lavardac for a day out, without their host.

Struck down, temporarily by lust; like a hormonal adolescent, Thomas was introduced to the tall full-figured, middle-aged lady on a very hot day. In an 'Alva Gardener' Panama sun hat, flatteringly shading her 'timeless' beauty from the ravages of the southern sun, she was wearing a floor-length cotton floral dress which had showed the armpit sweat. Apart from his cooking, which she had appeared to enjoy, with a creditable appetite and seconds of scallops, she had showed scant regard for Thomas or his re-modelled farmhouse. With no great harm to anything but his ego, their history together was short; a long email to her afterwards that was ignored.

Remembering only the first few bars of a Neil Diamond refrain, it would not stop repeating.

Red wine; red, red, wine. Buzet wine

After a customary dig about Thomas not drinking in the land of plenty, their host had suggested a trip to the local winemakers. Donald headed the most creatively dressed league table of visiting Englishmen in his relaxed summer style; a cheap yellow t-shirt with self-added bon mot, nylon blue shorts, hugging his genitals, and black trainers with nylon socks to his calves.

Sam's inspiration 'travelled' worse even than he would have dared write him.

Looking back with hindsight on a retiring Alice, she was quiet all day; and anxious.

The wineries were holding a summer sale of older vintages, almost run out.

Prices were very cheap, some just a few Euros a bottle.

The house could not guarantee some of the wine bottled thirty years before would have been drinkable. Though there had been signs everywhere in English and French explaining the policy, Donald had wanted to buy a case and had insisted on a taste of his purchase.

The dark-haired French woman, who had served him, spoke remarkably good English, was mortified at his belligerence. Embarrassed at the ranting, Thomas jumped in with his bad French to offer a compromise. They had agreed to buy a bottle of his selected 'poison'; drink it for lunch then return in the afternoon to buy the case. By then everyone in the large tent were looking at them.

Graciously, given the tough, fast-talking matriarchs, famous in the region of d'Artagne, she would reserve the case till the next day. Obviously shaken by his lack of dignity, she stood on her own; and produced a form, like all things French, in duplicate.

Thomas recalled he had given her his email address, never having memorised his French telephone number.

So, he had known people in Buzet.

Curiously, noted at the time, when the woman caught sight of Alice rejoining their party at the conclusion of business, Thomas remembered very clearly, both had given each other the same terrible look. Disconcertingly even then, he would have categorised it as pure hatred; one hundred percent certain he was witnessing their first encounter.

Such rage was completely out of character for Alice,

The bottle, duly opened at home, decanted, drunk; and declared a must buy.

Typically for a man with so little understanding of the way his actions affected his wife, Alice, had been designated driver of the hire car. He had fallen deep asleep in the car and no wine purchase had been completed. A week after, the drama forgotten, Thomas remembered he had received an email, notification from the winery that the wine was no longer on offer.

Red, red wine... Buzet wine......

Thomas's instinct was to go visit his house in France to see how Buzet might fit into the increasing enigma. After all, there was little to occupy him, bar worry, till Alice had returned.

.... *thedayafterthedayaftertomorrow.*

He had made the trip many times before.
For a day or two to check construction during the restoration.

Suddenly weary, he left his desk and headed for the maternal comfort of the sofa.

"From the light of the earth to the light of eternal day."

Thomas observed the peak-white shafts from a slow-moving Ra hitting the wall.

"Where the fuck is she?"

Not one erg of its energy helped solve this frustration.

In need of more sleep, his body was totally resistant.

"Should I go? Should I stay?"

Stressed by the short window of opportunity if he were to act, he canvassed the light's effect on the perfectly white-satin finish in front of his nose. The paint job had been achieved recently with Em's help plus two coats of eco-friendly clay paint; stirred into its over-thick emulsion with lots of gratuitous female cussing. Of which he suspected, guiltily, he once had been the teacher.

Currently, as self-pitying 'pater' felt as used as the paint rag, a once favourite frayed old blue shirt, she had used to cover more important ripped blue-jeans.

"This paint looks and smells like white dog shit pater.

What ever happened to good old fucking Dulux."

Using the wood window panel frame as its lighting 'gobo', he noted the triangular shape projected by the sunshine onto his bedroom wall.

"Khut the pyramid, the "light".

Before its carefully angled capping-stones had been removed by vandals at Giza, they had acted like a huge mirror reflecting the continuing waves of energy from the sun.

Laconically, with the shadow of his finger, he tried to discern earth's celestial movement utilising the technology of a sundial. Any shift in the world for an undecided decision-maker would not turn it any faster because he had willed it.

According to modern minds, the source of all power had been predicted to continue a billion more years. Before it burnt out into a 'White Dwarf'. To remain as such in space, till time's end.

316

"Eternity"

Like death, the unimaginable certainty
Wistfully, he mused for a few more morbid
moments on the word, once so terrifying to him as a
child, thrown about so recklessly by his theological
teachers.

Dressing and going downstairs, he switched on
the huge new smart Tv using up to date flat
technology infused into the screen. Through his
hook up, the received pictures where of better
resolution than the test of high def in a commercial
using the new equipment he had made for TV
Broadcast companies on his Time in America. He
had liked to boast about it; so conscious every day
of the results on his computer monitor.

"That after you seduced Raquel Welsh Papi?"

"His cameraman SiS."

"The one who married Liz Taylor?"

"No, the one with the Buddhist guy in Working
woman, I think. "

"She fancies George Clooney

"He's married"

Via the lunchtime news, feeds from cameras trained
on current subjects more worthy of attention were

allowed to invade.

Replayed a dozen times, the pretty young person, paid plenty not to wear out eyes in the monotonous repetition, explained an event that maybe could be viewed more carefully.

The colour TV was a newish purchase.

Last year, his old black and white faithful, which was a friend, had been sold on e-Bay for five measly pounds, after his daughters' discreet bullying.

"It runs on steam pater."

Sensing his argument for black and white media being more appropriate for news was not made.

Overnight, there had been the death of a high-ranking policeman on the Yorkshire Moors.

"On Ilkly moor bar tat...."

After recent events, the writer was ambivalent toward the long-established Bobby brand.

The man was killed by a single 45mm bullet from a police issue handgun found at his side.

According to the three assembled experts, the deadly projectile was aimed through his mouth.

"Poor sod."

The writer wondered why anyone would do such a thing to himself.

Wrestling with the image of gummy jellied fluids, and long transparent nerve fibres Thomas was inhaling the fragrance of fresh spring daisies. Laundered with a detergent, chosen because it had been unbranded and cheap. Flashing on the wisdom of a past generation, the once impoverished Fulham, boy remembered the donkey sperm rumour to have been an important ingredient in Camay soap.

"Made with perfume worth nine guineas an ounce."

Wearing brand new shirts and commentator ties, the panel of experts were exclusively male.

Because of a female sensitivity to goriness, he had assumed.

Before remembering such a malady never struck down the gorgeous fictional body-scientists on endless TV police autopsies, cultural imports from America.

He saw the programs, strangely enough, undubbed on channel one in France.

It had appalled him.

Shocked at how the French could swallow such rubbish, he was unable to construct a reason.

Like with other unexplainable fictions.

How it was now possible to see overweight people on the Paris subway.

The bullet each real medical, man had explained hit a vertebra at the top of the spine; the one which houses the internal marrow and carries the links to all bodily functions.

Ninety nine percent of intra-oral wounds, of which this was one, were self-inflicted, so effective death was instantaneous.
Not even half a breath was possible after the spinal cord was severed.

"Poor bugger"

Distracted, another time by their dress, Thomas wondered if these men were deliberately costumed; If they owned the shirts and ties, they wore.

In his old job as director, he was familiar with how his clients wanted his cast dressed.

But those were the days when a filmed commercial production, had budgets to finance such excess. Before 'video games' became 'scripts' and took the lead, in costs per second.

In his day, commercials were the most expensive way of filming, costing more than a 'feature'.

The comely 'anchor' had kept the pace moving.
Coupled with his blood alcohol level, the dead Bobby wore just his braided hat, white socks, and police issued black trainers.

They were the script writer deciders.

"Drink kills"

Recalling the smell of alcohol on Alice's, when they were eating each other on the sofa, Thomas never had seen any propensity for drink from her.

Before, when she was exclusively with Donald.

He wondered absently, if she was with him at present.

"I miss you so much. Please, please, be there Thomas."

Waves of jealousy effervesced like sodium bicarbonate bubbles in the close up during a hangover remedy commercial.

"How could she have sold the house and not told me?

Exasperated with inability, fatigued or not to resolve the issue, he needed to stop the endless flow of unanswered questions.

"Take a fucking action, man."

Sometimes, when he shouted at himself, the writer would shake out his lethargy.

A reminder, he always concluded; of the way he was instructed by his early teachers.

The sharpness of his tone was meant to pretend certainty.

One advantage, if he were to go, would be to check up on his house.

With such a late travel date he would have to swallow and pay the full train fare.

And hire a car.

But he would take his laptop along to write on during the journey.

In and out in two days it was possible.
He had done it many times before.
Ultimately, he wore himself out enough to smile,
Always a good sign his sense was returning.
Indecision, Thomas decided would certainly drive him back to drink.

Buzet wine....

The option to travel was made with no further prevarication.

One problem resolved, there was no end to the bad things the gods had held in store for him.

"Commander Patrick J Binden of the Northumbria Police Force"

For the first time since Thomas began to watch, a head and shoulders picture of the man who had committed suicide was transmitted. Decked out in the heavily silvered cap of a uniformed senior Police Officer it was flashed up as the highlights of a career in law enforcement.

"JESUS"

According to the anchor, part of the policeman's career was served fighting with the 'ethnic-cleansing' mobs in Bosnia.

"It's him."
Stunningly, Thomas found himself staring into

face of the big man who had assaulted him.

"A Muslim hater. He was a cop.

How in God's name had he got to Yorkshire to shoot himself."

Emphasising the event had occurred two miles from Keighley in Bronte country, the program compilers played on the idea it was an area with a long history of the occult.
Presumably because they were getting little information from the police.

Madame Blavatsky, founder of the Theosophical society once had lived there in the wacky, nineteenth century off shoot, the Society of the Drew and Light.
Their journal had been the Lamb of Thurt.
Hinting his might be some kind of ritual death, the unfortunate law man's minutes of news fame ended abruptly with the time slot, without any mention of undercover work.

"Poor shit."

The next news item in the wheel cycle replaced him.

Turning down the sound to wait, a more thoughtful Thomas mourned the death of another human. unexpectedly, he felt pity, not resentment toward his big-bodied aggressor.

Certainly, a little hopeless at his small part in it.

"Had they killed him?
Surely not? This was England for Christ's sake".

Then he remembered the recent police kidnaper rapist.
A bad wind lingered, rustling uncomfortable chimes.
Maybe he had not killed himself.
Had it needed consideration?
Maybe even action from him.

At that moment, worse than ever, he wanted to hold Alice.

Chilled, but not frozen with fear, he was ready for their reunion two days away.

Can a man ever rightfully take a life, even his own?
He was not worried for his own safety.
But the police must be told about the night with Alice.

What this man had done to him.

Determinedly, sitting up and reaching for his landline, he tried to reach McPherson.
The number of the policeman was on the card in his wallet.

To say for the next half hour, he had received the

'cold shoulder' would have been an understatement.

First it had taken an age for anyone to answer, even by todays excessive standards a long wait.

After more extended ones, he was shuffled around various offices.

"Not in our division"

"No sir not here."

"Have you tried special branch?"

"PC Jones you say?"

"Not Smith eh Jones you say?"

"Buxom and young?"

"Really sir?"

"She does not work here."

"We have no idea how to contact him."

Thomas never got to speak the Chief Inspector. Or even to PC Jones.

Apparently, they had, absolutely, no use for Thomas's information.

If they had not primed to give him the 'brush off', they had made a creditable job of it.

Eventually, one good citizen of the world lost interest. It was time to get on with his own life.

France.

CHAPTER THIRTY FIVE

When suggesting she had wed a Pakistani compatriot, the London parents of Patti Patel, had chosen well. Distantly related, he was raised in the North, in the far-off Lands of Newcastle upon Tyne.

After they had met, the silent rangy cobbler had turned an even quieter handbag manufacturer, instantly and everlastingly beguiled by the alchemy of the petite jet-eyed beauty.

Before agreeing to their betrothal, his in-laws had made an unusual demand for her hand; asking that her prospective husband move to the capital, into a house close to them that their daughter had spotted in Southall. In grateful return they would donate the ten percent deposit it had required; a much smaller actual amount than would be required today.

Over three decades later, the family still lived in the same good sized four bedroomed home: currently, mortgage free, due to his prudence.

In old age, munificent in laws had moved in and had died there a few years later; peacefully and sadly. But within twenty-four hours of each other in the bosom of their family.

Dan Patel's gentle voice was seldom raised in a household commanded by his adored wife.

The melodious ups and downs of his soft sing-song Geordie accent was tempered by the vernacular of the streets of the new metropolis he worked in; and by listening constantly to his London wife. At times, when he said something so softly, it sounded like he spoke in a whole other language, except to her.

The whole community, though at first sympathetic, were wary about the fanatics; universally frightened of their influence over the younger men.

When she told her husband about her son's mischief, there had been no trouble hearing her.

The painful treachery of their first born was devastating.

An unaccustomed coldness overcame a united couple, before the anger was flushed out.

A careful outcome had been speedily determined.

Following her return home from the doctors there was a raucous family confrontation, of hurriedly summoned brothers, with other close male friends and families. To tears, quickly at her blunt questioning, her youngest blurted out the whole story, desperate to regain love and forgiveness.

At first bemused, she was mortified that two of her children would do such a thing.

After a brief house search, rather less creative than his secret printing process, the hidden profits were found under the boy's mattress. Manifestly, they had been too difficult to bank; to explain nearly a hundred thousand pounds.

A confession had led to a bad beating for the eldest wayward son.

In this regard she was totally with the men.

Everyone in the family recognised, after Allah, Alice Patel was the law.

Suspecting Benjamin's brother involved in something so bad; the topic would become the only one discussed in the confines of their bedroom.

What should they do about him.

Loving Partners noted the trouble began with the demise of the two maternal grandparents with whom they had had a very strong bond.

Pati's notion had been to ship the boy straight to the police.

Her husband had fought hard against such a move.

In his experience the law makers were not a trusted group for their community.

A compromise was reached quickly with conscience, for her seventeen-year-old to be shipped to the family in Pakistan with a plan to install him in a business college paid for by his ill-gotten gains.

It failed he would be under the pain of much worse.

It was a threat, which she reasoned her family would carry out if it had been needed.

Desperately, she hoped this would straighten him out.

"He has to go tonight."

The boy had had a passport organised earlier in the year for a school trip to France.

No one argued her logic.

A cousin was in the bucket airline business, so the ticket was not a problem to sought out. They wrote them for the area every day.

They had the money in cash, and at an exorbitant investment rate they bought it through him.

After one long conference call to 'home' the thing had been settled legally

With even a bona fide application form.

Hopefully, they had acted quickly enough to avoid detection. Because if caught they knew it would mean a lifetime in jail for her son and terrible trouble for everyone else.

Regarding Benjamin, after forgiving his actions because he owned up, she was immovable.

"He stays with me".

She would defend him with her life, giving up the eternal one if needs be.

Again, no one dared to argue against such certainty because he was so young.

Frantically, organising the dispatch of their eldest was not a unique problem in their area.

Though a concerned father had never actually visited Pakistan.

Promising himself that he would one day, he had reassured his wife it was the correct choice.

The difficulty of acting was lessened by the speed at which they had to move.

They were able to, though felling traitors.

Happily, Nan was dead and had never to know.

"She had so loved the Queen."

Only, marginally, more experienced, Pati had visited for a three-week summer holiday.

Either way the eldest had needed to change.

"He'll survive. This will be his making.

He can return if they don't find out what he did, when he is a man."

Devastatingly, a scant ten hours later, he was gone.

CHAPTER THIRTY SIX

Emanating certainty, not showing her pain, Pati had decreased the hurt for the rest of the family. Unable to share the banishment of someone her body had created, she looked for ways to divert.

At least temporarily.

The others had thought the escape of her eldest was a certainty, when in the immediate hours following his flight, it most assuredly had not been.

But she added zilch against the idea.

Old urges, on seeing her Mentor, had promoted complex maternal feelings.

Overall, she craved to make an object.

To express concern in a physical way with her fingers.

One that he could see and appreciate.

Without the thought of another face to face, which she had abhorred.

When finished, if it were good enough, she would send it.

The idea to steady herself, necessarily, must remain her secret.

Begun that evening, while her husband watched the football for a few hours, submerged in a blinkered silence.

In a special school project, Pati had often visited Thomas's house, with his young daughters in attendance. So, she knew the address well where

Benjamin had posted the package.

No need then to question again.

Unnervingly, he had turned clinging, and desperate to be back under her wing.

Presently no one knew of the film pyrotechnic used, no physical hurt intended. Forces who controlled the information had continued to hide it.

Perhaps it would never be revealed.

In the private tutorials with her old teacher, Pati had grown to admired Cezanne,

But her inclination was for something quite different than the Frenchman's oeuvre.

Additionally, she would make nothing figurative because of her convictions.

Filling her art void presently, a highly proficient seamstress had helped at the machines if Dan got stuck on an order. She was responsible for everyday bag design.

Either way he always bought the prototype home to check it was approved.

So sensibly she would sew something for the family insulted Mr Maher.

Nothing that evening was available in her large kitchen workplace than the piece of cardboard she was to draw on, but she needed to start.

The ball point used in her process made feinter lines on the corrugations, but it had to do.

Her teachers amused bon mots were ingrained and too available.

"Turning the awful into the average. What an idea. Persevere."

On the oak table, with a clean tea mug inverted, resting on the cardboard, she had drawn around it.

The perfect circle to begin a journey into her mind.

Her blue biro converted it easily to an Islamic arch.

Deciding it need to be larger; she had fetched a small sandwich plate from the dresser, searched out a larger piece of cardboard from the recycling.

Reseated, repeating the circle motions several times around the plate, she wanted to make a heavier definite line. Drawn to that dynamic, it came to resemble a child etch a sketch. Fluently, she converted the upper section into the pointed arch. With an abandon tracking, she free- handed the perimeter making a satisfying asymmetric shape.

Absorbed in her art making, had covered the hour when her son passed through border control.

Recognised in her simple abstract shape, was a tear; surely the perfect non-denominational symbol to say sorry to her Christian teacher.

For no reason, as often occurs in the happen chance of making, with her needle threaded, she began to pierce the centre of her form, thinking about where she might embroider. After several pricks careful not to puncture herself, she had felt the protrusions on the reverse side of her work. Turning it over, the cardboard revealed a satisfying

333

series of worm spirals had begun to grow.

Excitedly the fragile medium in which to construct her sorry note had been discovered.

Next day, after a sleepless but alas wordless night for both parents, she rose early to complete her domestic tasks to leave the day clear. After a sad husband had left for work, content for a diversion, she had sought out the art shop in the mall. Finding a protective cover; the deep sided frame already with front glass had a removable backing.

Home again she cut four pieces of cardboard to size, to have four tries for her artwork; finally needing only, her efficient first try, impossible to copy.

Joyously interrupted by a call, she received word the boy had arrived; would be traveling on to Pakistan and his uncle, spending the next day there traveling to his new home by car.

Working for most of that day, she completed her curious pointillist tea-coloured tear, much as she had imagined. With silver thimble and several different sized needles, she had multi poked out the volume of her image. By the late afternoon the amazing honeycomb was finished.

Next morning with Dan all day at a supplier, she set and sealed artwork into its frame.

Timelessly, hung dripping, as if for all time, it lusted a creator's signature.

This was a tribute by a faithful wife of Islam, who

would have no personal ownership, letting content proclaim her message, relying on the receiver's expert sufferance to decipher.

As she knew he would

On the back, she had added two words.

"Maf Kama."

Essentially, sorry

Joy for the few minutes it was finished was astonishing.

"Another Patel masterpiece" as he had used to tease.

She packed it smiling in handbag tissue.

It had fitted neatly into last year's best seller box, labelled Black Patel, adding a second clue, emphasising preciousness, the commercial maker, not directly the giver.

Fifteen years preserved at the bottom of a wardrobe, and that many out of date, she pulled out the Norma Kamali dark suit. It smelt of mothballs but updated by the same fragrance bought frequently by a devoted spouse, she was able to squeeze smartly into it.

It took an hour though to summon courage to don make-up to walk the Fulham Street; having decided to deliver it herself because of the bulk.

With a stock of the appropriate carriers, she recognised the need to accelerate.

To be home before her husband's tea.

Supper, she had learnt over the years was not eaten North of London.

By bus and train in high heels was completely unremarkable. But very exciting.

Reaching the familiar front door, the scorching of the letter box was soul shockingly memorable.

Realising the rashness of her exposure, she was unconscious of the far-off spy camera.

Automatically, self-preservation had stopped her dead.

Measuring in her head for the opening, like others before she had not accounted the letter carrier.

Obviously, her offering would never fit.

About facing without a wait, the step seemed an inappropriate place to leave it.

So, she up for home.

Job completed; it had not been rejected.

Her walk back was ecstatic.

Totally free of guilt.

Benjemin would have it as a reminder of his youthful foolishness to explain to her grandchildren.

To his brother when he came back.

The real tear in her eye was for him.

Departed an hour earlier, Thomas was chumping

on his pain au raisin at the station, awaiting the
Eurostar. unconscious of the efforts of an
exceptional student,

He would never enjoy the work made with him in
mind.

By a woman, in apology for all the man-made
smoke.

Nevertheless, a work of genius which would live
on in her family.

Like the Koran page, already back on his wall.

CHAPTER THRITY SEVEN

Thirty-five minutes past midday, precisely, thirty seconds after her doors had closed, the laden Eurostar began its regal progress, strictly in line with international requirements. Using a tiny portion of the massive power available to its four-giant electric engines, topping and tailing both halves of the line of coaches, an endless caravan had slid out of the station.

Once a sanctuary of Edwardian expectation, Saint Pancras had been restored to the nation renowned for its weak railway tea and stale jam sandwiches.

Savaged of ageing grime in the face-lift of a long-neglected beauty, with each vaulting piece of cut stone, every fired red-brick and cast-iron rib, blasted back to its youthful blush. A technique that had spilled over onto newly rolled stainless steel, holding acre upon acre of etched glass, used to fabricate the shells of the shops along the concourse.

Modified to the consumer cathedral for a modern Metropolis, the space had been rededicated to modern needs. To hunger for expensive milky coffee, oversized muffins, elephant packages of sweets, bottled seas of chilled water, acidic lakes of sickly-sweet sodas and of course the continent of sandwiches.

Piled high in small cut down forests, other old travel companions had not been neglected. Competing in lines with the libraries of weeklies, monthlies and the capital's favourite 'dailies, laid out at the start of another exhausting new-fangled British walk about; devised by a once beloved Mr Smith, whose W.H no longer identified him as an honourable mister.

Reinvented to frustrate clients, by his devious marketers', to increase the greedy intake, it had wiggled and snaked on a lateral hike over the entire retail estate, forcing a pass of every single item it had on sale, replacing what once had been useful paper and pen newsworthiness, with a coke mountain of added sugar.

Suitably anxious, but otherwise submissive, expectant European travellers carrying the excessive weight after checking in, milled around at the glass departure gates; dwarfed by the Cambridge-blue load-bearing filigree of caste iron carrying the roof. Another Edwardian experiment in construction that would have flattened Notre Dame Cathedral to a massive pile of stones had a similar span been tried in the ancient church.

A thoughtful new fiction-writer on his frequent journeys to his French home, found it had been hard to recall exactly what this sleek-lined ascension had looked like, when it had been offering far less poison.

Having finished his two cinnamon-and almond croissants in quick succession, while casting aside his concerns with a chuckle, a reluctant post-modernist, licked his fingers guilelessly, to rid himself of the sticky mess. Amused with the whimsy of a departing Gentleman, an Empire to back up his arrogance, he looked out seated forward in a favoured aisle seat.

Unwisely, before he had left the house, he had rung to convey his dash to France to his daughters which had commanded attention.

Em had demanded the immediate conference call when he had tried lying to her.

"I'm on the train "

"NO YOURE NOT".

"He's gone senile".

"You've known her how long father?"

'And she dumped you".

'Why are you chasing her to France.'

Sensibly, he had not passed on any of the New York flight information.

"Make sure you get a prenuptial."

"And bequeath her the god chair."

The link had been abandoned by them.

Carefully he tossed the soiled napkin with exaggerated care into the little carrier supplied for breakfast. Reassuringly his Sun, Guardian and Vanity Fair were on his lap beside.

There had been another issue for the trip at the

surprisingly, uncrowded booking office.

All second-class seats on his connecting train were fully booked, so he had needed to pay for a first-class ticket to travel the other side of the tunnel. Passing through the French countryside in such luxury could hardly be designated inconvenience.

On the English side, laptop opened, set down on the table, he calculated it was fewer than two hours since he had decided to travel. Maybe his trip had been a crazy notion, but despite resistance he was content with his decision.

Quickly closeted again inside his travel cocoon, it had allowed the release of a thousand restraints applied by worry.

He had wanted to hope; to believe, there was a reasonable explanation for Alice's behaviour.

Half-closing his eyes, he sought to understand his urge for love; perhaps even of how to fulfil it.

Discomfited, barely a blink later, by a nudge and the smirk of a French conductress on malingering passenger duty, he was awake to a sure sign that he had been snoring again in public. Taking several shame-filled seconds to admit to the sounds of a busy City, were the Gare du Nord, it had been way too pacey for an advertised train journey lasting two hours forty minutes. Tasting nausea in his furred-up kettle mouth, wiping away the chin dribble, to confirm it, one frightening swallow of disgusting left-over London coffee, had rebooted his time clock to continental: without actively missing a second.

Up and off the Eurostar to his French train change, fractionally ahead of a clean-up crew with massive black plastic bags, he bequeathed his empties to them.

Thankfully, his hand luggage was flexible.

Milling providentially with the higher ranks of world society, he travelled to glorious Paris on the Metro.

Every time he made this move; he went straight back to unapproachable French exclusiveness on a first ever trip abroad. Travelling down d'Orlean line, he glided the history book; between Les Halles; Chateaux d'Eau; Saint Suplice; Odeon; Saint Germain des Pres; Cite et all, riding identical carriages to Audrey Hepburn in Charade. Efficient self-service chrome handled doors still opened and closed with a self-relieving hiss, expectant of his teenage Swedish crush to trip through, un-aged by spanning decades, wearing her virginal Saint Joan blonde crop to seduce him all over again.

Onto the wall of hexagonal shaped stone, before the arrival of the station name at Gare de Montparnasse, other signs had been posted in spray-can daubs of black, silver, and red. Birthing genes needing to desecrate any wall remaining vertical, as if by standing it had ridicule them. Unreadable names of unknown assassins, signed to attempts at self-harming, akin to urban suicide. Inane scribbles done by those who had to live among the desecration of the most beautiful city modern man had ever made.

Millennia before, Calligraphists had conquered gesture painting without spray cans, in the daily exercises of a soft inked brush in solitary marks on rice paper. Allowing no corrections, was the business of their craft, marks left where they had been laid, using skill to avoid any misplacement. Understanding daily changes to the human spirit, the skills indicated it in symbolic sweeps, perfect placement rarely achieved.

A religion much like Jackson Pollock's; pushing into spontaneous accidental territory to claim it.

An exciting state that lacked normal creative controls.

Rising, three-note cadence of the SNCF"s familiar indent on the overhead sound system, echoed around a platform, filled with another departing population, this time French based.

He wondered if the provocative effect of the female half-whispered chant with its over-cautious pronunciation of every syllable, was a result of using the same recorded tape country wide, editing in the station name and details.

Trying to decide which end to poke his ticket at the entrance machine, no longer an art Noveaux palace gate, to be certain, Thomas had fed both ends in. Heavily influenced by the design of the loathed English parking meter, it was enamelled in the modern French manner a bright yellow.

Beside what he hoped was his train, he strode down the 'quay, unease increasing with each stride. Glancing numerous times at his ticket he was concerned about the length of his walk,

It took a good country mile to reach his compartment on the very long TGV.

Ultimately passing a second restaurant car, he

found his first-class carriage almost at the head of the train. Inspecting through a line of the lightly smoked glass doors of spacious red-velvet compartments, each had four armchair-comfortable adjustable seats, backed with embroidered white headrests. Finding his aisle seat in the third one like the Paris Pullman's of old it was nothing less than elegant. Pushing lightly on the door handle it slid open electronically, to step into a welcoming new cocoon to travel the four hours South.

Bag stored above him, he was seated with his laptop on the extensive, not cramping table between the seats, breathing a little heavily from the walk to get there.

Not entirely yet used to the comfort, the sense of newness surrounding him, the automatic glass door slithered open again. It announced new arrivals with the breeze of their fragrances; both miraculous smells unrecognisable to a 'straight' man, who prided himself on distinguishing such things. Journey companions had joined him; a gay man and someone he assumed was his mother. Onto similar shelfs to his, above their heads on the other side of the compartment, they deposited a single, magnificent, mid-size black Dior alligator suitcase. Graciously, they took their places opposite him without a glance. Never envisaging, she would cross an animal-rights activist on first class French travel, the mothers matching skin and gold chained black handbag was set down beside her.

The delightful nosegay from two distinct sources, ensorcelled an infusion that transported the writer to

an exotic spice convoy from the Indies: quite
separate from yesterday's tube train experience.

Bumping gentle elbows in an accidental collision,
the duo divested themselves of light shawls
contrived to hang over each left shoulder.

« Pardon mama »

Pas de problem Ma Petit. »

His was in mannish rough caste grey cashmere
knit.
Hers, a silk and flowing floral flag with a
wonderful eagle head pin to fasten it.
Underneath, both wore perfectly fitted black suits,
each cut according to their gender station.
His deliberately, oversized and miss aligned with
tin pipe thin trousers a la mode; hers the
reincarnation of Coco Channel, with the petiteness
of a rich, well preserved single woman.
An ageing Monica Vitti rather than a mature
Catherine Deneuve.
Scarcely using the pretence of his illuminated
computer, Thomas gawked on.

In the way real Parisians find perfectly natural,
the two colluded without a single outward gesture
toward him; ignoring his attention as if he were a
hanging pull-strap.
Except once, later in their journey, when the
mother had wanted a cigarette.
She glanced the question at Thomas, who gave
his approval nod, passively.

Though it clearly was a non-smoking compartment.

Their combined nonchalance put him on his knees, begging for more.

It was a charming form of narcissism the English have admired, misunderstood and resented, since before the last time we had to give back Calais.

With the reputation as a nation of lovers it was difficult to imagine this pipe cleaner, thin delicately painted French mother, seeming to tread so lightly on the world, had ever engaged in the sweaty carnal undertakings required to spawn the equally lovely, discretely made-up hunk, who sat next to her.

It got Thomas to wondering; how it must be to love a man, physically.

Beautiful as most young people were in their youth, not unconscious of his attractiveness as art student, he had been pursued by a gay man.

They had become close friends.

Never once over their five-year friendship was a pass ever made; or the word same-gender attraction ever uttered. His mentor and friend had been living with a male partner.

From this relationship Thomas got to see the bond between a gay man and his mother.

Traditionally unbreakable; inevitably formed by the father's absence.

Once the journey was started, with cautiously orchestrated movements, the young man rose, effortlessly from his seat, miming sipping a cup to his mother.

She acquiesced.

He moved towards the cabin door; dark-hair greased back to increase the Latin look with the drama of a treacherous tango-dancer. The beautiful black clad fashionista was stopped momentarily in mid-flight by the door. Arching shoulders in the classic stance of a sword striker, he waited for the slow- moving glass to catch up to his pace, before dashing out in a forward glide.

A few stretched out minutes, shared silently with an obviously adoring relative, he reappeared with black coffee in paper cups and two petite pan-au-chocolate: to thrill with a demonstration of delicate food theatre. Outshining the ritual of a Japanese tea ceremony, no wayward crumb was spilled, each flake coaxed meticulous, with napkins into rouged lips; consumed like they were the Eucharist; with every tiny sip of their dark beverage enjoyed as if it had been the blood of Christ.

Disembarking at Nimes with their precious animal skin Dior's, the couple left Thomas with huge separation anxiety; determined to revisit the perfumery in Agen when time permitted, to discover their intoxicating secrets for himself.

Soon forsaking his laptop, Thomas changed seats to an empty compartment to stare out of the window after sensing the venom was running and snapped off the page about the painter; Incidentally becoming less and less like Donald in his writing.

347

Asymmetrical acres bearing the magical fruits of Bacchus, scurried hypnotically passed in endless rows; unremitting fields of dark-knuckled trunks to the height and thickness of a child's arm. Modern day wine growing required the green shoots to be tied at adult calf and shoulder height; then entwined for further growth on field-long wires, drawn taught between pile driven oak posts.

Adored by ancient decorative carvers in wood and stone, the vine tentacles grow the familiar five-pronged leaves, to cradle and partly disguise the elaborate necklaces of hanging green and purple treasure.

Less penetrable, other similar straight lines defined the limits of fruit forests not dedicated to alcohol. Currently, in anticipation of summer, roofed in a net gossamer, the fortresses a des pommes, a des peches, a des prunauxs; peak and dip in natural geodesic domes; effortlessly covering a hectare or more, defending against would be winged invaders.

Abruptly, from another separate more perplexing world, social process outside the window blurred to inconsequence. Seeking to distract a hassled trekker from his road to home, coincidence lay other nets seeking to entrap him.

Thomas's mobile began to pulsate in his right pocket on the arrival of an incoming call.

He dove to retrieve it.

Exasperatingly, the communication was from his

French service company welcoming him to France.

Clicking it off, he slammed the phone on the plush seat next to him.

Half anticipating others, since he was being tracked in France, no more than a minute later, the chip responded. This time the peels themed on the Marseillaise.

Again, a tired Pavlovian heart had leapt.

"Alice"

It was not she.

His first caller to France was more inappropriate.

On an illuminated pale purple screen under caller id was the name of her husband.

"DONALD?"

Bewildered, momentarily, Thomas let the national anthem of France continue to demand his full attention.

By the time he had decided to answer, the phone had stopped ringing.

Totally bemused; he was at a loss to know what to do next.

Resisting the temptation of testing the upholstery a second time, perhaps, if Donald were the repeat caller, he would leave a message.

Sure enough, breathless minutes later, the phone

erupted again.

This time with a sustained high 'g' that indicated he had a voice message.

Fumbling the keypad again, it took an age to get through to the call centre.

On a second go at the password, he made contact.

Then there was no mistaking Donald's recorded voice, broadcast to all and sundry not just Thomas. a melodramatic proclamation castigating married life in general but most especially his spouse.

"Due to my partner of twelve years who you all know as my wife but never actually was, whose sullied name I will never utter again, I have unwittingly been living in a relationship with person I know nothing about. That relationship is now ended as my life will be in a very few hours. I want only the worst for that treacherous bitch who has led me to hell. Those who own my paintings guard them well they will one day reward your investment. I trust we will meet up again in eternity and a far happier place.

Please don't send flowers; have a drink on me instead""".

Knowing Donald as totally self-centred, Thomas instantly understood him incapable of committing the ultimate crime.

"Could not do it. He would need her to pull the trigger."

Shocked by the selfishness of his antiphon, it appeared Alice's husband must not be aware of Thomas's part in the affair.

As yet.

Enormously helpful in regaining his equilibrium.

"All mouth."

Had Donald known, Thomas would have been at the wall in the firing line.

Cantankerously, he felt a little ignored.

She must somehow have confessed a lover, without naming him.

Replaying the extraordinary recording, idolise red tiles and verdant fields, abstracted by Cezanne e flashed passed, understanding no clearer.

"She must have said something.
Before she came to the house."

Obtuse, but not out of character, this guarded creature he was discovering had made the situation fractious.

But that was a step too far.

Quietly clicking off the phone, he replaced it exaggeratedly next to him on the seat to work out his position.

Worse than ever he needed to see her.

The house sale had been explained; somewhat.

351

Given what he had to face with her deceitfulness, he had turned and run.

They both had

The speed of the sale could just have been luck; it was a nice house.

The marriage breakup, or whatever it was, would lead to speculation about their relationship.

It was something he had to face,

But was not daunting.

With a shiver he understood he had liked it.

CHAPTER THIRTY EIGHT

Long anticipated, the train sound system clicked on abruptly to announce Thomas's French home station. Already down the internal step at the carriage exit, he was first in line to get off the train. Computer packed away, bag slung diagonally across his body, he held his mobile in his hand. Passport and car rental papers a bulk in his zipped inside pocket, wallet in the left trouser one so he could feel it against his leg, prescription Rayburns on his nose, as a safe way to carry them, and he was ready for anything.

He liked being on the move again.

The drift into the station took forever, he on a tight schedule to the rental.

With a huge ex-purgative hiss, the 'very fast train' ceased all motion at the appropriate coloured number on the station quays.

Miraculously, despite his worrying, it was two minutes off schedule; slightly ahead of time.

Jumping onto the platform after the compulsory wait, he was happy to be back in the familiar main town that was his home from home.

Fast walking a less grandly refurbished French station foyer in the twilight, he took off his sunglasses to lighten the gloom.

Outside under a powerful down-lighter on the

newly scrubbed cream-limestone walls, he pulled out the car hire order for a small vehicle of 'indeterminate provenance, solving why his same day booking had been allowed. Calamitously, he saw it had not been. The copy order he had printed out was dated, not for that evening, but for the following week.

Wincing he thought of Alice.

Then immediately of Donald.

It took time to permeate rhinoceros-hide reality.

Pushing panicky through the hire firms glass front door, to his relief in the darkened office he caught sight of the top of a male number one buzz-haircut, attempting to disguise early balding.
Oddly the Frenchman was lit by a flickering TV set, not a computer screen.

International tensions had mounted quickly from here.

Channelling a traditional adversary before he had spoken, the seated attendant, scarcely raised his look above standing waist level.
His unique English had a definitive American twang, sounding he had had GI training.

"Twenty hundred hours and fifty-five minutes."

Thomas's mobile was more accurate, it had

checked itself onto European time.

"Forty-five minutes to nine. "

Knowing of local intransigence, when they were rushed, Thomas understood he had minutes to convince an ultra-difficult agent to lease him the car; or his whole enterprise would be compromised.

Avoiding the direct lie in French, a desperate traveller chanced his arm in his native tongue.

"Maher, I booked it in England on the internet."

A quick glance at his screen, the man's response was clear and predictable.

The familiar firm head shake, followed by the single syllable exclamation, to any unusual foreign request, delivered with arrogant resolve, tempered by the pain of a martyr.

"Non."

Injudiciously, a seasoned continental traveller had only his computer printout to play; which he had, extravagantly waving it; arguing at the volume of a maligned French wife, with a pair of expensive soiled female underwear, never to have graced her loins.

"Get me a fucking car."

Increased by tiredness, the transference of Thomas's displaced anger was directed at a disgruntled front-desk clerk, rather than at his unreachable over-promising capitalist employers; fat cats who once had employed O.J. Simpson as their spokesperson.

In case he had not been heard the first time, Thomas repeated his scream.

The real blame for the mix up lay with him; willing to believe he could book a car at such short notice.

Surprisingly, and hugely against the odds, it had worked,

After only the briefest of long pauses, a bigger substitute vehicle for the same money, two series up, had been offered: reluctantly for sure, but with never even a glance at the mis dated order.

Promptly, its mouth similarly un-scrutinized, the 'gift horse' was accepted, with similar grace.

Maybe, as a National later counselled, the miracle was affected by dealing aggressively, albeit in a foreign language, with a French husband, unused to independent action, unless cajoled in the recognised spousal fashion.

He wordlessly completed consequent paperwork and the car inspection, at 'bat neck' speed. Besides the unmovable scowl, the boy had owned a completely unremarkable face, as he watched the football game. The mini-TV sat with the sound down at his elbow. Unwittingly, with reminders of home, Thomas had chosen a night for his adventure, when 'les Blues' were competing internationally.

Refusing to look away to meet his client's gaze, even when receiving his passport, credit card and driving license, the young man speed wrote every detail of the contract in long hand, the soccer match reflected in his glasses.

Thomas's replacement vehicle turned out to be a silver hybrid of a male he never discovered for the twenty-five hours he had charge of it.

Granted, it was racy, the profile was a new one to him.

In the darkening Agen station car park, built over a Roman forum by the first Italians to try take advantage of the Southern French, a steep natural hillside was half-enclosed. The mechanics of the vehicle's driving system were explained at even faster spoken foreign.

Musing, momentarily, why a hybrid was a petrol not a diesel combined with its electric, for that would have seemed greener, Thomas sensibly avoided voicing the question.

There had seemed so little time.

A few weeks old, the front left wing, already owned a gentle indentation, like an empty vacuum-formed container for a cup cake.

Made by a previous hirer it had not yet been

repaired, presumably because of the same lack thereof.

During their walk around the car, which, had never been washed the whole of its short life, the damage was noted but not remarked upon.

Again, Thomas just like the Frenchman wanted to be away.

Taking his seat on the left-hand driver's side, when he had ownership of the key, he abandoned his satchel and mobile onto the other side, to sink into surprisingly comfortable absorbent rubber contours.

Reminding himself what side of the road to drive on, he pinched his accelerator leg.

The last twilight had faded into black night.

Turning the key in the ignition, it had lit up the many internal dial lights burning so intensely they had hurt his eyes.

Scrambling under ski slope curves of the dash, he searched for the nob to reduce them.

"Teach you not to listen."

Eventually, he found an unusual wheel-like control, hard up against the door jam, disguised as a ventilator adjuster; in the meantime, researching the air-conditioning, he switched on the radio for a little incidental accordion playing.

Ultimately adjusting his car seat backwards to

accommodate his long legs, he strapped himself in.

Again, unintentionally, he turned the wipers on and off several times before he found the correct side of the steering column for the headlights, flashing them to full when he had control, to annoy the car hire man he caught in their beam as he locked up.

Thomas was driving an entirely appropriate, ditsy, transport, for his dash to the unspecified.

Able to crack electric window ed down a little, he could, make out the sounds of cheering at a full time whistle on the man's turned up mobile.

"Vive la France."

Aware, of his contributing to the misunderstanding between the two races, Thomas's smile was an instinctive response. Loving the country of his adopted second home, which bought him so much peace with its beauty history, and art, a true Francophone agreed with the old French President, when "doing a Churchill" on a recent visit to the English Parliament.

"When God created the French and the English he did so from quite different metals."

Then he membered Donald; uncomfortably aware of his guilt.

359

" Sorry mate."

Senses racing, he forced himself to concentrate on the other side of the road driving.
The sun already well gone; he was out of town lights into the pitch black of the countryside.

On the familiar highway to his French home, the next concern, considering his exigence, had not been planned.
 He would recce the address in the morning by his odds mobile; a simple strategy but lucky to be effective.

"Buzet"

The woman he had wanted to meet, might no longer be involved with the vine maker.

Nor was he certain to recognize her.

Sloughing a little, if had come to nothing, he would have checked the studio before autumn.

"The day after the day after tomorrow"

By not being in London, he was out if Donald got difficult.

The suicide harming seemed a brag.

"He would never damage himself."

Branching onto the main highway there had been no traffic.

Just two soft fingers were needed to turn the efficient power steering.

Wrapped in a driving seat so dangerously comfortable, he guided the eco-friendly missile, effortlessly, into the fast lane; Commander of his star ship; to between assigned dotted light lines, continuously, dashing passed and instantly reforming.

Increasingly, reflective 'cats-eyes' had made night-driving a near universal experience.

Combined with the cold Zenon head lights it was like playing a video game.

Thomas had liked the old yellow headlights, once the feature of international night driving; often in a contest with angry on-coming local drivers with the less powerful sodium beams trying to blind the English with their tricky switching.

Tranquilized by routine driving on a perfect tarmac surface, no need to expend mental energy, lassitude leaked in its invisible strapping.

Well established symbols, illuminated in the progress, began to fuse with internal blinking lights, spasmodically making it hard to recall which country he was driving.

Switching off the accordion playing on the radio, it had begun to grind,

Dangerous considerations asked from the other darkness.

What if he tried to cut out his own path.

Ever the egotistic agnostic, drifted, let go a little further.

Driving fast, temporal spirit lifted; sucked in to what he was not sure.

He was not running the universe.

A level of consciousness AA known as the second step.

Accepting what they were not.

Genuflecting time and time to powerlessness, in this humble space, Thomas earned a just reward.

Unconscious of suicidal urges, he nodded off.

Horrifyingly, the world displaced into a gushing swelter of remorse; back twenty years to a similar experience, driving the coastal highway between L.A. and San Francisco with heart break yearning for his family, thousands of miles away in London.

Reflex returned him from his lethal time-travel.

Luck held the car on a slightly deviant course.

Comforting, at the time of greatest danger, he felt the hurt felt of long ago.

"I'm sorry".

In speeded-up vision before a crash, the sensation of travelling too fast manifested as he hit the curve, the full force of gravity navigating to inches of the left-hand edge and certain death.

The hybrid gripped hard onto the surface, showing a racing pedigree, as he threw the steering back and forth in wild counter. Screeching through it for a few long seconds, it straightened. Then nonchalantly as if in a surprised Duck line of chicks, went rollocking back onto his legal lane as he had slowed.

Immediately his turn off to Lavardac was on him.

Able to sufficiently reduce to safe driving pace he made the exit.

Still totally alone on the road.

Slowing to a crawl, his heart was palpitating fast enough to leap out.

Pulling into a construction lay-by he had passed many times, he guided the car to a stop,

Turning off the engine he buried his head in his hands to help control his shaking body.

No tears would come.

In relief he almost smiled.

"I'm so sorry".

CHAPTER THIRTY NINE

Flooded at night by a single streetlight, his beloved Saint Germaine enclave was transformed into the isolation figured in the Hopper masterpiece, lacking only the last petrol station on the road before eternity; but adding a barking dog to hell.

He smiled curiously to himself to have been almost home without a peep from Tippy, Monsieur's dog.

Every rural family owned a least one of these beasts, most of which were not treated with the gentleness a Fulham boy had been accustomed. Certainly, he had understood no English, when sworn at in a foreign tongue for his endless barking before his master's call.

Tonight, he was typically obtuse with a silent welcome.

Slowing, when he had reached his turn off, the change from tarmac to the unmade surface, was full of holes and dips; left by him, the landscaper, to discourage casual sightseers from turning it into a short cut.

Erected by the French Utilities, a lone streetlamp shone at the top of the tree canopy from a moulded concrete pylon; more imposing than its simple function would have seemed decree. Alone in the darkness, its mellow beam picked out the electricity cables for several kilometres, looping the edge of the vine fields.

The little community had once been a single farm; detached by living into separate and private territories.

His, and Monsieur and Madame's.

Clearly by their efforts in the kitchen and the garden, they were from a farmer family. His job now was chief mechanic to the commune and would sometimes require a massive, combined harvester parked by the houses.

It was a position with status of which he was clearly proud.

The most expensive thing they owned bar two well maintained but beaten-up cars was a two-barrel shot gun, used all Sundays during the season in the nearby woods.

Thomas's restoration work had accentuated the old farmhouse, and its garden patio around which the hill had settled. In the years he had lived there, he had never been inside their house though he had invited them into his to admire his changes.

When the weather was appropriate, which was frequent, they eat outside.

A one or two down. Their daughter had the upstairs.

Thomas reckoned the privacy it had been a pride thing. Living in the smaller building.

He had bought his house from a couple in the village for an exceedingly small amount of money so understood theirs had been rental.

The lead up to the house and his front door was

on the upper level.

Avoiding the spreading Sycamore, he pulled up and parked dead in front of the old barn doors.

Climbing out of his 'fierce' transport, it was an automatic reaction to check his mail in the keyed post box. Some of his French house bills were sent direct to Fulham, but he had also banked in the village and online.

Only occasionally would he receive mail.

As it happened, an efficient local country post service had taken only a day to reroute a letter from Buzet to the Englishman, who had lived on a hill and liked to write letters.

When he caught sight of the American stamp dated four days previous on a buff foolscap envelope, everything else in an otherwise pile of junk mail was bin bound.

Under the cold light from a keen new moon, just arrived, missing only an orange lens filter to feign full photographic daylight, the details would soon be fixed for perpetuity in his mind's emulsion.

Returning to the driver's, side Thomas reached unnecessarily inside, to switch on the head lights to see if he had dropped anything, without letting go for a breath of the extraordinary package.

Anxious not to wake his neighbours, after the one-handed collection of mostly paid bills he kicked through double-wing seed pods of his tree sinking back down into the upholstered driving seat and switched off again.

Exhausted by the ten-hour journey, he felt pumped with adrenaline and hoped for its fizzle to subside. Having received part of the solution to his puzzle with Donald's phone message, he was waiting for the other, squeaky trainer to place down. With the car door still wide open to save the slam, he discarded the junk mail onto the passenger seat, to sit while the customary stillness enveloped.

He opened the letter.

CHAPTER FORTY

'' Dear Thomas
You probably think you don't know me.

" JESUS"

It would have stayed that way, if something momentous had not happened in my family, which directly affects you. Forgive me please from pursuing in such an oblique way, but the situation is so confusing, I could think of no other ploy to arouse your interest, which is imperative.

Please understand what a huge embarrassment this is for me, to have to reveal even these few facts. I have sent you three emails, and this letter with a copy to your house in France, in case you were there. Donald, who is well known to me, gave me the name of Buzet, as one he remembered in France, so I sent it to the post office there. I told him to say nothing as a surprise you might not want.

Yes, I know Donald. And you. Your gang at art school have remained very strong memories. As it happens, I used to live upstairs to Wini, and your family, when we were all very young. I remember, when your place, which I hear is now a mansion was divided into two flats. Before both our families grew too big, and they rehoused ours in a council house. I will go into any more details you require later, when in the hope I can do so in person.

I no longer live in England and my trip to you needs organising once you have agreed to meet.

I am an Attorney and a widow who had two children.

One was in the second photo with my mother at the Fulham baths.

Hopefully that will orient you to the facts.

The first photo is my mother much younger; to show the strong genes and family resemblance of our three generations. My likeness which I include here is not from our college days. Hopefully you will authenticate it in the flesh.

Unfortunately, both my son, tragically, and my mother, naturally, are both dead.

His death I will explain later.

My mother died rattling about in that council house, a decade ago, where she had bought up three children. My girl Alice is alive and healthy; of which you can attest to.

It's of no importance but you will probably have no memory of me, though my childish heart remembered our first kiss. I have followed you from afar. I was at Chelsea art school too for three years; but in your noted solitariness you did not recognise me even then.

I know I must sound like a freak; but it is imperative that you know the background to understand our family dynamics.

So that I can finally help my darling in a way I have so far been unable to.

That's all I can tell you for the moment.

I pray that you will see it in your heart to contain yourself for her sake a little while longer.

With much love. Sandra

"Jesus"

A speedy check of the contents made Alice's parent credible.

He read the letter for a second time.
Then a third time; seeking a missed nuance to make his trip to France less fanciful.
But there was none.

Judiciously, photographic copies of photographs from the emails had been included in the pen and ink letter.
Together with her own booth-style photo, cut neatly from a group of four passport pictures. The face of a lean middle-aged stranger who bore not one recalled feature. Or worse, any spark of remembrance.
A self-burnt disc, labelled on parchment paper in the same copper plate precision as the large envelope with American air mail franking, was another addition.
Someone in design he guessed, comfortable with the use of computers.

"She must have been a graphics student; not a painter like us."

"A tad theatrical perchance?"

She confirmed at similar ages, mother and

grandma had been remarkably alike.

To the son and grandson respectively.

The letter writer had chosen an eccentric way to half make her point.

Thomas, instantly, wondered about mothering skills.

How she had influenced her daughter growing up.

Half explaining, she was the author to the puzzle, Sandra had left out the clue to the unravel of its mystery, clearly not by chance.

Additionally, the extent of her contact with the brash painter was perfunctory.

His onetime friend Donald had never said a word to him, about this acquaintance from college days.

Before they had been more distant.

Grudgingly, he accepted, there had been no obligation for him to be informed.

Assuredly the announcement of the mother's arrival on stage as a cast member had not been included in any of program notes.

"Did Alice know about any of this?"

Too many more precious moments in the stillness, were long enough make it a struggle to get out of the car.

Reluctantly, shouldering his strap bag and computer carefully, he closed the car door; happily, with no urgency to lock it in redemptive isolation.

Clouds had dispersed completely overhead, to reveal the ceiling of stars.

The Great Bear was in its familiar position for that time of the evening; directly, above his kitchen.

Till he had bought the house, he had never properly understood how much the night sky shifts constantly.

Bathed in the three-quarter moon, his passage up the pathway was lit to his front door, till his movement activated the light switch, which blazed into a pool of yellow a few strides from home.

Wondering if Mother and daughter were together at that moment, it dawned on Thomas that to have arrived in his hand, the letter would have required posting from the US at least a week before. So, it would have been mailed well before he had bedded Alice. He had no idea what significance this had but currently he felt it might.

Flipping the envelope in the yellow light, there was a simple fact to check.

Clear markings of a date eleven days previously were visible. Absolution of the timeline, added to the weirdness.

"Why are you writing to me now?"

Thomas could not dare to consider another option which came to mind when he had mentioned it in his rant. The worst of all taboos; and surely without Donald's foreknowledge given his reaction to the current marriage crisis.

"Had he all those years ago been this lady's lover. And impregnated her? Making Alice his daughter."

Undoubtedly, that would have constituted the defiling of a sacred relationship in his voice message.

"Oh god I hope not. "

He trusted the thought was more paranoia that he had accepted he owned.

This woman's circuitous method had not been healthy for Thomas.

Automatically, his thoughts jumped to Em and Avi, kicking like a thrown brick.

Arousal or any sexual attraction to those small super humans, whose nappies he had changed frequently as babies, simply was not in his DNA. A healthy father recognizes himself, as the first male his young females will encounter, adjusting accordingly, to healthy curiosity.

The main building of his two-hundred-and-fifty-year-old farm was rectangular in plan, on two stories; the lower half, at some time before, the grain store, nestled into the hillside at the lower level. Struggling with his key in the door lock, it had turned, with the small heave needed, and the snug Frech turquoise painted front-door had sprung open.

Concrete facts he had hoped would bring relief, left him wishing himself to be under his duvet, delaying resolution of the mess indefinitely. Sandra was the person to send the emails, probably without her daughter's knowledge or consent.

Inside his familiar loved space, the slightly damp smell, from experience, would quickly disperse, flicking on the fuse box next to the door; the bag and laptop went straight down on the fruit wood table; bought locally at a place called Condom. Not a joke, according to the Aquitaine's, where they had been invented. Had a museum and everything to show off the early sheepskin sheeves.

Even with the head and shoulders picture, it was difficult to think of this Sandr Moss as the child he had known; save she looked like a freckled, fairer skinned, taller version of the darker Alice.

Chiselled, cleanly near the top of his life stone, when he had been six years old, just before her seventh birthday childhood memory was of another Sandra Moss. The one, under the cover of his play table they were using as a tent, showed him what was in her elasticated white knickers.

All her other faces had been blanked by that first look.

He tried wedging her into other pertinent events. Like the church graveyard on a sweltering hot summer day, at the queen of the May procession held it Saint Thomas's.

*"Oh, Mary, we crown thee with blossoms today.
Queen of the angels and Queen of the May"*

The childish love for the heavenly Royal, dressed in a virginal white bridal dress and veil, befitting the young spouse to Jesus. According to the child bewildering ceremony, she had been offered symbolically up as his wife. Yet at single digit age, Catholics already knew you were allowed only one mummy, unless you were a pagan infidel with a pointed helmet and scimitar. Or had lived in America in a big cowboy house in a place called Utah.

Again, he could clearly envision, the church and cemetery, where the crowning procession had walked, but not the magic of a face; vowing he would rummage back home in his archives for the old photos.

His orange glass tulip lamp was safely illuminated hanging from the pale, sand coloured, main beam of the room made from one tree, two, a half centuries before that he idolised. The peaceful spirit of the house classically, hewn with similarly wood-beamed braces, a vaulted ceiling in his enormous kitchen everyone understood had been his hook to buying.

'His own little Celtic chapel bless."

"With its own everlasting orange candle poppa?"

Only half a pace through that door, when Em had first visited with her sister, Avi had blessed herself in the sign of the cross with blasphemous timing.

"What time is communion?'

Regarding his working areas, Thomas would argue it was his choice alone, nothing to do with his upbringing, to set the long, free-standing counter on concrete bookends, free of re-pointed walls, and bared back to their glorious stone construction.

Sure, it had hinted at an altar; but that was coincidental.

Random sacrilegious armchairs and a new, large, wood burning stove, soften the purity, staving off winter; for the south of France could produce snow, to dips below zero.

"Where's the holy water font?"

"Obviously you haven't been in the bathroom."

If it was necessary to link his interior design ideas to religious antecedence, then his free standing, perfectly rectangular tub of granite, was more of a sarcophagus.

Even a non-professional joker had admitted.

"Bless".

Brick, plastered walls, deliberately had not reaching the timber ceiling, providing cover for the shower and W.C; leaving plenty of space for the stand-alone bath 'en-suite' into the bedroom.

The entire lower ground floor, made originally from earth, had been replaced with under floor heating and granite tiles, running the full length of the house.

Leaving the beams exposed, the second of the two areas made a large bedroom; a new window and double-glazed doors cut to take in the dipping vineyards beyond.

He was beat but the unpleasant task had been left till last.

"Call Donald

Flipping open his mobile, he went to the incoming call file and redialled the number.

It had rung endlessly; eventually cut out as expected.

He considering calling a mutual friend to check. *"No one called you Thomas".*

Digesting the simple callous truth, there seemed little else he could achieve till morning; save sleep.

Switching on the power to the hot water not the central heating; because it took a whole day to heat, he plugged in his phone and computer on the charger; and went downstairs to bed.

Most evenings just before nine thirty, a punctual dormouse, well known to guests, liked to speed up this wooden staircase before effortlessly scurrying up the rough stone kitchen walls, across the main rafter and through a small cap into the insulation. Presumably, after forage for its family he was one of the small delights of living in the middle field next to him. After a sudden absence from the almost nightly charade, the small character added a pervading musk of burnt flesh for a day or two to the kitchen smells. Before the circuit blew, and he was found electrocuted in the expansive but deadly new fuse box.

Deciding to do without much other than the clean top sheet already laid out on his chair Thomas grabbed at his double duvet and dumped down onto his bed fully clothed. In moments he was fast asleep on top of the mattress cover, tossing and turning into dormouse Purgatory.

CHAPTER FORTY ONE

Startled awake by a worrying rat-a-tat-tat, on his bedroom window, Thomas was on the defensive before his full day in France had properly begun.

Proven so easily led by ripe imaginings, all urgency had been sucked out by yesterday's astonishing communication. Foggily, determined to fight further intrusions by ignoring them, there was no one in the world he was ready to speak to yet.

Even his missing beloved.

Deeming himself asleep, if his eyes were not open by more than a slit, he lumbered out of bed, committed to returning there just as soon as his over full bladder had been emptied. Into colliding timpani, with base drumming at the window, the high-hat tinkle of his fierce stream of urine, not yet reaccustomed to rural wildlife, he had forgotten the two magpies who lived in the oak tree opposite marking the boundary a few meters from it. Sun-up would often catch a long-tailed trespasser perched on his sill. Always the male of the pair, startled by its own reflection, it would peck, aggressively, at the pane in angry puzzlement.

The bird's self-important disbelief matched the house owner's face of the day.

"" thieving bloody magpie".

Fortuitously, with better recalled foresight, only a bleary eyed, vision was needed to guide him into his carefully cited toilet-bowl; set high enough by him to accommodate his extra leg length seated.

When the female bird of the partnership flew overhead outside, the rapping at the window ceased, abruptly; as it always would.

Properly empty after a long night and the tympany concluded.

"The root of the penis is at half the height of a man."

Different proportions in sanitary ware for those of above average height, had been discovered while rebuilding, were not often catered.

Double sized in the seated position, inches needed to be calculated for comfort in half-time: like dog years.

"A palm is the width of four fingers."

Looking down, absently, even a discomforted adventurer could never ever have conceived a doctor slicing it open like fig; as required by transsexual males when becoming a woman.

Not overconfident of his size, why the posit arose at that precise moment was not clear.

'A foot is the width of four palms.'

Replete, but shaking off the final few drops,

Thomas mused comfortably about the size of things.

'A cubit is the width of six palms.'

Leonardo had tried to explain perfection by proportions via the human body.

As once the Egyptians had.
Twenty-five inches made up a sacred cubit.

"Dear Alice"

Eyes fully opened; it had taken a whole three minutes from waking before he had mouthed the name of his deceitful beloved.

After a day on the train, and a night on the bed, his clothes were rank.

Undressing, he turned to the shower, allowing time to get it up to the correct temperature; having learnt the lesson to test the water temperature of even efficient plumbing more carefully.

Long ago in his second house, all mirrors had been banned.

Except the one in his precious oak armour, the door he left slightly ajar, so it never caught his refection till he was almost past it.

Attempted only, occasionally, when he was returning to Fulham, shaving was accomplished with difficulty in the edge of a small- mirrored frame of his two daughters in New York.

He had already decided he would skip the chore

this morning.

Proud of his easy plumbing installed in France, water flowed away promptly into his fosse, down carefully checked gradients, hating to visit houses in any countryside with a problem in evacuation of effluent.

With a fascination for pentangles, but an aversion to sorcery, the design of the tile floor downstairs was an oddity, which even the originator would agree was extreme. Disdained by monsieur Besci his mason and head builder, Thomas had ordered his own body scale circle, cut into the grey slate tiles on the lower floor. Arms and legs spread in the cross of St Andrew, his pose on the floor was Leonardo's Vitruvian Man. A scaled sketch demonstrating the relationship in the average, male body. Measurements of the hand, the foot, the yard, and most importantly the ancient cubit were indicated to nestle into. The house owner liked to lie and to meditate in it after a revised Alexander method.

After the entire floor had been laid, but before it was grouted, the craftsman mason had devised a way of forming a flexibility compass needed to etch the circle. With a radius of about a meter, a hands width between, and had secured an electric router's wire to a two central metal weight. In an hour had cut the perfect smooth grooved circles subscribed inside each other for his hands and tors to fit into like holds on a rock climb. When finished it had exactly matched Thomas's outstretched dimensions.

'Fingertip to fingertip, exactly two cubits.'

Though appreciative of the job he made, the skilful craftsman was unable to understand its logic.

It was explained to him several times in bad French.

Concluding no doubt his client was a warlock or more likely in the land Cathar, a Free Mason.

The effect of the floor design was a subtle one.

Thomas found gripping the edges with his fingers immensely satisfying.

He liked to lie naked on the hard, chilling spacious, floor.

Arms and legs akimbo in a variation of the Alexandria method it allowed his skeleton to settle back to its natural balance with a book as his hard pillow at the base of his skull.

He used up his older harder back of Ulysses as his pillow.

Reading less and less fiction, every time he saw the book, he was fearful he might never open a novel again; let alone finish, the best-book-ever-written candidate.

Sinking down one handed to his knees he turned and lay flat in his circle with the thick tome the perfect, fat, support for under the back of his head.

Paying no more attention to the warnings precipitated, when the days already swirling centrifuge began to still, he stared up into the three-hundred-year-old tree main beam and the less heavy modern timber replaced by him.

Another question, which the letter had not

answered, asked itself.

"Why had the stranger at the wine fair been so
enraged by Alice?"
He had no clue.

Fully aware there was little logic to coming to
Buzet; like a magnetic needle to its north, the
unknown woman drew him there.
He resolved, capriciously, he would continue his
plan to try find her at the vineyard.
It would give him an excuse to doodle rift around
the area, always an inexpensive joy.
The earliest train from Agen was quarter to three
in the afternoon arriving home to London just before
midnight. Back to talk with Alice post-haste

Surely between the two of them they could
resolve the troubles.

*'There is no such thing as a nothing. So, you can't
paint it.'*

On learning of Sam's project on zero, ashamedly
disguised as Thomas's own, on their round around
the British Museum, Alice had offered her learned
take on the subject.
One and zero being the fundamental tools of the
binary system, zero was a concept.
With no physical existence in the real world.

" Doesn't exist in Roman numerals either darling."

Spreading out his arms parallel to the ground so they formed with his torso legs and head a cross, he paid homage. touching his toes in a stretch this was not the day to crucify himself.

All urges turned to coffee.

Up on his feet again, replacing the book on the small circular table under the window with a rough concrete top made with his own hands, he opened the page to see the talismans first words. However, many times he repeated them, he was reminded of one man's pursuit of the original.

Stately, plump.

Through the picture window his attention was drawn to the magpie. In its black and white Newcastle football colours, the bird was returning to the oak tree with twigs in its beak to add to the circular nest.

Presumably, his lady friend was secured comfortably inside.

Always soothing, no matter the season, the windows in his house owned a 'view' across the valley of vines; a landscape when in full sunlight aped many. He had learnt to accept the comparison in no way disturbed its natural balance. Progress was reborn through them morning, bathed in affirming inevitability.

He recalled how many times he had promised himself he would paint it; one day.

Perhaps the subject to tackle after he had

finished Ulysses.

CHAPTER FORTY TWO

Securing the house, with so much time before any train, the writer decided on the circuitous route; to a second breakfast at the café de sport; with croissant from Lavardac bakery. To say hi and goodbye.

Dressing with the near exact same second set of clothes from his bag, he repacked the smelly ones in the same way, to wash in London.

Carefully tidying the bed, he left on the hardly used duvet.

He made his first coffee from his kitchen store.
In an identical coffee pot to the one he had in Fulham.
When finished he washed them.
Left them to dry.

More settled, he packed Sandra's letter face up on top of the clothes.
pondering if he had sucked out all its information.

Happily, no cook cleaning had been needed since he had not eaten.

Perplexed, by the likely hood of huge, wasted effort, he switches off everything in his stylish space,

On another overcast morning, he had aimed the

dusty lifesaver for the perennially cultivated wine acres surrounding. At this time of year, red poppies grew the fields in abundance the primary carmen petals signifying remembrance.

Passing slowly through his small efficient village, which boasted three banks and as many hairdressers, without hope of an answer, he mulled over the demise on Alice's brother.

Passing the Marie, his local bank branch off Main Street corner was housed on the eerily 'Alles des Allies', the name always arousing thoughts of his own and war time blow from his pram on a hot day's bombing, Aways struck by why he was ever in the in the front garden, family wisdom had had it there were no day raids. He guessed, in those difficult times, for a mother who had to take over the chicken neck ringing from their sensitive father for the special Christmas treat, there had been other siblings to worry about.

Dome, something of a bike ride away, a village much like this, he had visited only once because its history was so disturbing.
 A plaque erected at s spot near their small Marie was where three partisans were hung from the first-floor balcony of the Hotel de Ville: executed by occupation Nazi's.
Given the tightness of the square, it must have been an awful experience; for villagers forced to watch, only generations ago.

Some like the Marie, he knew had still been living.

Not remembering Sandra in the picture of her as a grown woman, it was no sure a thing he would recognise the winery lady if they had met up.

Hand lazily on the steering, it became the wee gee-board that pointed itself at Buzet.

For a decade at least, unemployment for young people in the area was high.

Many, like his neighbour's daughter, approaching thirty, would never find employment; could not leave their parents rented home unless they had married.

Local disaffection had been heightened by a half ignored Muslim community, resettled in the village, decades before from the French territories. They had included his own magnificent stonemason builder.

The head scarf was worn by many older black clad women.

In wholesale immigration to the homeland, numbers had not been calculated because of egalitarian concerns. Asking the race question to a French citizen had not been considered French.

With the recent invasion for cheaper second homers like Thomas, after a history of battling had not benefitted the British cause; now in line right behind the hated Germans. Compatriots were silently blamed for the rise in house prices by people who would like to but could not afford to buy.

Non profiteer Thomas sought out Aquitaine to have a painting studio with space and light; resurrect by his hands and other locals and saving it from delinquency.

In the unavoidable slow meander, he passed by the Bastille of Vianne, his neighbour.

founded by a Brit during the invading crusades in the eleventh century.

An entire four-walled stone fortification intact after nine hundred years; a tribute to the continuing skills of the French mason; and his foreign pay masters.

Colonization from across the Channel then was not a new thing. Even this far south of Calais.

Alice's mother had taken the other way after the war.

To America.

Adding the snaps with the child, for certain she had lived in Fulham because she they had verified it.

Checking the time amongst the profusion of illuminated digits on the complicated dash, Thomas on a relaxed schedule, but caught up in his rambling thoughts, he had not meant to dally so long.

The surprise time suddenly caught on the dash made him anxious, halted further meanderings.

More urgently, he turned the echo traveller on a more direct path.

Maybe afterwards he would have his lunch in Agen. At the famous train side café.

He might even have time to revisit the cathedral restoration going on quite close to the station; to see if it had improved upon the 'cute' makeover of the twelfth century Gothic church interior he had loathed.

Supporting his radical theory, which having learnt to rap in their Latin-based language, deeply traditional Frenchmen might be shedding centuries of discernment. As any travel analyst who had eyes could avow, the most popular form of French house construction was not Thomas' s classical fairy-tale-country, but the brand leading Bungalow; one storey suburban disenchantment.

Bizarrely, without warning, shockingly mournful and mindful of too recent horrendous times,
a second war siren screeched out from high up on the winery roof tops.

Signalling the noon hour it was for the ritual of lunch.
An unforgettable sound, eternally arousing stress.

"Right side of the road Thomas. Easy on the gas pedal."

Proud of their new technology, but lacking the romance of their forefathers, les Vignerone de Buzet had built three enormous, corrugated hangers in the mid-fifties, to house their reformed label.

Impatiently, he turned onto its forecourt, Thomas slowed to a stop, to allow a for lunch.

Streaming towards their cars and home, several dozen workers had burst from the factory.

Some headed directly behind him to under the overhang gracious old châteaux, perched on the hill that bore its name. An additional block of flats had been added at restoration, creating an unfathomable juxtaposition. Next to the shaved fields of the river Baise, a disconnect that had always bothered him since he had moved there.
A monstrosity the responsibility of the maker of a red wine without the full body of a fine Bordeaux.
He had presumed, to house its workers.
A building that would not have been out of place beside his own council flat on a Fulham bomb sight after the Blitz.

While stationary, his luck had run out.

Following cursory glances, a Muslim woman approach, her cautious gaze not toward the stranger.
Turning his full body, revealed the person he had fantasised would solve the mystery of Alice.
Absolutely it was her, despite all previous concern, and the year since he had seen her.

She carried an addition to her wardrobe, a signifying head scarf.

Why this stranger's image had been burnt so deep into his consciousness he had no idea.

But there was no denying it had.

This was the woman from the wine tent.

Alone, but moving self-consciously, tying and retying the belt of her full gabardine mack, too tightly at the waist, she was interested entirely in her own endeavours.

Certainly not in Thomas's.

Headed for the flats, he was parked directly in her path.

Strapped into his driver seat, he played nonchalant but could do nothing to avoid a confrontation.

She advanced quickly, toward the bonnet of his car to pass by.

Then for no reason he could discern, she had turned to look straight at him.

Accentuated by the fabric capturing her hair, the indifference on her face disappeared, relaced, mesmerically by the glare with which she had greeted Alice.

A momentary look that had lasted, deliberately, longer than politeness demanded.

Arrogantly, it questioned why it had been returned,

Clearly the recognition had been mutual. Not the least apologetic for her obvious instant distaste, slowing her stride, she continued passed, her nose continued to be held higher in the air.

Overcome by dread at the secondary recognition of real terror, he turned to watch her walk away. Not with the svelte bounce of his young postman, but the fulsome waddle of a middle-aged woman.

Assimilating information that would not allow rationalisation, something felt, dreadfully, out of kilter.

Disappearing up an outside staircase to the flats, she reappeared a few moments later through the lattice work of fancy open brickwork, unmistakable a product of the period.

At each level of the climb, she was visible; until till she reached the fourth and top floor.

Here she stopped at a blue front door,

She unlocked it and went inside.

Obviously, her front door, it was beside a kitchen window with an uninterrupted view of the castle.

Thomas was anxious and felt the intruder.

He sat for a full five minutes to calm himself.

Eventually, he persuaded himself to go up.

To talk to her.

A compulsion so strong it became an imperative.

He owned not a notion of what he might say, when he met her.

"This is fucking cracked."

Out of the car, he flicked the key fob to lock.

Walking, almost behind himself, he made his way up her stairs.

It had needed no effort.

Hardly took a moment.

When he reached her blue door, all forward propulsion ceased.

Instinct froze him.

He talked himself into pressing her bell.

Directly in his eye line, the badly re-painted door had blistered under strong waves from the sun.

Turning merely a degree, the château eerily dominated.

Turning back, he waited with no idea what he would say.

A huge urge to flee enveloped him.

But he hung on.

He knocked again with his fist, routed to cheap pink floor tiles,

He had dared not sneak a look through the undressed window.

He heard footsteps behind the door.

Saw the vague hustling form.

Brusquely, the door had opened.

There she was.

Face even angrier.

Rooted like a skull cap in a Vermeer portrait, the scarf was held tightly in place, accentuating a face that could never have been called beautiful. Or even feminine.

Her coat was off, replaced by a full wool cardigan, in the warm air.

In an elaborate guilt frame hanging on the wall directly behind her head, a picture was visible for any visitor to see, in it the flag of the American Confederate army.

Side by side with a grey infantry man's hat with its

395

unique squashed concertina bowl.

First from the military memorabilia, then from the hatred in her dark eyes, Thomas's wordless stare went down onto a white knuckled hand, securing the doors edge ajar.

A strong hand with stumpy fingers painted in greenish nail polish to appear womanly.

Atrick beyond the most expensive cosmetic surgery to be anything but male.

Desperately, it forbade passage into her life, holding a hundred-year-old Smith and western long barrel pistol, seeming too old to function, but cocked for action, and aimed at his belly button.

The forewarned thunderclap sounded after the explosion, but only in Thomass mind.

Looking up he was staring at the hint of morning shadow on a face before his surgery had graced a man. This Muslim woman smelled of lilies of the valley, staples of our grandmothers.

At first obscene, apparently against our nature, senses can transform.

Intimate prejudice for the fluffy down on appetizing Alice's upper lip.

Eye to eye for the moment, the question hardly dared to be asked, answered itself.

Pure hatred, verbalised American disdain.
"Fucking limey."
Too assuredly not to be genuine, the hand left the door and flew up to salute derisively.
Reminiscent of a refugee from second world war

lost for half his following life in the jungle.
"Stop stalking me or you're a dead man."

The terrified woman threatening Thomas appreciated was once a man.

CHAPTER FORTY THREE

Isolated, and stumbling, into the pews with leftover dust- sheets, Thomas's despair had not been aided the taupe redecoration at the Cathedral in Agen.

Morosely, trying to digest his radical male shame, he sat for ages in supposedly holy space.

Not a single stray parishioner had interrupted to cross himself and pray, in the hour he considered.

Eventually he left for the station.
Trying to find the proper response when a lover had not revealed her sex at birth.

Was Thomas entitled to the truth?

Dare he say it; had he been lied to?

Paranoia sustaining, and losing the power to commit, he had driven back from Buzet?

He tried reconsidering every memory he had of her.
Weighed each for their normalcy.
But hardly remembered boarding the train.

Or returning the echo mobile.

Or the four-hour journey.

Till he had arrived in Paris.
to understand what had been unimaginable.

"You have been inside a man. "

Sunlight eventually would register again.

But never through the lead lights at his arrival
gates at Montparnasse station.
Or into a Monet fog from grimy steam
locomotives.
inspiring the genius, who had painted the gigantic
water lilies, which had foretold modern Art,
If they had not already been its Estate.

Changing trains the Art world's once capital city,
Cezanne's words tumbled out.

**"Treat nature in terms of the cylinder, the
sphere and the cone."**

Words that were swerving out of context.

Implied religious geometry had been ignored by
life, when Architects replaced the tall, gracious
nineteenth century glass at this spot, through which
a full steam locomotive once had exited after
someone left off the hand brake. It had rolled, to
plunge almost its entire length off the elevated track,
ending a famous nosedive out of it at forty-five
degrees to the street. Reflected in archive pictures,
always noted, when he passed, pre-dating Magritte
and his Surreal fireplace with a train crashing out by

399

forty years.
'Time transfixed.'

"Alice was once a man".

Homing in on a quandary, two lovely large, long hands had been used extensively for her well paid hand modelling career:
Big feet too, sometimes in the similar employ.
Then he reconsidered the Christ like scar on her side.
Like the one made by the centurion to see if Christs blood flowed and got only water.
Beautifully healed without evidence of stitching; simply a fine healed cut to run flat over pale the slim acres that he once had ravaged.
She had complained it a botched kidney repair.

Sure, her teeth had been replaced by porcelain, but who's in her day job had not.
Made by the same dentist used by the greatest chorographer of English ballet.
she allowed few to forget.

Shockingly after a little research, change of body Obour was common in HRT.
The smell so assiduously detested by her after sex, but frankly arousing?"

Of course, her androgenous look had ever been a curiosity was it a cause to wonder.

Descending the new building's three-part

escalator from the noisy upper track to the change
of stations, via the metro at the ground, the writer
routinely began the seduction back to Paris. Smells
of the city, highly evocative of forty years before,
when street drains, and cigarette smoke combined
in a more pungent bouquet; for him le Parfum de
Paris had never been a problem. Minus the full
olfactory of human manure from the plumbing of
ornate art-nouveaux urinals, a replicate mist drifted
presently by him from a navy-blue uniformed posse
of Galois smoking security. Dragged on by an
aggressive black Rottweiler on a not so leisurely
check for criminals, two rugged armed cops with a
tenacious police girl holding the dog, were moving
down a parallel electrified staircase. Looking up
passed them, from the natural angle of the lower
treads he spied a local miracle which had needed
deliberate attention to avoid. Following a long intake
of breath, he took no avoiding action to continue
with an unobstructed view up a minimalist pea-white
skirt, to a long smooth pair of impossibly well-turned
brown thighs, topped by a handkerchief size piece of
white lace intended as panties. Hardly anything was
disguised by an angel of these streets, where such
miracles were enacted daily. With the speedy, flick,
of a waving Pope's absolution, her downward drift
repeated past three separate turns of the escalator
as he gawked healthily. Reaching the bottom
several beats ahead; he reversed his confused start
in the wrong direction. The leggy creature with wide
nostrils of the Reunion Islands, easily caught up with
him. Openly swishing her oiled shoulder length
pirate ringlets, acknowledging his attention, she

401

rewarded with an unselfconscious twinkle, which encouraged his leer. Like any nine-year-old schoolboy caught peeking, he bowed his head, blushingly, as she passed. Enjoying the effortless effects of her display, the gorgeous Amazon bounced off in the direction of the new glass station front. A prefect cafe-Au-la complexion, strutted out on impossible red high heels, taking her to the height of a basketball centre pulling her small glossy matching wheeled suitcase behind, drawing legitimate perpetuation of Parisian a la mode.

Instinctively, disgraced by his sexuality, like the good relapsed catholic he always would be, Thomas laughed out loud at his sinning.

Then wished he had the beautiful Alice to kiss. Have her there to hold.

Was she always a woman disguised?
Would invisible female chemistry pheromones have been evident even while still a man?
Did hormone treatments contain the hidden girl gene.

" Just have to wait till you see her again."

CHAPTER FORTY FOUR

Research confirms, reaction time to sounds was faster than that to light.

Average auditory arrives in one hundred and fifty mile per second.

Visual stimulus in one hundred and ninety.

"What did he say?"

Once received, both take time to reach the brain,
Sound stimuli average nine-mile seconds.
Ocular average thirty.

"Did you see that?"

The differences persist whether the subject was asked to make a simple response.

Or have a complex thought.

Captive to his and future hopes, missing a significant replacement on the arrivals board, the airline announcement was incomprehensible to Thomas.

These were his second, and third major errors, on a special day.

The day after, the day after tomorrow.

From there on in, with an embarrassment of fortune, he would not stop counting.

Over the speakers of an advanced digital-sound system, hidden in the ceiling, with each, spoken syllable projected by an E.U. Purser, perfectly reproduced; to tumble around the bad acoustics of a busy arrivals area. Believing himself phonetically word perfect, the speaker in an English learnt from cockpit address systems and laminated passenger instruction texts, in his best pilot pigeon, massacred the beloved tongue of Byron and Yeats, in deep Slovak base.

"What did he say?"

The announcement was transmitted, not at some transcontinental out of the way location on a 'go-go' airline, addicted to planes arriving before they were due, but in the relative new Terminal Four, at the world's busiest airport, by a mainstream carrier.

Clearly, with the future threat of paying to use of air-plane toilets still hanging, the imperfect experience of budget travel had arrived at the Majors.

At five forty-five am, Thomas had just arrived.

Familiar with this New York flight, he believed he had been in time; anticipating whiling away a half an hour with a coffee by the arrivals point.

Like many men, everlastingly, not reading instruction thoroughly, this was his first.

Had he been able to decipher the audio, or had he seen the miniature arrivals board, an already anxious writer would have learnt much; several important minutes before he had.

The flight was the one pertaining to Alice'.

It had already landed at Heathrow. Because of favourable tailwinds across the Atlantic

It was thirty minutes ahead of schedule.

His 'beloveds' original timetable had her arriving at six am.

A convenient flight for him in the old days because it was cheap, allowing a full extra visit day.

So, perhaps he should have known better.

Following his return home, the day before on the Eurostar, not daring to go to bed in case he had not woken in time, he had spent several hours catnapping on his favourite spot on the sofa. According to sod's law of inversion, his careful planning had made him thirty minutes late for the over-anticipated rendezvous.

The day after, the day after, tomorrow

With a rush of emotion, a text on his phone had informed him of the landing.

His expected passenger was already through customs.

In by gone days this could have been relied upon to take an age.

"Am at the arrival point".

Using his road runner experience to avoid other pedestrians, he chased down the sparsely populated corridors to speed to her side. While he ran, he endeavoured fanatically to make out the rest of the message on his phone. Wearing brand new boots like the unbroke trainers, was not easing the tension after days of it.

The text message was equally annoying; and inscrutable.

For some reason it had a New York area code.

"What are you wearing?"

On the previous day, the question was one which had bothered him, immensely.

But not now.

On his way from Saint Pancras, he had taken up most of his morning shopping for the entirely new wardrobe he was wearing.

"I have on a pin; I am sure you will recognize."

His I phone explained in written words.

Of the pin, he had no clue.

His updated coat was in a colour, which could only be described in sales literature as light black. With a high cut collar, it was made from a fibre, the sewn label indicated, able to survive a nuclear explosion; but had not mentioned the wearer; who of course would not. Shoes had been updated to zipped Chelsea boots, the socks back to the favoured orange.

The whole thing had cost about as much as his computer.

At least everything fitted as he sprinted to her.

Haplessly, with the start of the day after the day
after, already passed, the third or fourth person out
of an uncrowned collection point, bearing luggage
with a New York sticker was not the slim dark hair
sex pot he had been expecting for ever.

A tall woman well dressed and wearing a golly pin
in her lapel was holding two iPhone's.

Clearly, she was on business.

Yet she seemed to be smiling, tensely, at him.

Alarmingly she had headed in his direction.

In the warmth of her endless handshake, he half-
appreciated he might not be seeing Alice yet awhile
es he continued his search for her over the woman's
shoulder.

"Thomas?" Sandra"

Nonchalant, there was not a single marker about
her face or figure which seemed familiar.

His unconscious mind expected more; from
someone he had known since the beginning of his
life. Providence, then started to rip the soul of a
sensitive lover, who had tarried far too long.
Subliminally, he recognized the 'golliwog' enamel,
once more precious to him than diamonds, but not
the orange-topped football socks, which he had
offered in a swap with his brother.

"Sandra Moss."

Eventually, comprehension dug all the way in.

The letter writer had superseded his beloved's arrival her mother.

Efficient chic, and an astonishing large handbag carried over shoulder seemed her only familiar baggage.

"Remember the pin you gave to me?"

The copper backed copy of the black wool doll in its black and white striped waistcoat, was pinned to her bosom in the place where American patriots usually kept their stars and stripes, which was displaced, to her other label of a fine chalk stripped navy jacket.

The forgotten gift of his Maher family trophy was his present to this stranger on her seventh birthday and she had kept it ever since. A family, not a personal treasure, because the only way to get one had been by saving a dozen paper replicas from under the lid and before the grease proof paper that sealed the communal Robertson jam pot.

Offering itself as proof of his perpetually transient heart, the enamel functioned as her pass key.

Following a dark war and not used to the idea, gifts were forever, he and his brothers had mourned the passing of the pin. It had taken a whole year to collect the paper 'gollies'; a time span much great then than it had been to an older man. In later life, memory of it had helped the writer's understanding of brand loyalty in his commercial film career.

"Sandra."

"You got my letter and my emails?

There was something close to panic in her tone.

She was reassured by his nod.

"Don't worry she is coming to meet you later.
This was the flight I could get here to arrive on time and get back.
I had to talk to you first as I'm sure she told you."

No, she didn't.

The words were muted in his head.

Indicating the morning would end catastrophically.

For a moment, half-turning in a dazed attempt to appear mobile, Thomas considered offering to buy the broach back for his brother in New Zealand; who no longer spoke to him; disregarding the suggestion as too trivial at such a serious time.

"To protect my child".

Assuming a pretentious English public-school education, an accent he never had had, just like his misguided brother, it replaced his transatlantic whisper.

"Oh right. Good show."

But the bomb was dropped.
By him
He knew not why.

"I know.... Sandra."

She paused; not answering directly.

His approach was unexpected.
For both

"What do you know Thomas?"

Had he looked less superficially; he would have
seen the feelings of a distraught parent; the terrible
strain on her face.
A twin expression to her daughter's often worried
frown.
Had he been more perceptive; and less self-
absorbed, he might have recognised the hope
engendered by his remark.
Unsure, he reinforced his statement.
As if he ever had been in possession of such a
wanted metal.

"... the truth."

Brown eyes darting around in search of any sign
to explain his comment, she looked for confirmation

for several seconds.

A poker player analysing a raised bet.

Or the good lawyer, she would later own to being.

Waiting for her witness to fully express his thoughts, she gave no indication of what hers might be.

"Let's find the transit lounge at BA and talk. I have a VIP card."

One of the essential pleasures for the rich, who need to travel on commercial airlines, which Thomas had always appreciated, money helps to insulate. Trade on regular airlines in first class and expensive hotels, exists in his view, because of the servant master relationship. Enslavement Thomas had enjoyed guiltily, when he had but had not tasted much since his rerun to his homeland a decade before.

"I only have a few hours, and I will leave before my daughter arrives.

I visited to talk to her and her husband a week ago.

I can't afford more time off."

Hardly a single thing about this woman was expected.

Till Thomas chose to see the good.

To look deeper at someone who no longer was a

graphic artist.

"Them. What Alice and Donald?"

"Yes. To see if I could help with their marital problems, but to little avail.

I just can't afford any more time of work; but I had to see you first to explain."

They finally exchanged grateful smiles at the discrete looking V.I.P. door a few careful yards away.

Behind it, both had relaxed into a privilege world.

After showering in the 'rest room', expansive even by her high standards, Sandra swapped her cream, silk half sleeve blouse, for the same one in white. It came from the unusual travel sack, which contained all her short stay requirements; including the two phones placed in strategic matching pockets in the top.

Wearing no makeup but with well-dyed lashes, her fair complexion shone with tan of a healthy diet; and expensive pampering; probably with some sort of outdoor life; sun bed or bottle assisted.

Noticeably, taller than her daughter, she lopped back to the table; a strong toned filly released back into the fields to trot. Approaching, firm brown unclad calves suggested a runner.

Looking much younger than years, Thomas knew they had numbered two more than his own.

"Quite a facility you have back there."

A more tolerable wait, after the early rushing, encouraged him to calm his worries; to look forward to the special things to happen on the day, after the day, after tomorrow.

"You look fit."

Instantly, her discomfort was palpable.
She was overly defensive at the compliment.

"Do I indeed?"

Negating an effusive disposition, a darkened tone denied any relationship, then the concerned mother and her daughter's doting, suitor. Despite personal things she had already shared, she wanted no woman compliments.
Granted he was meeting with an attractive woman of his generation, who claimed to have been a long-term fan, thoughts of anything but Alice were far from his mind.

She had smelt great too, but he had not told her, respecting the boundaries.

Quickly she explained her return flight.
"There's no time.
I'm due to leave in two hours."
"Wow that is quick."

Intelligibly, there was little time together to waste on small talk.

Opposite each other in comfortable armchairs, across a small round table, covered in a white heavily starched cloth, he scratched the fabric, nervously, with his fingernail.

"Won't you be exhausted?"

"Flying's a lot of sitting really. I can never sleep on a plane. I exercise which helps."

Carefully, she began to unpick the puzzle she had helped knit.

"I'm running a woman's half marathon in the park next spring."

At the very least their tastes coincided.

"You run too I hear?"

"Yes, I do; sometimes with her."

It was a 'her', rather than an Alice, a deliberate choice not a slip of his tongue.
Lest, in hindsight, it might be misinterpreted by anyone as his view on her womanhood.

All attraction denied up front, Sandra's conscience was liberated, allowing her to be fulsome.

"She knows I'm here to try and help."

Searching, green, rather than black, eyes were directly on him; irrefutably, reminiscent of the daughter he adored; believed once to be a man. Guardian of so strange a secret she continued her story, waiting, perhaps, for a more appropriate moment to address the subject.

"I'm an attorney."

Instead, she ordered green tea, some ice, from a waitress with only one other customer to serve; dressed passably, as an airline hostess.

He ordered a black coffee for himself.

"I've worked for Congress most of my life. It means a lot of travelling."

Boundaries established, slim arms were across the table, both hands held those of the man, she believed had loved her daughter.
Unconsciously, taking on the changes of local inflection her voice had become the verbal amalgam Londoners often adopt, when living in New York City.
Obviously, concerned at the way she had contrived their meeting, Sandra wanted the writer to know all about her daughter; conscious of the precipice along which they had dawdled.

415

Despite her earlier embarrassment, they were soon deep into each other, like lovers themselves.

It caused him regret, when her gaze switched to the arriving green tea tray.

Difficult to understand this mother's power picking off only the burnt currents from the bun, she drank her own water poured into the glass of ice; then had sipped on the green tea.

Refusing to let him tip as the breakfast had been free, she put down a twenty-pound note.

"I left the art field a long time ago.
Waisted a degree really."

Sandra had an expressive way of speaking, so that one sentence was a definitive break before the other began as if she was following court notes.

"Had to start again from scratch to get a job that made money.

Her husband had been an attorney too, in the military.

'He helped. Normal; but so, kind.
Liked to say he was Mr Average.

"Average?"

'Short'

Another method by which to encode wholeness.

He had not known it, but Thomas was batting an average.
A fifty-to-fifty average.
A two to one, against.
For both sides.

"She had everything, when she was young but my time."

Time, the mathematician Tits had argued the third dimension was added to the calculation of the base of the pyramid to account for ambient electromagnetic storms during the sun's fierceness, when the earth's movement changed distance to it.
The ancients wanted their monument to be a perfect physical demonstration of what they had known astrological in every dimension.

Two, zero, six.

"You guys; my old art school mates always fascinated her."

It would have felt heartless for Thomas to have reminded her how distant they had been at college.

It was Donald who had been her mate.
Not he.

The Cubit throughout the Great Pyramid had been a constant.
It had equalled 20.6 inches.

Thomas repeated this certainty in his head.
It helped him to remain calm.
He used the magic number, when running as a pacing mantra.

"She hardly knew her father.
He was away so much before he died.

American Japanese."

Interested to know the ancestry passed onto Alice, yet Thomas had not ventured to ask; thankfully, he no longer had to lay the parentage anywhere near Donald's door.

The truth was the truth coming from the mother's mouth.

"With my career I neglected her.
He was an army man.
We had two babes in quick succession.
He died in Vietnam after we moved to the US."

Two, zero, six.
Certainty for sure.
'The King's Chamber had been ten times the Cubit; or 206" inches.

206 had been a Saturn number sunk into the wholeness of the chamber.

"I never married again. She found three old photos of me with you guys.

Made a little altar out of them. I had not had the
heart to object.

Do remember how handsome you all were?"

Thomas never consider he had had that attribute;
but at college time Donald was devastating, dark
and surly hansom.

"Made me tell her the stories of you and Donald
over and over".

What Thomas was hearing was not reassuring;
making it seem if they both had been stalked.

There had been 206 original courses in the body
of Cheops Pyramid.

In 206 years, there would be 7 orbits of the planet
Saturn.

Then it came, instinctively, from nowhere.

"I know she was a man, Sandra."

He had wanted to say it first to Alice.
But still it felt good.
He could not carry his guessed at secret any
longer.

Forward posse Sandra had come to negotiate
terms.
He was making things easy for her.
And for himself.

419

Yet the wait for her answer was endless.

Unfathomable.
But confirmation enough.

Sandra stared on without flinching.
Not relishing the moment but knowing hesitation and no denial would confirm the truth.

An averaged stone from the floor: 206" x 412" = 84,872 square inches.
The number of square inches in the average stone, 4243.6 divided by 10 is also the same number the Common Cubit squared: 20.62 = 424.36.

"She was always a girl Thomas.
Even when she was tiny.
Despite that silly penis."

His shiver was not anticipated.

Certainly, no worse than if it had been.

"How clever of you to see it. She tries hard to hide it.'

Truthfully, part in him was overjoyed by the telling.

"Such a relief Thomas."

"I think we can live with it."

His words.

He had needed to hear himself speak to them.

A mother's smiles were radiant.

Beyond grateful.

She squeezed his hands, tightly, for an age.
Passion expressing feelings strong as an orgasm.

Secure, she had fulfilled her mission.

Before it was properly begun.

"You have been inside a man, he had not said.

Absolved by a presumption.

No terrible shock.

Nor outrage.

Just coming together.

"She came to me and told me.
She could no longer be a man."
She tried it, till her thirteenth birthday."
I tried to persuade her.
Her brother had killed himself.
Over the same concerns.

Two people from my womb who could not live in their male bodies."

Thomas felt the pain, as if he were a brother.

But stopped her there.

Called a halt.

She was grateful.

Really, there was nothing left to say.

"You've done enough; the rest must come from Alice.'

"We'll be friends Thomas."

"Yes.

And I love her".

Again, the smile; the look; the hands.

But words; words they were ended.

Thomas steered the conversation back to steadier ground.

"So, she was with you in New York then the past few days?"

Alas a simple question shook the world.

After harmony, his terrible luck came rolling back down the hill.

No Thomas she's here."

A fact naturally to rock him.

"In London... all this time?
Alice had to be somewhat devious to survive what she had been through,

He had never expected this shiftiness.

One hundred percent he had her in New York.

Again, she had played him.

"Didn't she call you?"

His change in equilibrium was evidence enough that she had not.

"I told her too."

Sandra's response was hardly sensible.

"What in London?"

"Yes, when I left her at the hotel a week ago."

New facts toppled in on an unwary several.

"Paid for her to stay till today.
She had nowhere to go till they got house money.
It's supposed to happen this week."

The silence to follow crushed life.

"Oh my god what has the silly bitch done this time."

Immediately Sandra had wanted to try reach Alice.

Thomas stopped her.

He would deal with it from now on in.

"Is she coming to the airport at that time she said."

"Yes. But why didn't she call you?"

The announcement came of Sandra's flight back.
She insisted she would stay.
But he was firm.
He had needed to sort this one out for himself.

"Its hours to wait till the rendezvous."
Sandra saw the sense in that.

But no
After receiving two long distant work calls back-to-back, she left looking distraught.
"I do have to go Thomas I'm so sorry.

Are you sure you don't want me to wait."

She gave Thomas her child's number and her own.

Insisting, he call her, immediately, after he had met up with Alice.

They walked speedily together upstairs to the departure gate almost in silence.

Finally, she tried to give him the golliwog pin, but he refused it.

After a huge hug she was gone.

In the days that followed he tried Alice's number numerous times

She had not picked up.

The average top surface area divided by 20 to find the average stone's top surface is 4,243.6 square inches. Translate the number of square inches into the number of square feet by dividing by 144 equals 29.469444 square feet per average stone, the number of Earth years in Saturn's orbit: 29.469444 years.
The average top surface area divided by 20 to find the average stone's top surface is 4,243.6 square inches.

Average numbers, like opinion polls can be very

425

misleading.

When people said fifty percent of couples get divorced after marriage, it left the same percentage still married. Despite all research into the complication of the human spirit by mathematicians and artist alike, the relationship between them remains uncertain territory.

From the outside, after a trillion words in marriage two people can be unfathomable.

Thomas had waited for Alice of course.

For two hours,

Even after the Air India flight she said she was on had touched down.

She had lied, to her mother. Who would always forgive.

More coffee,

Thomas understood that Alice would not be coming.

CHAPTER FORTY FIVE

Accepting, free mood music from the radio, a fanciful librettist had attempted the move toward resolution of his enthralling operetta. Worked in effortlessly earlier, between his words, the distressingly later stages of his score, refused to carry a tune. The ending imagined called overwhelmingly for the cords of an unpaid church organist, disputing it frantically with a Yiddish fiddler, so that the wind of change might not rustle forever in shaggy ends.

Anything really. Bar the Verdi requiem, repeating endlessly on his DVD player.

"Did this actually happen pater?"

Syntax insisted that the named writer ponder different solutions, maybe using a Haneke like film character, about-turned high up on an unsupported tree bough, cutting with a power saw, while imploring readers to let him idle a while longer in the third person. The voice change was so radical.

"Of course, not sis, it's a story. An allegory."

"What's that?"

"A story about a story little one."

"Oh right.
So, he's a bigger friging liar than she was."

F'ing without swearing, to make the point of her distress.

Comfortable with expressing anything in their endless banter, an elder sister had got unusually serious; her pause much longer than expected.

But yes, Alice had dumped Thomas, quite unreservedly.

"How is it possible to tell a happy story. It's not. It's possible only to tell of its preparation and of how it was destroyed".

"Andre Gide me thinks."

"We've heard it all before."

"SEVERAL TIMES"

"It's depressing Pater."

Considering the huge funk in which Alice had put him, it was worth saying that Thomas' had been hurt by male female distress. Made him want her back. Desperately. Everything that had happened felt unfulfilling, made more complex by the gender change or not.

Yet it had not seemed logical not to tell his girls all the facts.

Just yet.

"Went back to the husband evidently."

"Do we need to change locks?'

"No, it was a friend."

"Ah lucky thing then.
Him stealing off a friend."

"It lasted a whole two weeks".

"Fourteen fucking days does not a heart break make."

"Is that more Gide?"

"No. It's a sorry card.
I am his sorry card.
They always rhyme such things."

Though much had happened in the time, in truth the affair with the painter's wife had been started and concluded between two Sundays.

"So, no history, huh, according to your head guy Barbara eh father?"

"What head guy Av?"

"His shrink, Em."

"He has a shrink?'

"Had

Actually, it was a gal not guy?"

"Same thing in Anglo Saxon."

"Had a shrink long ago.
To get over leaving us."
"And you never told me?"

"Christ Em do you need one too?
Look at the state of him."
Eventually, after comprehensive discussion of the
pain, sympathetic daughters had thought about
taking more professional advice.
"God yes he does look awful.'"

CHAPTER FOURTY SIX

Alice was a beautiful woman.

Just not classic.

 And highly cantankerous.

Candidly, she had never been confident or comfortable around sex, hardly ever allowing her painter husband to look at her naked.

She could justifiably have been labelled prudish.

Tricky for someone married to a painter and a disciple of Hopper.

His infamous wife was his main painting model, notoriously insisting it was part of her job for life.

Many years married; the less famous painter couple of late, had had intercourse only rarely.

Grumpily one day, Donald had said something nasty about Alices lack of desire.

Instantly, riled and spitting poison, she had threatened to leave him.

Worse still, with the blood drained from the perfect olive complexion, she rashly swore to sell the house. Bought with her family's money, never repaid, legally she had owned it outright, making it a dangerous proposition. Live ammunition in a prop gun?

An 'acquaintance' from the pub, ignorant of the facts, over- hearing the grumble had gossiped house prices. Missing only a bone-carved cane top for full dandification, the flashy trainee realtor, had got into the painter's head, building up family tensions considerably. Resonating in familiar vowels indicating a paid education, the man had been unable to take his private public schooling any further than two 'O' levels. Carrying a massive deficiency in the 'grey matter', much to the shame of his titled father, with identically plum sonance, and little more nuss.

On walkabout during a customary stand-off, Donald had sought only to scare her. Thinking he had partnership rights, when he had bumped into the agent a second time, he had been delighted by an offer to sell.

With one immutable condition.

It had to be done quickly.

When Alice had been told about it later in the day, she had voiced no concerns, cussedly, ready for a fight, knowing she had the paperwork.

Another couple, identified too quickly by the man's office, amongst several elbowing their way to the front to get into a desirable school catchment area, both applicants had good annual City bonuses. Instantly, an irrational sized deposit had been posted in escrow by engorged realtors, increasing complications at an alarming speed in a crazy market.

Becoming more than ever her usual awkward self, calls started to come straight to Alice, targeting her on discovering she was the money.

Still vengeful at the stinging of spousal afront, enjoying the battle, she had given out her bank details. Not signing anything but knowing such a release would result in a deluge of paperwork.

At this moment an innocent Thomas had pounced into the starting stalls.

A lively favourite to block out the race to the bottom.

Even by chance to satisfy her growing needs.

More words of encouragement had been exchanged, when informed by others of a partners footing.

Belligerently, enjoying the fight she had refused to surrender,

Cutely she had asked more money.

Not with a signature on paper just verbally.

Even she was not that crazy.

A day later, the sale signs were up together with the property security-watch inaugurated; their erection suits-boys current and lowly job in Property. The first to know of such sales, he had long fantasised about using the information, Donald had been the first duck in line, lifted by hook and rod from the water of a fairground game.

In jactitation of a once ruling class, no longer with the power to facilitate the promise, the sale was offered to be completed within the week.

Total nonsense of course.

While overall, an incredibly wise investment, the property had more than doubled in value since purchase. Facts easily checkable on the internet. As many had on hearing the whispers.

For a wife to continue the game, free to sign she had to hustle, husband free.

So, she had moved Donald stuff out into his painting studio. Before sunset.

A renal punch to maintain her high, which was considerable.

but which lasted only an hour when reality dawned.

Profound consequences cooled things from there.
Each partner had begun to acknowledge their own
recklessness.
To themselves if not to each other.

   Those responsible for the legal work saw the
moron in charge was attempting to milk his money
cow jerking its udder with a hand gloved in rough-
grade sandpaper. Time might have cured the paper
mess as she had agreed the sale verbally. The lack
of it had been total. A notoriously, difficult local
council had turned the agent's paperwork to
garbage and binned it.

   Alice became daily more nervous but had not
even needed to back down.
   Whether she had meant to go this far had never
been determined.
   The bets were on not.
   Evey thing OK then. Save from the panic of a
homeless a husband in huge freak out and an
introspective lover drowning in his sea of love.

   Curiously a new realist husband had drawn first
breath. Worked out all for himself that on a slower
time scale the house sale it would be a doddle if
both had agreed to it. He would get his part if they
had remained coupled.
It would have set them up for life if they downsized.

It was a depth, discovered in hardship, which could

never have been guessed at with Sam.
Donald became solicitous.

The physical was not obscured, but he had lived
unknowingly with it for a marriage.
Why would her change, well before they met, be a
problem for him.
Plus, the real-life artist had huge concerns about
spending later life alone after decades sharing her.

Certainly, he had loved her in his own way.
Admired by all for his artwork, he had the creative
ability to launch himself, wholeheartedly, into an
attractive project; however, off radar it might have
seemed. Had bitten deep into the fleshy, forbidden,
fruit. Alone, he had awoken aroused a couple of
mornings in his messy work surroundings, the image
in of his wife before with an unwanted extension. An
excited Donald had begun his epiphany.
Her secret had not changed the woman he loved.
 A selfish line of reasoning but a path to a better
understanding of the real world.
Though not of how others might like to explain its
workings.

Conversely, becoming additionally Solomon like,
regarding the surrender of his mortal self, the
resurrected creative decided guilelessly on life.
Speedily cognisant, that he had no interest
whatsoever in spending an old age in penury, he
had needed to see her. Putting aside issues of trust
for the moment, she had always been the person he
had consulted on critical issues, he picked up the

phone.

Happily, for him, he had her correct mobile number.

CHAPTER FOURTY SEVEN

Alice had answered his call, its number displayed on her screen, on the fourth attempt; each try sieved through the levels of acceptability.

Shocked by the gentleness in his new voice, given the previous days of constant aggravation, with hints at self-harming, she had thawed. Quietly to herself. Like Thomas, she had been certain he would never have made good his threat to do away with himself. Replacing the receiver at the end of their conversation, as usual, issues with confrontation were at the core of most of her problems. In the rush to make ready they were cast, almost casually aside.

During extensive preparations after checking the marks on her arms were gone from four days ago with Thomas, she had shaved her legs shinny.

Essentially, motivations for a duplicitous nature were based upon fear, her mother would, readily, confirm and what Sandra had tried to explain to Thomas at their meeting.

A Thought full mother had as usual had tried to cure the problem with money and left her at the hotel she had booked into on her first visit; paid the weekly for her stay in Chipping Norton. It was world class spa, the reason for its choice. And by American Express way of payment.

Alice had no need to go home immediately.

Sandra had been told of the prospective house sale. She had been wholeheartedly against it. So essentially no harm yet had been done.

A meeting between the estranged marrieds had been agreed between them later in the day.

Remembering Donald's homelessness and happy at the perspective beauty pampering a softer Alice had been recalled. She asked the reception if she could have her husband stay with her in till the weekend. Not entirely unconscious of how such a move might be perceived, a few moments later she had added a cot to the request, feeling the happy with more cover. if Thomas were to find out about the stay. Not a busy time for hotel visitors, the elegant Italian manager, part of the hotels Capitalization revenue share agreed for the extended price of a weekend stay, postponing the obligatory suite clean to be include and included it on her mother's tab. Left as an Amex bill, stamped with her card but not yet totalled it would be a cost to her. Believing Sandra to be a Congress woman, rather than his lawyer, the hotel gave her a huge discount; thinking to use the word-of-mouth publicity in the summer, a boast already used when they had been flooded with American guests.

Alas and alack, the first night of the gratuitous hotel extension was actually 'the day before the day after, the day after, tomorrow'.

No-one had told Thomas.

On reaching the tempestuous age of forty there was the worry not a unique one, that she had missed out on something.

That she had never found her soul mate.
The one big love.
Alice needed to be wanted.
Totally adored by a man.

With Thomas the requirement had not been transferred to pleasure in his bed. Entirely blaming him for mishandling the business to fulfil her, and just as needy, when the physical part had not sent her into space, she suspected it might have been a masculine hang over in her psyche; a thought that had allowed her to see a sluttish side.

Looking her astonishing, good, self, and almost edible after the spa treatment, in identical but green set of heels to those at the Westbury, having spoilt herself with two pairs, the painter had not needed the glass of his favourite Poille Fume laducette she had opened to conjure an entirely sunny view of married life. Seeing his beautiful, theatrical wife again, dressed entirely in a tight black everything, an imaginary Mfyt sliced away any sienna shade chiffon, left hanging from the painter's eyes.

Uncharted in the incomprehensible averages telling why the fifty percent of married couples hang together, a well-scrubbed beast turned into a very mobile sexual animal of quite a different stripe.

The explosion to procreate entirely lawfully had happened before a very good room service supper was even uncovered. Once begun the ravaging had continued, feverishly, through most of the evening much in the fashion, when first she had devoured Thomas, but the results hours were longer and astonishing. Head lights of her partners wanton stare focused on her, she became a happy hare in the glare; able to dash and dither girlishly, whence she had come, releasing herself to fate when he had caught her.

Alice had insisted to herself she had loved Thomas,

After twenty years odd years of fantasising about him this new thrill was quite a different turn on with the man who had the correct paperwork to do anything and clearly the intention of using it.

The designated hour at the airport, Donald was snoring beside her as a result of his workout.

Sore bruised but satiated, she would dare not wake him lest he began his exhausting ravages over again. Yearning so long for another man whilst married and the physical part had always been satisfactory. But no longer.

Hence the real conundrum.

She might still have loved Thomas to her mind she had clearly loved two men.

Her history more understandable she believed it was not the strange experience society suggested.

CHAPTER FORTY EIGHT

"She called you Pater?"

So, against what seemed logic and her actions, Alice was not ready to release her captive yet a while, after so many years in pursuit. Considering how the lack of a house sale had affected his love life, it seemed right to her logic that Thomas received a proper airing of the story.

Nor surprisingly it was a stance which had genuinely flustered most everybody else.

"They spent a 'whole day' on the phone together.

"What a witch."

"Why call him?"

"Wanted to say sorry I suppose?"

"So, you can be best friends fore ever HUH?"

"Kinda."

"The creep."

Obtusely, Thomas had sworn to his writer conscience, Alice would never be exposed to his book until he had gained her permission for using her name.

An unwary universe interrupted, to deliver another astonishment.

Mercifully, the recently to be divorced couple, still allowing conjugal visits, had teamed up again and sought out professional help for her.

Eccentrically, and made entirely, without a speck of embarrassment or contrition, Alice ordered her close writer friend, stroke ex-lover into the proposed therapy with them.

'Hippies'

'Playing sharing beds again'.

'Really'

'I'm shocked'

Feeling responsible, despite all the obvious dangers, Thomas had agreed to get involved with huge trepidation. The apprentice wordsmith understood he was in no position to say no if he ever wanted to get his book printed. Indeed, the new situation could turn out full of virginal copy potential.

In a single surgery visit, to an imaginative therapist, found on the web, quickly the trio discovered an unmatched compromise. Second visit with the Israeli woman, a clinical therapist with a name none the three could pronounce, Alice was asked if Thomas' book was so important, why she had not written one of her own. The easy reply had been to say she was a mathematician, not an artist like her two lovers. A blunt therapist had called her on this; explaining the three lead writers in the Simpson's had master's degrees in Math. Insisting woman were all closet artists; if only with their continual manipulation of proven facts, the professional truth teller had scored a blind hit, on the soft essence of a hurting soul. Alice quite simply had adored the doctor's response; deciding there and then to do a book of her own experience. Donald helping with pictures.

Days later more in homage to the tones of Monet than to Degas, after the spoken account of the efforts of the American admirer, but with Alices expensive shoes kicked off at the door, according to house rules, she was painted up a touch too perfectly for the spring morning, and full sunlight. Entering through the colourful stained glass front door, she mumbled an idea, a touch too speedily, when ushered into her newly reunited friend's minimalist space. Expectant of male attitude at the start at their forth coming meeting, organised by herself and for her benefit, she added a wide armed embrace, which made no contact with an anxious host.

Thinking in preparation about perching himself on the arm of the over stuff sofa to be casual, Thomas stopped himself and stayed on his feet, wary of being sucked into the soft silk prison. Close enough to pheromones that intoxicate, he was stubbornly deaf to any flattering dictum to weave his own silent avoidance, miming half an air kiss and redialling the phone at his ear. An overt display of brand-new technology barely a day out of its box and he was on a panicky search for Donald, the new printer and other prospective attendee to a book conference. The resurrected ex was turning out to be an unexpected support in the project to assist in her attempt at a book as its printer. One with pictures

Unable to find his spiky plastic hairbrush earlier after a morning shower, Thomass long grey hair was electrified by a towel dry; making it impossible to groom the city bison mane to match his spanking new brown-corduroy-ensemble, which coordinated the treacle-coloured floor. Loathing to clothes shop, but extra fussy again about how he looked at the delicate get together, Thomas pushed nervously at a tangled lock on his forehead, in anticipation of the encounter with two friends, once married to each other and apparently had resumed in their union.

"He'll be here."

Her answer was to a question, obvious but not yet made.

Hardly a gulp later, the recorded front doorbell tolled a second welcome of a classic favourite.

Deceptively childish, but adultly Channel pink toed, Alice shot to the door across highly polished maple harder than glass. Ever the fleeing dancer in her amorphous, well-cut-street chiffon, witting strides, had quit her previous celebrity foraging for mundane impatience. She had believed the push on the doorbell was her ex. Head inclined like a teenager furious at an unfair, parental grounding, perfectly matched manicured digits tugged open the primary-coloured glazed portal as she made ready to growl. Onto the scrubbed- door step, rather than her expected, stepped post girl Zuleika. Roaming his high carpet-less Fulham plains a safe distance from the dressing down that seemed inevitable, the home'-owner's shouted hello was pleasant enough but made without interrupting his attempt to find the errant printer.

Effulgent in permanent expectant mobilisation, the postie's astonished guffaw, perfectly expressed the surge of adrenaline shooting between two attractive women a generation apart, meeting for the first time.

"Who's the doll, Mr T.?

Zu engaged a passable New Jersey accent; encouraged in her youth by a taxi driver father who had worshipped Frank Sinatra.

"You know I'm into older dames."

A year after Thomas was caught accidentally bath-naked by her at his partly transparent front door, the regular letter carrier would occasionally still break up on him about the incident. Swearing it had been the funniest moment of her post career to date, she intimated she would never reveal it to a soul; neither had believed her.

"You're 26 Raddock ain' t you darlin?
I'm your mail man too. "

Offering the small pile of mail directly to his lady friend, translating occupation, then gender, she matched her southern drawl and she super-sized her order to lascivious entice.

"Shall I come over and lick you a few stamps".

Casually, loosed by default into the fray, the only cover Alice could rustle for her sudden girlish timidity was to try ignoring the cheekiness. An excited tidal flush was rising.

The first conference for the project suggested by the e therapist was specifically mid-morning to benefit Donald's schedule.

He had not arrived yet.

Having taken so long to get him out of her house, his ex-wife had not wanted to organise it there and risk another scene.

"Call him again".

A notorious bad-early-riser, Donald needed to travel on public transport from his new flat in Dalston, which would have taken an age in the rush hour.

The day before this an etching printer had arrived there and been set up professionally. Hyper alert to his constant tardiness, suffering in silence was no longer an option for Alice.

Clearly affected by the gorgeous youngster, she tried her best to effect distance.

Attracted to exactly this kind of domestic drama, judging from the fun in her eyes, Zu hovered

enthusiastically at the open front door.
Her delivery officially made; she upped the levity.

"Wonderful bum Mr T.
Even perter, when she's mad."

Acknowledging the letters with a wave, Alice tried
to return the ennui that she was not a mistress of.

"I'm forty-two young lady and married".

"No problem sweetheart. Got one at home
meself.
And call me Zu.
Watch out for this one though. Bit of an
octopussy."

"We are waiting for my husband".

In search of some standing, Alice neglected the
detail which 'Good friend' Thomas added, seeing the
course of events and adding to the whiz.

"Ex husband"

A well-practised south London hunting roar filled
the sunny hallway as Alices full blush arrived.
Not an unpleasant experience, it was an unusual
one,

"What's its name Mr T?"

Compliant Thomas, dodging behind his ex-lover

for safety, was hesitant but happy to assist.
" Alice"

"Nice name Alice. Kind of regal "

Pirouetted on a leading cowboy booted foot, in allowed elegant post wear from China, which had never been within ten degrees latitude of the great Texas Divide, one lovely "mail maid" beat her speedy retreat.

The disciplinarian to new world order, tried to remain queenly quiet. Holding protective custody of the open portal door, the gorgeous child had slid off. It took ages to ease the door closed behind her. Thoughtlessly, looking into the distance, to check down the garden path for Donald, through one of the clear door panel framings, the astonishing profile turned again on her. Fully, aware of the attention she was causing in a carefully, crafted 'over shoulder' Zu mouthed back Alice's name with half closed eyes; as it swallowing a tasty soft centre in time to an exaggerated, rear end -swagger, perfected at her Tuesday night salsa class.

Perfect comic timing to witness the final seduction, Donald appeared from around the corner hurrying for the house. Any day on Thomas's Garden path would have been special with a beauty making flirtatious contact with Alice, but a sudden left, Zu reached the market to disappear with her empty letter carrier.

Momentarily, Alice was bereft at the loss.

Condescending smiles rippling and Thomas joined her at the door; with three empty glasses and a bottle of celebratory non-alcoholic fruit wine and his phone.

Several more static moments ensued, before it was safe for her to let go the latch.

"It would be good to have a girlfriend "

CHAPTER FORTY NINE

On that unfortunate day, both of Thomas' children had been in contact with actual worries, not conscience flashes to check he was breathing.

Only one pointy finger press, and hell had exploded into flames of news of the fire they had bought was presented.
Many conscious minds than theirs that morning had been blown by the huge mushroom of smoke and melancholia that once had been Notre Dame Cathedral. Its roof space crackling like newly lit fire logs in a way never imagined possible on live tv, the unsponsored commercial for the second Apocalypse burned eternally.

Christ finally had died again and risen according to prediction.

Haplessly the shocked lady mathematician was let into his space, not for book talk but to spend the next hours weeping, appropriately or not, sunk onto the timber maple floor in front of his screen.
Her hand into the illusory tv flames, it became pink edged.

Unnervingly, once more Thomas was at her command.
Despite silent warnings, she became again his person of importance.

Assuming he could make such a thing happen, it felt it imperative he stop her tears.

Futility superseded him.

Continuous feeds factualised the ancient church burning at a speed seemingly casual for an event of importance.

There should have been more bluster.

Like later

A mistaken workers incompetence sounded too insignificant, for destroying so much importance.

Donald tried to add muscle to the lift.

Arrogantly, both her men had assumed they could shoulder the burden.

The new print maker checked in to hear the dreadful news.

She continued to be destitute trying to assimilate the catastrophe.

"We can't grow that grade of timber again.

Curled a little into Thomas, his words convinced sometimes.

She liked his story.

Experiencing the fall well after he understood he had tripped, he had drifted,

before hitting something substantial.

It was benign.

Acknowledging he was too close to the pale skin,

not indifferent to the prompting of her incredible thighs, he carelessly brushed the stubble on a hairless face to tasted salt in the tears.

Close up after an absence, her smell was headily consuming.

Then came the separating scratch because the woman he loved might have been a man.

The tick was alive.

It reduced him.

Alice oblivious, was shut out in her pain.

A certain amount of material existed she had argued to make the world.

New develops from it.

Thomas was watching, senses electrified.

The match struck,

It burns and was charcoal.

Death the certainty

We rationalise.

"I don't want a child.

It's not necessary to prove I am a woman".

Soon an impatient ex-husband was in the room.

Two tongues sought nourishment from any available feast.

His shoes respectfully off he too looked hugely pained.

Shocked and unrequited Thomas moved way.

Saw the danger in his passion.

The shame in losing.

He understood he should not be there.

Donald held her.
Resistance was for a friend,
His roughness excited

Passion flamed forgetting.

Arbitrary familiar peace

Thomas went outside.

Sat on the seat under Mr Kent

Later without blame, taking comfort from each, three close friends sat across the table in the Tate modern.
With view of the much younger dome, St Pauls still standing.

They had come via St Pancras station.
On the tube
To remind themselves again of a magnificent span.

Revealing the missing rose quartz and diamond engagement ring, once supporting the engraved tungsten wedding band, both had been sacrificed that afternoon to finance his printer.

A new life.

Asking Thomas for helping words for big ideas in the pictures.

CHAPTER FIFTY

Recognising her husband's, evangelical tone, as the prolusion to more rage, Alice sighed. Soon she would be hearing one artist's name, castigated above all others: in the pub, at a party, or on some other social occasions. To all sorts of people, mostly, unrelated to painting.

"Bloody Creedy."

Giving him a nickname made the artist seem like a long-time friend.
But Sam never met Martin Creed.
It was his Avant Garde reputation that had upset so hugely.
One work was the most despised.
The 'piece' with which 'Creedy' had won a Turner prize.
Early on in his discourse Sam would explain this 'piece of 'sh'art'.
Should never have been credited as art in first place.
That would have required craft and an illuminating idea.
This had possessed neither.
In his humble opinion.
The easy, even legitimate beef against the man's pretension, the flavour of the Sam's truths was too often drowned in red wine.
Like the five contestants in line for the Turner prize, the Conceptualist winner was given a

whole gallery at the Tate to display his winning work. Cussedly, he had chosen to put nothing into this large empty white space with beechwood floors, settling for fiddling instead with the over-head electrics. He worked it so the studio would automatically illuminate, when someone walked into the room, would turn off again, when the same visitor left.

Maybe, this was a visual pun of the sound of one tree falling in the forest.

Or maybe not.

The artist himself had muted the theory.

He had refused to commit to it.

Insisting his piece was whatever people wanted it to be.

Asynclitism to irritate not just the painter but a whole commonwealth of art lovers.

The prize money, twenty thousand pounds, in huge cheque form was delivered to the winner after an appropriately specious speech, by an arrogant and tardy Madonna; arriving thirty minutes late to an event on real live, TV. She was living in London at the time, with her English director husband before they divorced; a choice as presenter, perfectly exemplifying the Galleries marketing approach to Art, loathed by Sam.

"Burn down the house it secures."

Gossip claimed it had been the ceiling writing at the top of a ladder required to reach it, with *which conceptualist Yoko Ono had first bewitched John Lennon.*

A big Beatles fan himself, Sam had seen her original show all those years ago.

Even in the flesh he was never able to understand how her work seduced his idol. later shot dead in New York. How much more appropriate he felt, if Sam's paintings were to receive the gratuity and the acclaim, if he was young enough to get on the list.

These days entry to the Academy to get a picture hung for the Summer Show was a cattle market, unless you knew someone on the selection committee.

This year's exhibitors to another ridiculous show, included old men who once had earned the title of professional artist and were his teachers at Art school.

Men to whom he had listened and carried their advice into his work.

The vapidity of their exhibited pictures made him shiver with fear and disillusionment.

Flicking off his studio lights, to save 'juice' on a dark autumn evening, Sam made his way angrily to the kitchen, for a glass refill and 'a bite to eat'. Annoyingly, the delayed trip off his overhead studio light, took on the acoustical rhythm of a Creedy. A reminder, sour as the milk he had poured into his morning tea from a mistaken carton, Alice had put aside to make yoghurt. His thoughts jumped to Government sanctioned and expensive new light bulbs in place, everywhere in his home bar the studio, were not helping his mood. Could other people not see the light they produced was on an entirely different colder, colour?

Why, like in the introduction of digital projectors at all cinemas was there no street insurrection?

Were audiences blind to the change from film to digital projection?

The bottle was on the kitchen table and not hidden; in case Alice wanted to check his intake. More importantly, he guessed, to shame him into moderation.

Dispensing with his Hopper influences, Sam was trying to make another portrait.

This time of just a woman's head and nude upper torso against a simple dark background imitating the favourite at Kenwood.

He had been working on the face for some time, positioning.

The painted image on his canvas at the far bottom right looking out in.

The composition was not obvious, but he felt good about it.

Making him feel a painter, merely, by sitting on his beautiful antique easel, any picture on it seemed to gain importance by its reassuring presence.

Some days, when he ratcheted it up and down, with centuries old antique brass mechanics still in perfect running order, he *talked to the support like a friend.*

Trying to work again from a photograph, his subject was the result of a great deal of negotiating with his wife.

The wine bottle was one of her caveats after a surprising approach to him.

Ostensibly, she seemed to be avoiding him more and more of late.

They no longer eat together by mutual agreement.

But of her own volition, she came to him two weeks before with an idea right after her early supper. Knowing he wanted a model to paint she suggested a girl she got talking to at her evening class.

Why she spoke out he could not even guess at.

But she had.

The agreement was made quickly for the girl to visit for tea. If Sam liked her, Alice would take a photo with her cam, and he could work from that.

At a final live sitting Alice would supervise

When the sitter had arrived, it transpired she was still in her late teens.

Dressed in a halter top and jeans she had short boyish hair.

Sam immediately saw her attraction.

Together they made one good snap with Alice's digital still camera a new appliance his wife handled with acquainted ease.

459

Sam had never seen it before; and certainly, never contributed to its purchase.

He wondered why and how she had come by it.

But of course, he had never asked.

The girl was accommodating.

overly so, smiling throughout Alice's fuss around her.

The resulting picture was something he would enlarge and print-up.

She would also come later for a full sitting for him to get final details.

Alice got her to strip down. The experience though exciting, he was conscious it was a test.

The girl stripped down while Sam left the room to return a few minutes later.

Wanting to make her likeness recognizable, especially as she was not known to him as a friend, for days he had struggled. Where he hoped to be inspiring, her reproduction though careful and accurate was disappointing, utilitarian even and academic.

While he was labouring on it, Alice had knocked on his door, before the usual call. His supper on the table without the usual following announcement the kitchen it was free for him to occupy. He went to the door but only on a second knock. Unlocking and opening it, aggressively, he found a worryingly vulnerable looking wife, actions so out of character, he beckoned her inside.

Hesitantly, she came in seeming awestruck to

460

be in his 'holy of hollies'.

She flopped down onto the sitter's chair, the only one in the room bar his stool.

She barely glanced at the picture of her new friend.

He gladly would have accepted her opinion on it, but she sat in silence. an indolence that was mystifying. She hardly knew why she was there. Also, it became clear to him that she had been crying; he a husband, uncomfortable around tears. It was no better here.

He never knew what to say.

Concern rising with every noisy heartbeat, she sat without speaking.

To break the uncomfortable void, he thumbed toward his picture.

Still removed, she turned her head toward it very slowly and stared.

Without enthusiasm he mimed her friend's name.

Not spoke it but mimed it.

She seemed to mumble something.

He asked her out loud to repeat what she had said.

Electrified by his tone, all her pacifism vanished.

Like an umbrella snapped into rigid place; limbs and body became taught.

Seated in the chair, she screamed at him without looking, deliberately continuing to study the well varnished floor. So loudly it was difficult to understand the words.

She had wanted him to know she had been 'dumped'.

Her same few words shot out; half a dozen times; without diminishing their passion.
To make certain he had understood.
By whom she was dumped she would not say.

Then, not instantly, but turning to him, curling up like a cat, she leapt up from the chair going for his bewildered face. An air born leap with nails and teeth, quickly drawing blood. Trying to save himself and to shake off the rabid possum she had become, he half shook, half flung her toward the door. Releasing her tearing at his cheek, momentum carried her to the open-door stumbling passed it. Grabbing the handle to right herself, forward motion continued, she closed it on herself. Leaving an eerie, comical, void. Shaking with shock, Sam stood, disbelieving for a few moments in pain, waiting for the door to open; her to charge in and restart the attack. But it never came. He was safe from her after he had turned the key. With a paint rag to help stop the bleeding, he was startled to hear the front door slam shut.
It was the last evidence of her till morning.
After a whole nightmare night out, looking

pale but composed, she had come home;
seemingly resigned to her fate. All other
compulsion repressed; she had apologized.
explaining, she too had been drinking.
Regarding whom dumped her was still not
offered?
   Sam was too much a coward to ask.
   Thus, things had stood.

   Understanding the ways of the world, frozen
by the silence for another whole day from his
painting an emotion he could not identify by the
next evening overcame him.
   He was ready to follow her in his car when
she had left for her class.
   In front of the group of a dozen people, which
included the face he was painting, the reaction
of her teacher, when Sam was guided in by the
janitor it became clear what was going on.
   Dazed, and with the marks on his cheek and
neck, he about turned unable to look at the man
clearly messing with his wife.

   Final confirmation came from her in his
studio, but much later.
   She returned home after the long bus ride full
of trepidation reeking of sherry.
   He heard the truth, stoically.
   She offered divorce.
   He heard himself saying no.
   It surprised him.

   Alice knew, he could not live on his own

463

without her.

She had not the heart to kill their life, completely.

She left the studio; this time with excessive care closing the door on him.

He understood she would not leave.

With the realisation came the pain.

For moments he was gasping for breath.

And so fearful.

Then came his anger.
It had needed to be released.

His revenge again was like with the porn picture, this time more careful with anger.

Soon he made his way to the floor with messy hands coloured in her multi coloured streaking blood. When he looked up at the picture the effect of his watery daubs was astonishing; not this time to become abstract yet her image refused to disappear; and continued smiling.
He ran more pale colours onto his brush into the pigment already on the canvas, but the features were disfigured.
With more paint and more water, she was fainter but would not be disappear.

From incarnate Belsan, he heard Alice call out his supper was ready.

She was going upstairs to bed in the spare room.

Such a defeat needed medication.

Safe to move around the ground floor again with her upstairs and with sticky paint hands he had no taste for food but for a second bottle of red wine.

He returned to his den.

Out of necessity and sheer habit.

Studying the hated picture now half dry and she still was smiling.

> *After a few damps of his paint rag damp, a glass of red wine and with drops of his own blood after clearing off a few of the worst unsightly blobs.*

> *Voilà it was another completed finished picture.*

> *Still quite recognizably the girl had been made, it seemed of a rainbow of tears.*

CHAPTER FIFTY ONE

One final incident, a relative few days later, stubborn instincts had refused to die quietly.

Raising past spirits there had been a long ring on the Van Morrison.

Reflex, not out loud, it had been outdated and sensationally incorrect.

"Alice."

Thomas had been reading his Guardian before consuming another cheese fondue simmering on the hob.

Over time, his spotless sofa, where he perched had lost the scent; to be replaced by a Dior fragrance bought to refresh it but had never risen to expectation. It had cost one hundred pounds, so maybe similar virile donkeys had been used its preparation and paid homage to the original concoction.

"Alice"

He had told himself they were over.

Finaly, he knew they were.

Confident, after so harsh a warning, his alter ego would never allow a repeat involvement in anything so unusual as her thereafter had been so painful.

He had he promised, when feelings were less bruised, T. H. Maher would continue his book.

Certain he had much data from the experience to finish it healthily.

Less interesting perhaps than what had transpired, but that too had to be accepted.

Currently, another obvious stunner had appeared to be standing in front of the stain glass.

According to what he could make out without opening it, which he delayed deliberately, the diffuse image seemed dressed as a sherbet lemon sunrise. Familiarly opening the door when he had worked out who the beauty his soul ignited, his eyes directed to the level of the half-exposed bosom of his personal postal delivery person. In high, high heels a great deal of the long, polished, leg had been showing.

"Zulieka."

"Hello mate, sorry to trouble you on a Sundee but we have a question."

A 'sunflower floribunda rosa', he recognised from his Guardian Garden catalogue was in her hair, for the night coiffured under a passable black wig. The distinct odour of civilian medication suffusing, he had guessed at rum. It took several joyful moments before he was able to take in everything. Including the young woman standing behind her, dressed like a Tango Argentino dancer, unusually in yellow tap shoes.

"No offence mate but we are in a hurry."

Just on or way to a competition.
Get to go finals in Paris if we win and they pay the coach ticket."

Eh this is Laura."

Hiding in her shadow was a pretty, lean woman, who stepped forward dramatically with heavy, natural black eyebrows, dressed in a superbly fitted, man's midnight blue tuxedo with tight striped trousers. Generally similar Argentinian dancer affiliation, the outfit was topped with a black fedora. Wearing a high-way robbers mask covering the rest of her face, happily she carried no pistol.

"Show the tash babe.'

Laura whipped the mask down, as if mooning her face, to reveal a truly lovely, unmade-up job with a pencil thin mustachio draw in eyebrow pencil above her upper lip. Striking the second pose of the west Indian runner who had taken all the gold sprint medals at the previous Olympics, but with longer outstretched extension, she sparked wickedness.

"You never said he was my father's age Zu."

She was at the most ten years older than Zu.

"You sure he can still manage it babe".

Much laughter followed as the pose reformed.

"Ignore her mate. She's just a common tailor.

"Like her suit?"

Again, came the coordinated arm flashing on the other leg with the girl's nose to nose.

"Her friend made my dress. I chose the fabric."

Other enthusiastic strikes in opposite directions, and everyone was having a really good time.

"She has agreed once I've seen Paris.
I can't go through life without having had it.

Get my gist mate?"

Already Thomas's mouth was open.

He had a notion of what she meant.
Frankly, flabbergasted, even if they had been playing.
Unabashed, the well-rehearsed comedy duo continued its routine without pause.

"She wants a baby."

"All we know are girls and few gay boys from Oxbridge."

It was a horror beyond his wildest fantasy.
But funny even sober, he had had to admit.

"She wants someone normal as a donor, not one of her clever friends."

"Saw yours once and we thought of you."
Closer to the floor, holding arms around each other, the accompanying the roars increased.

"We need one."

At this point they lowered voices,
To a stage whisper, but not to spoil the pleasure for the rest of the street.

"One nice big one."

Unable to hold the pose, they held each other up, temporarily, their mirth was so extreme.

"I think I wet myself."

"So whad ya think? Me for an hour no strings. A melange et tois."

"Just so she can see what it's like."

Thomas was speechless; but joined in the fun.

"What now?"

It was certain an amount of alcohol had been talking.

"If you ain' t up to anything. She'd be OK with it".

"Had to be someone mature."

"And no longer than an hour"

"Like the pros."

"What'd you reckon."

He had had to say no.

But it hardly slowed their fervour.

"Shame"

"You're not serious?"

Zulieka turned coquettish.

"Half."

"We had been talking it over but finished off the bottle of rum."

"And we look so great we just had to show someone."

With that they had waltz off. Or rather tangoed out of his evening.
"Bloody men."

One final pose and they were gone.

The End

Printed in Great Britain
by Amazon